# A Winter's Wish

ALSO BY JUDY SUMMERS

*The Forgotten Sister*

# Judy Summers

# A Winter's Wish

WELBECK

First published in 2022 by Welbeck Fiction Limited, an imprint
of Welbeck Publishing Group based in London and Sydney.
www.welbeckpublishing.com

Copyright © Judy Summers, 2022

Judy Summers has asserted their moral rights to be identified as the author of
this Work in accordance with the Copyright Designs and Patents Act 1988.

A CIP catalogue record for this book is available from the British Library

Paperback ISBN: 978-1-78739-947-1
Ebook ISBN: 978-1-78739-946-4

Printed and bound by CPI Group (UK) Ltd., Croydon, CR0 4YY

FSC
www.fsc.org
MIX
Paper from
responsible sources
FSC® C171272

*10 9 8 7 6 5 4 3 2 1*

# Foreword

I have been really looking forward to Judy Summers' second novel about the Shaw family, *A Winter's Wish*, and I have not been disappointed. Judy is a natural story-teller and in this book we follow the trials and tribulations of Delilah, the eldest daughter, who is a determined and feisty girl – she certainly needs to be for her courage and resolve is severely tested at times. All the characters are well-drawn and believable (even her alcoholic father) and again the research has been carried out meticulously into Liverpool in the 1840s and is very skilfully woven into the fabric of the book. I'm certain this will make an ideal book for holiday reading should you be fortunate (and brave) enough to be taking a holiday. Keep them coming Judy, I can't wait to find out what happens next . . .

Lyn Andrews

# Chapter One

The baby was dead.

This was only the second of her mother's lyings-in that Delilah had attended, but even from her place in the corner of the room she could see that the tiny, lifeless figure was very different from the squalling bundle that had appeared last time.

Ma had finally ceased shrieking, and was now emitting low groans and panting noises as the three women bustled about her. 'What was it?' she eventually managed, hoarse with exhaustion.

'A boy,' replied Ellen Jenkins, their next-door neighbour, wrapping the baby up in the swaddling cloth that was lying ready. The cloth that would now act as a shroud. She sighed and stroked the little face with one gentle finger before covering it.

There was a sudden exclamation from one of the attendants by the bed; the sad little group of neighbours who had helped with the birth became active once again. 'Delilah,' said Ellen, 'why don't you go downstairs? The others will be better hearing it from you, and your Pa will be home soon. Leave your Ma with us.'

Delilah cast a worried look over at the new bright blood appearing on the already soaked sheets, then made her way down to the main room. None of the boys were in, but Meg was stirring a pot on the fire and Rosie was in the corner rocking baby Annie on her knee. Annie was not yet one and a half, and Delilah wondered if Ma having another pregnancy so soon had resulted in the stillbirth. But some of the others in the family were closer in age than that, and babies died all the time, so who could tell?

She broke the news to the girls and comforted them all as they cried. It was the third baby Ma had lost altogether, but familiarity didn't make it any easier.

The door banged open and William entered, dropping his school books on the table before making his way over to Meg. 'Smells good!'

Delilah smiled sadly as she looked at them both. The single year's difference in their age was beginning to look much greater now that William was growing like a weed while Meg was as petite as ever, hardly taller than Sam.

William noticed the sad faces. 'Oh. Has Ma . . . ?'

'Yes. She'll be all right, Mrs Jenkins says, but I'm afraid the baby was born dead.'

William did what no other male in the family would think of doing, and embraced her. 'Are *you* all right?'

Delilah had somehow managed to hold back the tears until now, but that made her cry. Fortunately she'd managed to wipe away most of the evidence before Pa and Jonny stamped in.

Pa looked at the table, saw nothing but William's books and swept them away with an angry gesture. 'Where's my tea?'

'Ma started her labour this morning, and she's been lying in all day.'

'So? I'm a working man, the head of this house, and I'm entitled to see my tea on the table when I get home, no matter what.'

'Meg's made boiled potatoes for the rest of us,' said Delilah, trying to keep her voice level, 'and I've sent Sam to the pie shop for you and Jonny. We didn't have the chance to cook anything else.'

'He'd better get back soon, then.'

Delilah was irritated enough to talk back. 'Aren't you even going to ask?'

'Ask what?'

'How Ma is?'

'Well, I can't hear no screaming, so it can't be that bad. She should be used to it by now.'

'It's already over, Pa.'

'Well then, what you making a fuss about? Boy or girl?'

'A boy, but it's dead.' She couldn't keep the hurt out of her voice.

Pa looked like he was going to say something, but then didn't, for which Delilah was profoundly grateful. You never knew with Pa: on any given day he might react to the same thing with a smile or a vicious cuff to the back of the head, and she didn't have the energy to cope with such unpredictability just now.

Jonny, meanwhile, had spotted the chink of weakness in his eldest sister's voice. 'Oh dear,' he began, in a mocking tone. 'Is poor little Delilah upset about the *bay-bee*? Ahh.' He poked at the remains of the tears on her face.

She slapped his hand away angrily. 'You wait until Ma hears you talking like that.' She drew herself up. 'And anyway, I'll have your wages for the tin, seeing as she's not here to do it herself.' She held out her hand.

Jonny glanced at Pa, who nodded, and then reluctantly dug his hand into his pocket. He handed over a small pile of sixpences; Delilah counted them and then gave one back.

Delilah then turned to Pa, who poked through his own shilling pieces, laboriously counted out half and passed them over, and then re-pocketed the rest. 'I'll need to get out the house this evening, what with all this women's business going on.'

Jonny, bored while he waited for his meal, turned his attention to the younger ones. As Meg walked past him with plates for the table he stuck out one foot; she tripped and only narrowly avoided being sent flying, plates and all. When she returned with the teapot he tried it again but this time she evaded him, leading him to hiss in annoyance and loom instead over Rosie, who cowered and tried to shield Annie from him.

Delilah stepped in front of him. 'Leave them alone.'

Jonny almost raised a hand, but although he was by now much larger than she was, Delilah's additional year of seniority still held, especially here inside the house, the women's domain. She stared him down until he retook his seat at the table, tapping on it impatiently.

Further trouble was saved by the arrival of Sam and Jem carrying two hot pies. 'About time, too,' said Pa, biting into his straight away without waiting for anyone else to sit down.

Jem sidled forward to put the second pie in front of Jonny, skipping back as soon as it touched the table to avoid the expected clip round the ear. Having missed his target, Jonny crossed his eyes and made imbecile grunting noises at his youngest brother.

'You stop that,' called Sam, furiously. 'He's not stupid.'

Jonny made a derisive noise and turned his attention to his pie, making much of its meaty taste in the full knowledge that his siblings would eat only potatoes.

Delilah ushered the rest of the children to the table, aware that nobody had come down from the bedroom yet and trying not to worry about Ma. She motioned Meg to a seat as far away from Jonny as possible and watched her take Annie on her knee, mashing up her potato and feeding it to her little by little, not touching her own until it had gone cold.

Once the meal was finished, Pa pushed back his chair. 'I'm off to the pub.'

Jonny did likewise. 'Me too.'

'Oh no you're not, boy – not with me, anyway. It's bad enough having you around all day at work – the pub's for real men, not half-grown lads still wet behind the ears.'

He walked out, leaving Jonny humiliated and thus even more dangerous to anyone unlucky enough to have witnessed the put-down. Fortunately he took one look at Sam's smirking face and stormed out himself, shouting something about finding his friends and slamming the door much harder than necessary.

There was a collective sigh of relief. Meg began to stack the dishes and William reached for his school books.

'You go off outside,' Delilah said to Sam, 'while it's still light. Take Rosie with you and stay in the street here.' She turned to Jem and motioned the signs he used for 'outside' and 'play', pointing at Rosie. He smiled and took his little sister's hand.

As Delilah and Meg washed the dishes, Delilah couldn't help her attention straying to the stairs. Eventually she crept up and knocked at the door. 'Ma? Ellen? There's tea in the pot if I can bring you some?'

The door opened a crack. 'Don't you worry about your Ma, love. She had more of a bleed than we were expecting. We reckon she'll be all right now, but we'll stay a while longer. A cup of tea would be nice, and put sugar in hers if you've got any.'

'Won't James be needing his tea?'

'He was home at dinnertime today so I told him he'd best get himself something from the bakehouse or the pie shop tonight. He won't mind – he knows your Ma and me are good friends.'

Delilah was jealous on Ma's behalf of a husband who would make no fuss about that sort of thing, but there was no point dwelling on it. Pa was no worse than many others.

She poured the tea and took it up, then returned to settle in a chair and catch up on the evening's mending work while there was still light. Most of it was due tomorrow, and they would need the money. Besides, it looked like she would have to do all Ma's laundry work on top of her own sewing for a few days – the last thing they needed was customers going elsewhere because Ma was too ill to work, and then never coming back.

Ma had seemed to struggle more with each pregnancy, or at least those that Delilah could remember. They'd been so many and so frequent that it was hardly a surprise she looked worn out sometimes. Delilah was sixteen, Jonny fifteen, William twelve, Meg eleven, Sam eight (Delilah smiled as she recalled that he would note hotly that he was 'nearly nine', as though that made him a grown man), Jem seven, Rosie four and little Annie not yet a year and a half. And there had been two stillbirths as well – three, she corrected herself, counting today's – so Ma had been almost perpetually expecting or nursing for all those years. Poor Ma. And she was still young enough to have more; how much longer would she be able to keep her health and strength, at this rate?

Delilah shied away from thinking about what they would do, how they would manage, if Ma was no longer around. It was just too terrible an idea to contemplate. Best to keep busy to take her mind off it all, and Delilah could at least help by taking on extra work and allowing Ma to rest before she had to get back to her daily grind.

She was still going with her needle and thread some hours later, her fingers and her eyes sore as she looked blearily at the clock on the mantel. The house was quiet; Pa and Jonny hadn't yet come back and the little ones were all in bed, Meg, Rosie and Annie in the girls' room upstairs and Sam and Jem on their mattress over near the fire down here. The boys were sound sleepers so wouldn't be disturbed by the candle that burned on the table between Delilah and William, or by the two of them speaking in low voices.

Earlier William had been doing arithmetic. He was the only one who had ever been to a proper elementary school, rather than just free Sunday school for a couple of hours a week, and it cost them precious pennies out of the household budget to send him up to St James's every day. But he was brilliantly clever and had always been Delilah's pride and joy for that very reason: when Pa or Jonny bullied him about it she stood up for him, backing up Ma in her argument that he should be

9

allowed to stay on, even at an age when other boys would have left, so he could get an education. They had won their case so far, Pa grudgingly agreeing to the expenditure on the basis that it was an investment in the family's future: if William could get a salaried position as a clerk it would mean a guaranteed income each week that was not dependent on precarious daily paid labour at the docks. Besides, as he had always cuttingly added every time the subject came up, it wasn't like 'little Billy', as he always called his despised second son, was much good for anything else, pale and weedy as he was. And so William had his books and his daily respite from the rest of the family; and his teacher, pleased to have such an unusually able pupil, helped and encouraged him to study over and above what was necessary.

William had now put aside the columns of figures and was looking at some pages of text. Delilah had been to Sunday school with the others when she was younger, and she knew how to read – if a little haltingly – but as she gazed at his book she couldn't make out any of it. 'What's that you're reading?'

'Latin,' came the enthusiastic reply. 'I'm translating a passage from Cicero.'

'Who? Oh, never mind, it doesn't matter – just make sure you've put all that away before Pa gets home. You know what he thinks about it.'

'Latin?' said William, in a passing imitation of Pa's outrage. 'What use in God's name is Latin? That'll never get you a job. You learn your reading, writing and arithmetic, boy, and get yourself a position so you can support us when we're old.'

Delilah smiled, but before she could reply she heard the sound of the bedroom door opening and several pairs of feet descending.

Ellen gave her a tired smile as the other two local women nodded and left. 'She'll be all right now, I think, but she must stay in bed for a good few days, you hear? If that bleeding starts up again it might not stop.'

'I understand.'

'I've piled up all the soiled sheets in the corner of the room. You'll need to put them in to soak and then do them with all your other washing, else they'll never get clean. You know what you're doing, don't you?'

Delilah looked at the baskets of dirty linen that were already piled up, these ones from paying customers, and sighed. 'I'll get up early to make a start.'

'You're a good girl.' Ellen hesitated for a moment. 'I've left the . . . the baby upstairs in the room. Do you want me to call in at the church tomorrow morning?' She looked close to tears.

'No, thank you,' replied Delilah, in a voice she hoped was steady. 'It's family business so it's my responsibility while Ma's poorly. I'll deal with it. But . . . thank you for all you've done. You know we're grateful.'

Ellen managed a watery smile. 'Your Ma and me, we've been best friends since we were younger than you are now. We look out for each other.' She patted Delilah on the shoulder. 'I'll be off now, then.'

Delilah saw her out the door and then returned to her chair to sew and to contemplate what the morrow would bring, and the days after that.

\* \* \*

## September 1847

'There's been an accident at the docks.'

Delilah wasn't halfway through the day's backbreaking laundry yet, and these weren't the words that she wanted to hear. She straightened to see the worried face of their next-door neighbour, and was immediately sorry for her selfish thoughts. *We look out for each other*. 'Oh dear, has something happened to James? Do you need . . .'

But Ellen was shaking her head. 'No – it's not him, he's fine. In fact it was him who ran up to bring the news. No, I'm afraid it's . . .' She trailed off.

'Pa?' asked Delilah, her heart sinking. 'Or Jonny?'

'You'd better get down there,' was the only reply.

Ma was in bed. She'd gone down with the childbed fever soon after the stillbirth in May, and been so sick that it was a miracle she'd pulled through at all. She was more or less recovering now, but was still weak as a kitten and could hardly manage an hour at a time at her chores. Delilah was just about managing to keep up with both her mother's washing work and her own sewing piecework, although she never stopped while she was awake and hardly slept, dragging herself through the days in a fog of exhaustion. Luckily Pa and Jonny had been able to get plenty of work over the summer, with ships coming into the docks every day and needing their cargoes unloaded. But if they were injured and couldn't work for days, or even weeks . . .

As she accompanied James Jenkins the short way down Brick Street to the docks, skipping to keep up with his long strides, Delilah tried to get some information out of him. He didn't speak much even at the best of times, and all he'd say now was, 'Maybe it's not as bad as it looked – we'll see when we get there,' which only made her worry all the more. She hoped against hope that it was minor, a broken arm or something, and Pa would soon be back to—

Delilah stopped dead as they rounded the corner of a warehouse and she became aware of the two unmoving, covered figures on the ground. It was as though she'd hit a wall. She was gasping for breath. But there was no choice: she forced herself to push through it and make her way forward, slipping like a ghost through the crowd of gawping men.

'Pa? Jonny?' Her voice wavered.

One man broke off from the group of onlookers to approach her; it was Mr Bradley, the dock supervisor who was responsible for picking men for each day's work. 'Delilah,' he began, barring her way with one arm and then curling it round her waist. 'Don't go any closer, not just for a moment.'

'What happened?'

'A whole cartload of barrels came loose and fell right on top of them.' He paused. 'I'm not sure how it happened yet, but it looks like Abraham might have been slack. I'm sorry.'

A man was kneeling next to one of the prone figures. His shoulders went rigid for a moment, and then he got to his feet. Delilah recognised Abraham, a dark-skinned American who was one of the few dockers to treat her with respect whenever she brought down meals for her father and brother, instead of unleashing a constant stream of lewd comments like all the rest. Indeed, he'd sent a few younger men packing in his time, when he felt they weren't being polite enough to her.

A WINTER'S WISH

He looked at her with those hazel-green eyes, so unusual in a man of his colour, and spoke with a quiet but firm courtesy. 'That's not true, Mr Bradley. I checked those ropes only this morning.'

Mr Bradley snorted. 'As if I can believe anything your sort might say.'

Abraham ignored him and turned those sorrow-filled eyes to Delilah. 'I'm very sorry for your loss, Miss Delilah. Your Pa might make it through, but I'm afraid Jonny is dead.'

As if in a bad dream, Delilah tottered the few extra, unsteady paces towards the scene that would haunt and shape the rest of her life. Mr Bradley's arm slipped away as he looked at his pocket watch; she heard his voice as if from a great distance as he told all the other men to get back to work and start clearing up the mess of broken barrel staves and spilled cargo.

Delilah knelt first by the body that was completely covered.

'Are you sure you want to see?' asked Abraham, gently. She nodded, and he folded back the sacking from her brother's face.

Jonny was big and strong for his age, but when all was said and done he was a boy, just fifteen. Now, in death, he looked even younger than that. Delilah's

15

feelings were in turmoil, churning, changing almost every second. She mourned him. But she couldn't mourn such a vicious bully who had terrorised the little ones. But she should feel guilty for thinking like that. But it would be such a relief not to have him back in the house. But that wasn't a Christian way to think. But how on earth were they to manage without the wages he brought in? And . . .

'You're shaking,' said Abraham, who had remained by her side. He took off his jacket and draped it around her shoulders. He'd always been so kind to her, making her feel safe whenever she was at the docks, and asking politely after Ma and the younger ones. And if ever Delilah needed a bit of kindness, it was now.

She reached out one hand, her fingers cold despite the warmth of the day. She left it hovering a moment, unable to bring herself to touch Jonny's face. Then she remembered the cheeky toddler he'd once been, and that gave her the courage to pluck the little flower from her shawl and lay it on his chest before smoothing his hair.

She sat back on her heels. 'You can cover him now,' she said, hearing her own voice as if it came from someone else. 'I'll have to arrange for him and Pa to be brought home.'

'I can do that,' came James's deep and sympathetic voice, 'if you'll allow me to borrow a cart for an hour, Mr Bradley.'

'Anything to ease the lady's distress,' replied the overseer.

Delilah moved to Pa. He was lying on his back, quite still except that he was fluttering his eyelids. 'Pa?' she said. And then, a little louder, 'Pa? Can you hear me?'

His head jerked and there was a tremor in his arm, though nothing from his legs. Delilah looked at Abraham, who grimaced. 'It was a fair weight that fell on him, and more on his back than his head and neck, like Jonny. He might get the feeling back and he might not – there's no way of telling just now.' He paused, before adding, 'I shouldn't be intruding my concerns on you, Miss Delilah, not when this has just happened, but I swear I checked those ropes earlier and they were properly tied.'

Between him and Mr Bradley, she knew who she believed, and nodded without speaking.

'Is your Ma still in bed most of the time?' came Mr Bradley's voice.

Delilah stood up and brushed the dust from her dress, composing herself before she turned to him. 'Yes.'

'Why, that must be three months now.' He added something under his breath that might have been 'Women!'

Delilah didn't catch the word, but she did understand the tone. 'She nearly died, Mr Bradley,' she said, with some asperity. 'We're lucky she didn't. And she'll be up and about as soon as she's able, you can be sure of that.'

She shouldn't have spoken to the overseer like that, she knew she shouldn't. There were so many men vying for work at the docks that anything could be used as an excuse not to pick them, and the family's women talking back to a male figure of authority would be near the top of the list. But it didn't look like anyone was going to be looking for a day's work any time soon, so what did it matter? Besides, Mr Bradley seemed only amused. 'I like to see a girl with spirit.' He licked his lips. 'So, in the meantime, you're going to manage without help, are you? Your Ma and Pa both ill, and – what is it, six younger ones to look out for?'

Delilah nodded. 'Yes, yes I will. They're my family and my responsibility.' She looked the faces of the three older men around her, feeling young and inexperienced and scared and *female*, but she took in a breath and drew herself up to her full height, pulling her shawl around her. 'And now, if you'll excuse me,

I have to get Pa home, break the news to my Ma, and then arrange to bury my brother.'

*   *   *

## May 1848

Delilah watched as Ma laboured in the bed, writhing in pain and letting out an occasional groan. Poor Ma. Following the accident Pa wouldn't be fathering any more children, but it was just her luck to find out soon afterwards that she'd fallen pregnant already. Delilah was under no illusions about how babies were made, and she was ashamed that Pa hadn't been able to leave Ma alone even when she was still bedridden after the stillbirth and the fever. She'd been unwell through the whole pregnancy; thin despite her swelling belly, hollow-eyed and dragging herself around in an attempt to keep up with her washing so that she could take some of the load off Delilah. It was a far cry from the hearty Ma, face red from the steam, who shared raucous chat and jokes with the other women in the street and who dealt out hefty slaps to children – her own or anyone else's – who gave her cheek or who got too close to the boiling water.

Despite – or perhaps because of – Ma's pregnancy and illness, she and Delilah had grown even closer over the last few months. Life had been very hard indeed with so much less money coming into the house, but their solidarity, the idea that it had been the two of them acting together against the world, had helped to get them through. Delilah felt that she had grown up and assumed a new position in the family: no longer one of the children, needing Ma's care and attention the same as the others, but rather Ma's friend and supporter, helping her to care for the younger ones. And once this baby was born Delilah would love and cherish it along with all the others, helping Ma to recover in the certain knowledge that she'd never have to be pregnant again. The old Ma would return and everything would get better.

The labour had been going on for a long time, and Delilah tried to remain positive by wondering if the new arrival would be a boy or a girl. She didn't mind, really; another little sister would be nice, but a brother would be useful later on to help support Ma and Pa when they were older.

She sighed, thinking of their financial situation both current and future – something that had been a constant nagging worry since the day of the accident and one she couldn't ignore even while she watched over Ma. Pa had survived but his legs were crippled and he couldn't work; all he did these days was drink away the money the rest of them brought in and lash out at anyone who came near enough for him to reach. They'd lost Jonny, the other breadwinner, and the others were so young. Poor little Jem would probably never be able to work anyway, for who would employ him? So that only left William and Sam plus whatever she could bring in herself, helped by Meg, Rosie and Annie when they were older. But women never got paid very much, no matter how hard they worked.

Ma groaned again, a harsh, animalistic sound. Delilah wiped her face with a wet rag, making soothing noises and hoping Ellen would come back soon. Ellen had been sitting with Ma for much of the day, but the labour had come on so suddenly that she hadn't been able to warn her husband; she had to make sure he had something to eat after a hard day's work heaving coal, so she'd gone off temporarily to cook his tea and would be back later. Poor Ellen had nobody else to leave her chores to; she'd never had a child of her own, helping out with Ma's lyings-in one after the other without ever needing such help returned.

Delilah thought of their own meal that evening; it would be bread and jam with a drink of tea, so she could safely leave that in Meg's hands, and they'd have it as soon as William got home from school. The others were playing in the street, so at least they would be spared the sound of Ma's pain in the meantime. Pa, of course, was out, having dragged himself on his crutches to the pub earlier in the day.

Everything would be better once Ma was back to her old self. Delilah kept repeating that to herself over and over, partly for Ma's sake and partly for her own. She couldn't keep this up for ever: she'd been washing, drying and ironing during the day and mending long into the night until she couldn't see properly and she wept with the tiredness. She was worried that if she kept it up much longer she'd end up with coarsened skin from the hot water like Ma, meaning her hands would be rough and useless for fine sewing. And on top of all that she'd had to cope with Pa's drunken rages, the children and the rent man, longing all the while for this birth to be over and wishing – God willing – for Ma to recover more quickly this time.

'Delilah?'

She was brought back to herself by Ma's voice. 'What is it? Do you need anything?'

'Only to lie quiet a moment. The pain comes and goes.'

'Shall I fetch Ellen?'

'Not yet, love. The pains aren't close enough together, though they do feel even worse than usual.' Ma managed a tired smile. 'You'd think I'd be used to it by now.'

'Everything will be fine,' said Delilah, as though she could make it so by the firmness of her tone. 'Do you think you'd be able to manage a drink of water? Or some tea? I've kept the last bit of sugar for you. You need to keep your strength up.'

Ma shook her head. 'Listen. It won't be long before the pains come back, and I need to talk to you now, while I can. I've got something to tell you.'

'What?'

Ma hesitated, as though not knowing how to begin. She'd just opened her mouth when footsteps were heard on the stairs and Meg put her head round the door. 'William's home, Delilah, and Sam's asking can we have our tea now.' She gazed fearfully over at the bed, her eyes huge. 'Are you all right, Ma?'

'All the better for seeing you, my love. Don't worry about me – you just go and see to the little ones.'

'Yes,' added Delilah, 'you have yours now. I can't leave Ma until Ellen comes back, but that's no reason for the rest of you not to eat.'

'I'll put some aside for you,' said Meg, 'and keep your tea warm in the pot.'

When Delilah turned back to Ma she'd laid her head on the pillow, but she was smiling. 'My girls,' she said. 'So grown-up, now.'

'Meg's twelve, Ma – not all that grown-up.'

'And you're seventeen, my love.' Ma sighed. 'Seems like only yesterday.' She reached out a hand to tidy a stray lock of Delilah's raven-black hair. 'I remember when you first opened those beautiful eyes and looked at me . . .'

Delilah kissed Ma's hand, seeing as she did so that a new shadow of pain was appearing in her face. 'What was it you wanted to tell me?'

Ma looked past her at the door. 'Oh, nothing important, my love. It'll keep for another time. Just . . . if anything happens to me, make sure you look after your brothers and sisters.'

'Of course I will, Ma, but you'll be up and about soon.'

'Yes, yes I will.' Ma's face creased with pain. 'I think it might be time to fetch Ellen back, and send Sam down the road for Mrs Smith as well, if she can come.'

Delilah moved to shout down the stairs, then returned to hold her mother's hot – too hot – hand while they waited.

* * *

Some hours later, Delilah was downstairs staring into the embers of the fire when the screaming from the bedroom reached a fever pitch. The mending lay unheeded on her knee as she gripped William's hand; his homework lay similarly discarded. She'd sent all the others to bed. She had no idea if or how the girls might sleep in the second upstairs room with all that going on, though she could see that the noise hadn't kept Sam awake; he was sprawled on the mattress on the other side of the room next to an equally oblivious Jem, whom no sound could ever disturb.

William grimaced and clutched at her hand with every shriek he heard. Of course, he was a boy so he couldn't be expected to know about these things, so she smiled at him encouragingly. If he'd been a little older or a little more robust she might have sent him out to the pub on the corner, the normal hiding place of the Brick Street men whose wives were in labour, but she thought better of it.

'I don't remember it being this bad when she had Annie,' he said.

Delilah made no reply, but that was because she knew he was right, and the worry was gnawing at her guts. What if . . . ? But she had to keep telling herself that everything would be fine, and wishing she was right.

And then, just for a few moments, it was. One last scream was followed by an unmistakeable high-pitched wailing. But Delilah had hardly managed to exchange a relieved glance with William when she heard a panicked rushing overheard, incoherent shouts about bleeding, hurried footsteps on the wooden boards. Ellen's voice: 'You stay with me, Margaret Shaw!' The baby's crying continued, but all else gradually fell silent, and Delilah felt the weight of darkness beginning to settle on her shoulders.

The silence seemed to go on for ever, but Delilah was frozen to her chair, unable to move. If she didn't go upstairs, if she didn't go into the bedroom, maybe it wouldn't happen. She could put off the moment a little longer. She could retain the last dregs of hope.

At last the door opened and heavy, tired footsteps sounded on the stairs. Ellen descended; she was carrying a bundle and there were tears pouring down her face. She sobbed and sobbed, collapsing into a chair.

Finally she recovered herself enough to speak. 'Delilah,' she croaked. 'You have a new baby sister, but I'm afraid your Ma is dead.'

# Chapter Two

*August 1848*

'I'll have that rent by first thing tomorrow, or you're out.'

'You'll have it.' Delilah tried to keep her tone level and confident, for any hint of weakness would see them out on the street right now, she knew.

The rent man grunted and turned away, throwing the words, 'Last chance, do you hear?' over his shoulder as he stamped up the hill in the morning sunshine to his next unwelcome call.

Delilah shut the door securely behind him and leant back against it for a moment until her heart stopped racing. Then she made her way upstairs to where she'd hidden the money – a necessity these days, for Pa would take anything he could get his hands on and spend it on drink. He couldn't manage the stairs, though, so it should be safe. Yes, there it was, under the mattress that now lay on the floor, the bed having been sold some weeks ago. Delilah already knew exactly how much there was, but she counted it again just in case it had miraculously managed to increase itself. Unsurprisingly it hadn't, so the stark situation was confirmed: she had barely half what she needed.

There was just one chance. Downstairs was a basket of pristine sheets and clothes, all washed, dried, ironed and mended by her own weary hands. It was due to be delivered today, and if the bill was paid in cash then it would give her enough to stave off the threat of eviction. There wouldn't be anything left over to buy food, but they had a bit of bread left from yesterday, and if William managed to get half a day's work later then he should bring a couple of shillings home this evening.

William was just coming in as she descended. He looked up at her and shook his head; after failing to be picked for labour that morning at the docks he'd decided to tramp round a few pubs to see if anyone would pay him to unload carts or sweep floors, but it seemed he'd had no luck there, either. All was not quite lost, for word up and down the street was that two more ships were due in at around noon; he could go back then. The problem was that there were many, many men doing the same, not only Liverpool natives who'd worked at the docks all their lives but an increasing number of Irish immigrants fleeing the famine in their own country, and most of them were bigger and stronger than William. Personally, Delilah didn't see why the Irishmen shouldn't be entitled to look for work the same as anyone else – after all, they were just people who had fallen on hard times, which as she well knew could happen to anyone – but many of the men were resentful, and Pa was particularly vicious in his condemnation of the incomers.

Delilah looked at William's pale face. He was not yet fourteen, which meant that even when he did get work they would only pay him a boy's wage, not a man's, and he was so thin and puny that he didn't get picked very often anyway. Delilah suspected that he only got work at all because Abraham – one of the few full-time employees at the docks – put in a good word for him and because Mr Bradley was sympathetic to their plight. Indeed, the overseer had been more than generous, calling at the house several times to check up on Pa and to see them all, bringing gifts of food and drink each time.

Even after all the disasters that had befallen them in the past year, Delilah had tried and tried to keep William in school, eking out every penny for the fees even though it meant going hungry herself. But as they had gradually slipped further and further behind it became obvious that the situation couldn't continue. Still she had held her tongue, unwilling to be the one to shatter the dreams of the only member of the family who still had them. But then one day William had gone out as normal, returning in the evening not with homework but with three shillings; he had quietly left his beloved school behind and found a way to contribute to the family income. That night Delilah had shed even more tears than usual.

Now he was reaching into his pocket. He pulled out a shilling piece. 'I saw Abraham at the docks this morning, and he said he'd remembered that he owed this to Pa. But he said to give it to you, not him.'

Delilah took it and frowned. 'Are you sure? Pa never said anything, and you can be sure he'd chase it up if anyone owed him.'

'Who knows what's in Pa's mind these days? Take it, anyway – Abraham will be offended if you don't.' He paused for a moment and then added, 'I think he still feels guilty about . . . you know.'

Delilah knew he was referring to the accident. Mr Bradley continued to blame it on Abraham, but she wasn't convinced. He'd always been hard-working and careful; a black man didn't keep his job for very long if he wasn't, and Abraham had been at the docks as long as she could remember. *Safe* was the word that always sprang to Delilah's mind when she thought of him; safety in more ways than one. There was no way Abraham would have done anything to put Pa's or Jonny's lives in danger. Fortunately Mr Bradley didn't have the authority to sack him, as they were employed by different companies, so he was still there to keep an eye on William and to invent fictitious debts so he could help out the Shaw family without fanfare.

William was now looking at the basket of washing. 'Shall I take that? I might as well be some use rather than just sitting here.'

Delilah shook her head. 'I'm not sure that the rent man might not come back, even though he gave us until tomorrow, so I'd actually rather you stayed here with me. Sam had better take it.'

William nodded and pushed himself up out of the chair. 'I'll go and fetch them.'

Sam and Jem both came in after a few minutes, barefoot and filthy as ever despite her best efforts to keep them clean.

Sam sported yet more bruises, and Delilah sighed. 'Why do you always fight boys bigger than you?'

'Wouldn't be right to hit anyone smaller.' He shrugged. 'Besides, you just put all your weight into it so you're hitting with your shoulder as well as your fist, then it doesn't matter how big they are.'

'So who was it this time? And what about?' She cut him off before he could answer. 'Never mind, it doesn't matter. I need you to take that basket up to Mrs Millet's house in Great George Street – you remember where that is? Knock on the back door, give it to the maid, and don't leave until she's given you the money, do you hear? It's important we have it today.'

'Got it,' said Sam. He turned and made a series of gestures to Jem.

It was astonishing how they understood each other. Jem wasn't dim-witted – despite what the other children in the street might say – but he'd never been able to hear and so also couldn't speak clearly. He could make sounds, but as nobody except Sam and Meg understood them he didn't bother most of the time, although he had made more of an effort since Jonny wasn't around to mock him for his attempts. Delilah worried about Jem, about his future: he was a cheery little thing for now, but as he grew older and found it difficult to get work, what would become of him?

It was just one more thing to fret about, of course, a single item on a long, long list. For now all Delilah could do was make sure that Jem was housed and fed; he was happy enough being Sam's shadow and giggling with his little sisters. Sam was fiercely protective of him – as his frequent injuries showed – and they seemed to be able to communicate without the need of words. Sometimes they didn't even need gestures; a look was enough.

With a final admonishment to keep the washing clean and to get the money, Delilah saw them out the door. Then it was straight out to the back yard, for there was no time to sit idling.

By now Delilah loathed the very sight of the copper over its fire, the wooden dolly, the wringer, the clothes line – all of it. This was Ma's life, not hers; her ambitions and dreams lay in a very different direction. She touched the flower tucked in her shawl, picked from a crack in the pavement that very morning, for luck. Flowers. That was the work she dreamed about and wished for. But now was no time for wishes, was it? With a heart as heavy as the wet cotton, she picked up the first dripping sheet.

'Shall I help you with that?'

Delilah smiled at William as he came out. 'Women's work? You'll get laughed out of town if anyone sees you.'

He shrugged. 'Who's going to see? Besides, work is work, and I can't sit down while you're out here doing this.' He allowed the ghost of a grin to play on his lips. 'I won't try to do your sewing, though.'

'Probably best.' Delilah felt herself almost smiling for the first time in many weeks. 'All right. You turn the handle and I'll feed it through. Not too fast, mind; slow and steady is the best way.'

They began to squeeze the water out of the sheets. 'We'll be able to hear if the rent man knocks again,' said William, 'and Meg's inside anyway so she can call us.'

Delilah had almost forgotten that Meg was at home – she was so silent and withdrawn these days that she was barely noticeable. Since Delilah had been obliged to take on Ma's work as well as her own, all the regular housework had fallen on Meg's shoulders on top of the care of Rosie and Annie, and she got on with it all quietly and efficiently but in a buttoned-up way that didn't allow anyone to know what she was thinking or feeling. Another sibling for Delilah to be anxious about.

The worries all came flooding in again. Money; it all came down to money. Delilah wasn't greedy, had no wish to live in a big house or laze about while someone else did the work, but was it too much to expect that a hard-working family should be able to have a roof over its head and enough food on the table? But for that to happen, the family needed a breadwinner – a *male* breadwinner. Nobody could survive on what anyone was prepared to pay a woman, no matter how hard she worked.

And that was the long and the short of it; they were losing ground. There were not many more hours in the day that she could feasibly work, and those hours would get shorter as the autumn and winter came on – she couldn't sew unless she could see, and that would mean the use of expensive candles. Even if William got a full day's work every day, the cost of food and the rent on this house was too much – and that was before she even accounted for Pa's drinking habit. Sam would have to be the next to try and find work, but as he was only ten he was not likely to get anything other than running errands for a pittance. No, the writing was on the wall; this house had been their home for all her life, but they would have to leave it. She would put it off as long as possible, hoping that something would turn up, but she was only staving off the inevitable. Miracles didn't happen in real life.

Later, Delilah was indoors and starting to heat up the irons when the clock on the mantelpiece struck two. She was alone; William had headed back to the docks as soon as the first ship had been sighted and Meg had gone out to check that Rosie and little Annie were all right. Children played in the street all the time without supervision, but Meg was particularly protective, like a mother hen to the little ones.

Delilah looked at the clock, one of the few household possessions she hadn't been able to bring herself to pawn as Ma had loved it so much. It was past the time when Sam and Jem should have returned. She wasn't particularly worried about their safety, thinking they'd dawdled or run into friends on the way back, but she was starting to be annoyed. They should have brought her the money first and then gone out to play afterwards – what if they lost it?

She turned in relief when she heard the front door open, but then looked on in horror as two dirty, tear-streaked boys entered, dragging with them a basket of muddy, filthy sheets.

'Don't start!' shouted Sam, as soon as they were inside and the door shut.

'What happened? And where's the money?'

'Haven't got it.'

Sam sounded stubborn and Delilah lost her temper. 'We needed that money for the rent! If you've been larking about—'

She was interrupted by Jem tugging at her arm. She made as if to brush him off, furious as she was with Sam, but he stood in front of her and stamped his foot. Then he made the sign he used for 'listen' and pointed to Sam.

'All right. But this better be good.'

'We were nearly at Great George Street, and there was a lot of traffic. I was carrying the basket so I couldn't hold on to Jem at the same time, and he went out into the road without looking properly. There was a great big brewer's cart belting towards him, the driver shouting, but he was still facing the other way and he didn't see it.' Tears began to roll down Sam's face, making new tracks in the grime, and his voice rose to a squeak. 'It was going to *kill* him, Lilah, it really was – lots of people started yelling. So I pulled him back out the way, but I had to drop the basket and it all went in the gutter and it got run over, and I'm sorry 'cos I know it had to get there clean, but it was our Jem. Do you understand? It was *our Jem*!'

He had to stop as he was overwhelmed by the sobs and the shock of what had nearly happened. Suddenly, despite all his usual bravado, Sam looked like what he was: an upset little boy.

Delilah moved towards him but he stepped back, rubbing his knuckles in his eyes. 'So don't tell me' – his voice cracked – 'don't you *dare* tell me I should have saved the washing and let my brother die!'

Crying herself now, Delilah knelt and swept them both into her arms, holding them tight. 'Of course not! Of course you did the right thing.' She kissed the top of both of their heads. 'We're family, and that's the most important thing by far. Never mind the washing – I've still got Jem and I've still got you, and that's all that matters.'

She stayed hugging them, repeating over and over again that everything would be all right, until their sobs subsided and they began to squirm. Then she sat back, wiped their faces and sent them out to play before looking through the ruins of the basket, at the sheets and clothes that there would never be time to wash and dry again before the end of the day.

\* \* \*

It was not yet dawn when Delilah opened the door. She put a finger to her lips and beckoned to the others, counting heads as they all slipped silently into the street, followed by a half-conscious and bemused Pa dragging himself on his crutches.

There had been no possibility of paying the rent, and Delilah knew that the rent man wouldn't allow any further extension – he'd be back with a gang of tough, frightening heavies as soon as he knew the money wasn't going to be forthcoming. Unable to stand the humiliation of being thrown bodily out on to the street, Delilah had decided to take pre-emptive action. They had packed up anything they still owned that was movable, and everyone except Pa and Annie was loaded with baskets and bundles. Sheets, blankets and clothes were wrapped around their few items of crockery and cooking equipment, to keep them safe, and Ma's precious clock was safely stowed. All Ma's laundry equipment would have to stay, as it was far too heavy to shift, but Delilah hoped it would count to pay off the arrears they already owed so that the rent man wouldn't chase them. Besides, he wouldn't be able to find them; Liverpool was teeming with the poor and homeless and one more broken family could easily disappear without a trace.

Delilah tried hard not to cry as she shut the door for the last time on the house that had been her home since the day she was born. The house where they had shared the good times and the bad and where Ma had lived and loved them all. But, when all was said and done, it was only a building; what was more important were the children around her. She turned to the sad little knot and held out her arms to pick Annie up, settling her on one hip.

Rosie tugged at her skirt. 'Lilah? Why are we leaving?'

Delilah just about managed to smother the multitude of thoughts that bubbled up in her mind. *Because the world isn't fair*, she longed to say. But what use would that be? 'We're going to find somewhere else to live, darling,' was all she allowed herself.

'All of us?'

'Yes, all of us together. So there's nothing for you to worry about, you hear? You've still got me, and I'll look after you. All of you.'

She turned her face from the door and led them up the street as the sun began to rise.

\* \* \*

It was strange how much could change over such a short distance. They were only about a mile and a half from Brick Street, but this part of Liverpool was very different indeed.

The half a week's rent that Delilah had already saved and not paid at the old house, added to the money William had brought home after an afternoon's work at the docks, enabled her after some hours of searching to secure them a single room in a partitioned house. It was situated in one of the courts that proliferated in the area of the city bounded by Scotland Road and Gerard Street, where hundreds of dwellings had been crammed together in the space behind the buildings that fronted the main roads. After some haggling – and, for once, Delilah had been glad of Pa's menacing presence at her shoulder – she'd agreed that her available cash would cover two weeks' rent, paid in advance. That meant she had only Abraham's shilling and a few coppers for food, but at least they would be left in peace for a brief period while they worked out what to do next.

They were now following the landlord through a maze of narrow alleys, a rabbit warren of a place where very little sunlight reached street level, and where openings no more than three feet wide gave on to courts of varying levels of cleanliness. As Delilah peered into them she could see everything from scrubbed and polished doorsteps to heaps of rotting rubbish with leaking privies oozing out their contents while children skipped over the filth to play.

The court into which they were led was, to her relief, not one of the filthiest she had seen, though it wasn't the cleanest either. Their guide pushed his way roughly through a swarm of little girls and into a house on the left about halfway down. Immediately inside was a staircase, but instead of ascending he pushed open a door on the ground floor. 'In here.'

He stood back as they entered, the smaller children putting down their bundles with relief. 'And furnished, too – you should count yourselves lucky.' He held out his hand; Delilah passed over the coins, and then he was gone.

Delilah surveyed the room, which smelled damp even in the summer weather. She looked at the cracked windowpane in its rotting frame, the black mould on the walls, the broken-down sofa and a mattress in the corner that she didn't really want anyone to touch.

There was a long moment of silence.

Then, unexpectedly, Meg came to Delilah's rescue. 'There's a fireplace, at least,' she noted, in a businesslike manner, 'and we've still got the kettle.'

'There's a water pump in the yard,' added Sam, who had already been back out and in again.

Delilah nodded, put Annie down and flexed her aching arms. 'Well, it's noon and we haven't had anything to eat yet today. Some bread and tea will do us all good, and we've brought the scrubbing brush and the last few coals from the old house.' She rolled up her sleeves. 'Let's get started.'

# Chapter Three

Paying the rent in advance had bought Delilah a little time, but not much. After a day spent cleaning their new room, working out how they were all to sleep in it and learning their way round some of the alleys and streets, she went out to find work.

What she really wanted, of course, was to be employed in a flower shop – these had proliferated in Liverpool in recent years as the railway meant that fresh blooms could be brought into the city every day. In fact, not *a* flower shop, but *the* flower shop. The one on Dale Street that Delilah often passed while she was out collecting or delivering washing for Ma, and any other time she could find the excuse to go near it. She always lingered outside a few moments longer than necessary; the smell of it was heavenly and she looked in envy through the window at the girls in their pristine white aprons and caps as they served the stream of smart maids and liveried footmen who came in. The servants would take away armfuls, basketfuls; some of the richest houses in town must have rooms filled to bursting with colour and fragrance.

Delilah had dreamed of working in the flower shop since the very first day she'd seen it, but that was all it was – a dream. A wish that evaporated into the Liverpool air. A girl like her, from a family subsisting on daily paid labour at the docks, was never going to get a job in an upmarket establishment like that, and now that they were scrabbling to survive in a filthy one-room court-dwelling the chance had disappeared for ever.

And so it was that Delilah, with a heavy heart, stuck to what was more realistic and decided to apply for a job at the big laundry off Scotland Road. She would hate it, she knew, but it was the best chance of bringing in money for her family. They had to come first.

The laundry was easy to spot, clouds of steam bursting up from the many washing coppers, and Delilah simply walked in and asked the nearest worker who was in charge. She was pointed to a large, red-faced woman who was currently berating a tired-looking girl about something. Delilah stood politely until she was finished, and then stepped forward.

'If you please, ma'am, I'm here to enquire about work.'

The woman looked her up and down. 'Hands,' she said, peremptorily. Delilah held them out, toughened from the months she'd spent doing all Ma's work. 'Hmm,' said the woman. 'Experience?'

'My Ma took in washing, and I've been helping her all my life. I took over most of the work a year ago when she fell ill.'

'Why aren't you doing it now?'

'We had to move, so we're too far away from our regular customers now.' Delilah had been expecting the question, or something similar, and hoped that the noncommittal answer would be enough.

'How would you get blood out of white sheets?'

'I'd make a paste of starch and cold water, ma'am, and spread it on the stain with a knife. Leave it to dry and then shake it off, and repeat again if necessary before putting the sheet in the wash with the others.'

'Scorching?'

'Mix soap and milk, and boil the article in it, if it's not too bad. Or onion juice and vinegar, boiled with soap and then applied cool. Not that we ever scorched much, ma'am, as we were careful with our ironing.'

The woman nodded. 'You know something, at least. All right. Be here at seven o'clock tomorrow morning and you can have a week's trial. Four shillings a week for six days' work, Sundays off.'

Delilah gaped. It was much less than Ma had brought in working on her own account, and barely a quarter of what William could get for a week's work, even allowing for the lower rate due to his age; Pa had brought in five shillings *a day* when he laboured at the docks. The terrible struggle of a household without a male breadwinner couldn't have been laid out more starkly.

The woman saw her hesitation. 'Take it or leave it,' she snapped. 'It makes no odds to me – there's plenty of girls looking for work.'

What other choice was there? 'I beg your pardon, ma'am. Thank you. I'll be here on time in the morning.'

Their dire financial situation haunted Delilah all the way back to the court, but she tried to put it out of her mind in order to familiarise herself with the route so she'd be able to find it in the dark once autumn and winter arrived. The main streets had lamps, but there were no such luxuries in the alleys and courts, and a lost girl on her own would be easy prey for the drunks and idlers who congregated menacingly in the twilight gloom.

Once she was back in their room – she couldn't bring herself to think of it as 'home', not yet – she was

46

greeted by a couple of grinning little boys. 'You two look like the cat that got the cream. What is it?'

Sam, it transpired, had found work. 'The railway station's only a hop and a skip away from here,' he explained. 'You know there's that big wide street in front of it, and that fancy hotel down the road? Well, I'm to sweep the crossings so the ladies and gents can keep their feet out of the mud and dung on the road.' He puffed out his chest.

Half of Delilah was proud of him, as proud as could be; the other half was dejected that she had to rely on a ten-year-old to help keep the family afloat. She couldn't let on to him, though, and in the light of the pittance she would earn herself, anything Sam could bring in would be very useful. 'I'm so proud of you, Sam,' she began, before a thought struck her. 'But what about Jem?'

They both looked at their little brother, who had started playing some kind of game with Annie that was making her laugh. 'He'll want to go with you,' continued Delilah, 'but he can't possibly work in the middle of the street. What about all the traffic? It's far too dangerous.'

'I thought of that too,' replied Sam, with a hint of scorn. 'Of course I did. I wouldn't go anywhere without our Jem, would I? As well as the crossing sweepers there's people selling things out of baskets, and some boot blacks who shine the gents' shoes. I spoke to an old fella and he's going to let Jem help him – he says he don't like boys in general but he don't mind one who keeps quiet. Probably Jem won't get any money, least not for now, but it'll mean he's where I can keep an eye on him.'

Delilah told Sam again how wonderful he was, and he beamed. 'I can't wait till William gets home, and I can tell him I'm a working man now too!'

Delilah smiled at him, and then at Meg, who was slicing bread on the rickety table under the window. Was it just possible that their financial situation was going to be manageable? That they could live without debt, or even start to work their way back up? She had never been particularly good at arithmetic, which had not formed a great part of the girls' Sunday school education, so she would wait until William came home and ask him to add it all up.

While she waited, she picked up William's spare shirt from the mending basket. She hadn't yet managed to source any new local clients for sewing – she would have to get on to that, squeezing in some hours of mending each evening when she got home from the laundry – but her own family provided plenty to be getting on with. They might have come down in the world in terms of their living space, but she refused to see them in rags if she could help it. Besides, any slim chance that might still remain of William getting a clerking job would rely on him looking smart as well as being clever. Such jobs were for *respectable* young men, and Delilah was going to make sure he remained among that class, at least as far as clean shirts and un-frayed cuffs were concerned.

As she stitched, her mind turned to the missing member of the family.

Ellen had told Delilah more about Ma's last moments. Her final words about the baby whose birth had killed her had apparently been, 'She looks like Jem, bless her,' and Delilah had been able to see the resemblance herself in the sweet, contented little face as she rocked the baby in her arms throughout that dreadful night. In the absence of any instructions left by Ma, or any interest at all from Pa, Delilah had decided to call the baby Jemima. But what to do with her was the question; they couldn't feed her and she would soon die without proper care. Delilah felt a fierce, protective love for the tiny scrap that was all they had left of Ma, and didn't want to let her out of her sight, but she knew that her own first duty was to keep Jemima alive. With a tearing sense of loss she therefore agreed to Ellen's suggestion that she and James should take the baby in for now, finding a niece who was in milk to nurse her. To start with Delilah had seen this very much as a temporary measure, but as the weeks had gone by and their financial situation had worsened, the idea of having another mouth to feed, and one so fragile, had become more and more terrifying. Moreover, she could see how much Ellen doted on Jemima, her maternal feelings finally unleashed after all these years.

And the neighbours were financially better off, of course, thought Delilah, as she stabbed her needle through William's shirt with more vigour than necessary. Like Abraham, James Jenkins was an employee of one of the companies that owned a warehouse at the docks, so he worked and was paid all year round without the need to stand in line every morning trying to catch Mr Bradley's eye, or to wait for a ship to come in that needed unloading. With only a wife to support and no children, he had even managed to lay some money by, something almost unheard of in Brick Street and the subject of much gossip. When little Jemima was weaned, there would be good food for her to eat and a safe roof over her head. Delilah's heart tore in two at the thought, but she knew that Jemima was better off where she was. She longed to have her smallest sister with them, but if it was only to see her starve then it could not be done. Or at least not now.

But Delilah was allowed her daydreams, wasn't she? What if . . . ? Anyway, she would talk it over with

Ellen whenever she next got the chance to speak to her – she might be able to walk over there one Sunday while she wasn't at work.

Delilah began to hum as she sewed.

Her optimism was not allowed to last long, however, as any hopes of an upturn in their situation were dashed that evening. They all crowded round William as he went through what each of them was likely to earn compared with the cost of rent and food; he added it all up twice, just to be sure, and then shook his head. 'I'm sorry,' he said. 'If we're lucky then we might barely manage as we are, but no more than that.'

He started to point at the columns of figures, but Delilah interrupted him. 'Just tell us in words that we can all understand.'

'All right.' He thought to himself for a moment. 'If I get some work, if you keep working at the laundry every day and Sam can bring in his bit, we should be able to cover the rent as long as it doesn't go up. For us to have coals for the fire and anything to eat, I'll have to get work for at least part of every day. If we want to eat anything except plain bread or potatoes, I'll have to get work all day every day, the morning and the afternoon shift.' He paused, looking at the disappointed faces around him. 'And that doesn't account for any of us being ill, or for Pa spending anything at the pub or the gin shop.'

That was the killer blow, of course. Expecting Pa to spend nothing was unrealistic in the extreme; he was so deep in his cups these days that he'd moved on from beer to cheap, nasty gin that got him more drunk for less money. And he took every penny he could find to pay for it.

'We'll have to find somewhere to hide all our wages,' said Delilah, once the shock of William's words had worn off a little. 'We've got no upstairs here, so Pa can get round the whole place. If we're going to manage at all then we have to stop him taking it.'

She'd spoken while facing the smaller children, so Jem had been able to understand her. He tugged on her sleeve and pointed to the far corner of the room.

'What is it?' she asked, but she didn't need Sam this time to tell her what he meant. Jem pulled her over to the corner and then knelt down, scrabbling at the bare bricks of the wall. One of them was loose and he slid it right out; he pointed to the space it had left.

She kissed him. 'Well done, Jem.' She spoke seriously to all the others. 'None of you is to tell Pa about this, you understand? It's important. Promise me.'

They all gave their solemn word. 'Good. Now, Meg has saved some of the bread and jam we bought with Abraham's shilling, so let's sit down to it.'

There were only two chairs at the little table, so the girls perched precariously on the sofa while Sam and Jem sat on the floor. All was calm with Pa not around, and Delilah knew a brief moment of peace as she watched all her brothers and sisters eating. *No, not all*, she reminded herself – but one day maybe they would have Jemima too, and then what remained of the family would be together again.

\*   \*   \*

After that they fell into something of a routine. They got up early; William for his now much longer walk to the docks, Delilah to start at the laundry and Sam and Jem to scamper off to Lime Street. Pa, if he had bothered to come home at all the previous night, would still be snoring on the sofa. Delilah knew from Meg that he couldn't stand to be cooped up in the room, so he went out whenever he got up – though she didn't know where, or what he was doing, or how he kept getting the money to come home stinking of gin. All she knew was that his temper had got worse, and he was more volatile than ever.

Meg was now nearly thirteen, and Delilah would have to see about getting her a job too as soon as Rosie was old enough to be left in charge of Annie; but for now she'd have to stay at home. Besides, she was tiny and Mrs Baker at the laundry would take one look at her and laugh – great physical strength was needed to work there all day. So Meg looked after the little ones, kept the room as clean as she could and did the shopping and the cooking, such as it was. She did have the knack of making even a few boiled thrown-out vegetables taste like a decent meal, for which they were all grateful.

Work at the laundry was hard, even more laborious than Delilah had expected. A great deal of washing came in every day, for there were many better-off households in Liverpool who lived in townhouses; these were large enough to contain servants as well as family, but without the space for a dedicated laundry room. The mistresses – and no doubt the cooks and housekeepers – didn't want their nice places all hung round with wet linen so they merely stitched a distinguishing mark on every item and sent it all off, paying for the convenience of having it returned washed, dried and ironed without them having to go anywhere near a tub.

Mrs Baker wouldn't keep her business if her customers weren't satisfied, so her standards were extremely high. Every batch that came in was carefully sorted to separate the wool and other delicate fabrics from the rest, and then treated accordingly in different parts of the laundry. As a new employee Delilah was not trusted with anything other than the cotton and linen, the least specialist work but the heaviest labour. On a rolling schedule everything that came in was checked and treated for any bad stains; it was then all put in to soak before being squeezed through a wringer and then transferred to another tub filled with hot soapy water. There each item had to be kneaded and pounded to release the dirt, an exhausting task that made her back and shoulders scream at her. Then it went through the wringer again before being immersed in warm rinsing water, followed by a third wringing and then boiling in a copper for half a day. Mrs Baker then insisted on no fewer than three more rinses (in hot, warm and cold water), with blue added to the final rinse to avoid any yellowing of the whites.

What all this meant in practice was that Delilah spent her days in a blur of drawing, lugging and heating water, standing over steaming tubs, and pounding, wringing and carrying wet linen, all while getting soaked herself and trying not to be scalded. Somewhere in the laundry there would be the less messy work of drying, ironing and airing, or washing delicate lace, but she didn't see any of that. She staggered home each evening hardly able to stay on her feet, freezing and shivering as the chill air hit her wet clothes after the steamy heat of the tubs. Surely this was labour as hard as anything classed as 'men's work'? So why was it paid at less than a quarter of the rate?

Delilah generally had no time to worry about such matters, though, as more labour awaited her at home. The children wanted her time, of course, to tell her all about their own days, so she spent a precious hour with them. Once they were in bed she picked up her needle and began sewing, carrying on until the day's allocated candle or half-candle was finished, before an uncomfortable sleep on whatever chair or corner of the mattress she could commandeer until the morning came and it all started again.

But it still wasn't enough.

They spent money on nothing but rent, coals and food, but still their combined earnings wouldn't stretch. Then the rent went up, the excuse being that there was so much call for rooms, what with new immigrants arriving in Liverpool every week, that such a hovel was somehow 'worth' more than it had been last week. What it really meant, of course, was that the landlord could charge what he liked and nobody could complain or they'd find themselves out on the street.

Mr Bradley – who had somehow found them in their new abode – continued to call round at intervals to see Pa. Or, at least, that was his stated reason; whenever he was around he actually spent most of his time looking at Delilah, in a way that made her feel uncomfortable. It was he who suggested the idea of parish relief, noting that although what he called 'outdoor relief' had been abolished for able-bodied men and their families, they might qualify because of Pa being a cripple. What that meant in practice, Delilah learned, was that they could continue to live in their room but that the parish might give them money to help support themselves, just until the younger ones were old enough to bring in a wage.

Delilah, like most respectable working-class people, had a horror of 'charity', and to start with she wouldn't hear of it. But later, after Mr Bradley had gone, she had to weigh that feeling against the sight of the pinched, hollow faces all around her. She swallowed her pride and decided to apply.

The office wasn't open on Sundays, so it meant an afternoon away from work and the lost wages that would entail. Still, if it resulted in any help from the parish then the gamble would be worth it. Delilah told her story to a bored-looking man who agreed that a crippled widower *might* be eligible for outdoor relief, but he'd have to interview Pa himself and he'd need to visit their home, 'to check you don't have any assets that should be sold first, before you turn to the parish'.

How much would he expect them to do without, Delilah wondered, as she led him through the maze of alleys. Would they be allowed to keep their one remaining cooking pot? Bowls to eat from? Blankets for the bed? From his attitude she expected that he'd class pretty much anything except the clothes on their backs as 'luxuries' in order to avoid having to pay out. She'd already suffered the wrenching loss of pawning Ma's precious clock, and there wasn't much else left.

In the end, it didn't matter. The first thing that caught the official's eye as he stepped into their room was not any of their remaining possessions but Pa, snoring on the sofa in a fog of gin fumes. 'You called me out here,' he began, his voice incredulous, 'when you knew your father was a drunkard?'

She tried to make the best of it. 'He does like a drink, yes. But it's the children I'm worried about, sir. Four of us are out at work, labouring every hour, only my little sister left here' – for once she gave thanks for Meg's tiny stature as she hovered – 'to look after the two youngest. But without a breadwinner we can't put enough food on the table for everyone.'

The parish officer looked down his nose at her. 'A breadwinner, yes. A man is the head of his family and the household is judged on him. Your father may not be able to undertake manual labour,' he added, pointing to Pa's crutches, 'but he is making no effort to be respectable. If he were sober, and perhaps looking for any work that he could do even allowing for his condition, you might have a case; but, as it is, there is nothing I can do.'

He was about to leave, but Delilah stepped in front of him to bar his way. 'You mean, because Pa's drunk, his children have to starve?'

'That is precisely what I mean,' came the officious reply. 'His children are his responsibility, and if he can't stay sober enough to at least try to look after them, that's on his head. Good day to you.' He didn't exactly push her out of the way, but he walked deliberately forward, forcing her to move or have him run into her.

Delilah knew she should have more pride, but she tried one more desperate plea even as she was forced to move aside. 'And there's really nothing that the parish can do for us?'

He paused on the threshold. 'You're not entitled to outdoor relief, based on your circumstances, but indoor relief is open to you just the same as it is to everyone else.'

'I'm sorry, I don't understand what that means.'

'It means,' he threw over his shoulder as he stepped out, 'that you can seek admittance to the workhouse.'

* * *

From there it was all downhill. Delilah dragged herself to work every day, and so did William, who was growing gaunter and frailer-looking at every successive pre-dawn start. Meg became even quieter, Rosie and Annie cried with hunger, and even Sam and Jem seemed to lose some energy.

Delilah could feel herself becoming more and more irritable with them all as her exhaustion and hunger and guilt increased. William made what was probably meant to be a light-hearted comment about how things would be even worse if Jonny were still here, because at least now they were all on the same side, and she nearly bit his head off. Her furious reaction was, she knew, partly due to her own feelings of guilt; deep down, she too was relieved not to have Jonny's malevolent presence to deal with, and she grieved that she should feel that way about a dead brother.

Even the smaller children weren't immune from her fraying nerves. Sam, on looking one evening at the meagre slice of bread he'd been served up after his day on the streets, suggested quite seriously that he should go out and steal food or money, and she lost her temper entirely, boxing his ears and screeching words that she couldn't even remember later. And then, to top it all, one day she gave Meg some hard-earned and hard-saved coins to buy food only to come home and find that she'd lost half of it in the street. By that time Delilah didn't even have the energy to be angry; she just stared at the wall in silent hopelessness.

On top of this – and as if anything worse were needed – Delilah suspected that Pa was starting to be violent whenever she wasn't around. Meg, Sam and Jem all began to exhibit bruises that they tried to hide from her. If she could be in their room more often she might be able to prevent it – she was the one member of the household Pa still minded, occasionally, perhaps as he thought of her as taking Ma's place. But, of course, she couldn't be in the room because she had to be out at work earning money to put towards keeping the room. If she wasn't so tired she might laugh.

Delilah had put off and put off any thoughts about the parish officer's words, but as she looked around at her hollow-cheeked, battered family, she was forced to face it: the workhouse was now the better option. If they continued as they were, some or even all of the children were going to die, and it would all be her fault.

# Chapter Four

The chilly October day on which Delilah took Meg and Rosie to the workhouse was the worst of her life. Worse than the day Pa had his accident; worse even than the dreadful evening of Ma's death.

It was temporary, it wouldn't last for ever, and she would come and get them as soon as she could. That was what she kept repeating to herself all the way there, and what she told the severe-looking and evidently disbelieving matron to whom she signed them over. It was just for the winter, while she and William worked and saved and scraped to get the family finances back on track. She would come and get them in the spring, she promised. Until then, they wouldn't be able to see each other at all; the matron told Delilah that visits weren't permitted.

They had all entered the Receiving Room together, but soon it was time for Delilah to leave without her sisters. Rosie held on to Delilah until the last possible moment, but Meg stepped away in that buttoned-up way she had, refusing to be embraced, and Delilah didn't know which was worse.

Her own tears flowed as she stepped back out into the street, and she didn't care. She wouldn't be the first person who'd ever walked away from the workhouse crying, and she surely wouldn't be the last. Other people, she reminded herself, sent their children there during temporary periods without work or when times were particularly hard, and picked them up when finances allowed. Their life inside wouldn't exactly be a bed of roses, but they would be fed and they'd have a roof over their heads during the winter, which was more than she could guarantee her sisters at the moment. They would be able to look out for each other, too, kept together in way that wouldn't have been possible if she'd sent one boy and one girl; Sam, as Delilah might have expected, had resolutely volunteered to go along with Meg, but she'd refused on the grounds that they'd be separated anyway – and besides, they needed the pennies he brought in.

She, too, would be resolute. Her little brother and sisters had shown a bravery that could not be matched, but the least that Delilah could do was work to deserve them. She would work and she would wash and she would sew. She would even take on Pa and get him to mend his ways, insofar as that might be possible at this stage.

Unlike any of the younger children, Delilah could actually feel a glimmer of sympathy for Pa. She could understand, as they perhaps could not, that his work at the docks had been his identity, his dignity – his manhood, even. Being the breadwinner who came home with money and doled it out to his wife for the maintenance of his children was a source of pride and a marker of his status. And that had all been taken away from him in a matter of moments through no fault of his own. During the long weeks of his recovery it had become ever clearer to Pa that a return to labouring was a door that was shut to him for ever. Was it any wonder that he brooded, that he turned to drink, that he sought out the company of other men once he was able to move around, even if they could now only be found in pubs and on street corners rather than at work?

Of course, Delilah's sympathy only went so far. Pa's accident had caused hardship for all of them, not just him, and surely one marker of a man was how he responded to adversity? Perhaps if he'd tried to focus on what he *could* do, rather than what he couldn't, life might have been better. It certainly would have been an improvement if they'd been able to keep all the money they earned to feed the children, rather than having him claim it to take to the gin shop.

These were the thoughts that filled Delilah's mind as she made her way down Brownlow Hill, but gradually she became aware of a commotion in front of her. A group of boys had surrounded a girl and were pushing and teasing her. As she tried to get away from them her shawl slipped from her head, revealing a wealth of beautiful copper-coloured hair, and this only seemed to encourage them more; Delilah could hear shouts of 'Paddy' and other, less polite, terms that the local youths used for the Irish immigrants.

Delilah was exhausted, she was distraught about having just left her sisters in the workhouse, and she was fairly sure the boys were just passing the time of day and would soon get distracted by something or someone else. A small part of her just wanted to walk on by. But that wouldn't be right. How could she possibly leave a girl in distress like that?

Delilah moved towards the group, assessing them with an experienced Liverpudlian eye. The girl was about her own age, the boys younger and presumably out of work or having not secured any for the morning. In fact, one or two of them looked familiar.

Confidence was the thing. Delilah took in a deep breath and tried to imagine that she was Ma. 'Stop that, all of you!' she cried out as she barrelled into the melee. 'You should be ashamed of yourselves, acting like that on a public street!'

The crucial element of surprise was on her side, and they had all drawn back from the girl in consternation before they realised that Delilah was not, in fact, a hefty Liverpool matron. But by then it was too late; she had them. 'And you, Jack Smith, you get away from here right now before I tell your Ma and Pa what you've been up to. They're respectable people and you'll get the belt if they hear you've been causing trouble.'

The boy in question had already taken a step backwards; sensing his weakness, the others now turned on him instead of the girl, mocking him, 'Ooh, what will your Ma say?' He tried to regain his standing by making out that he was minding Delilah only out of respect for her family; she heard whispers about 'Jonny's sister . . . their Pa . . .' but it didn't matter. They were melting away from the girl and soon they were gone, off to find an easier target to alleviate their boredom.

Delilah turned to the girl. 'Are you all right?'

She was wary. 'I'm well, thank you.' Then, as she realised it really was over and became a little more confident, the hint of a smile appeared. 'That was a fine thing to see, truly.'

Despite everything, Delilah found herself returning the smile. 'They like to think they're tough at that age, but they're still manageable if you go about it the right way. It's the grown men you have to look out for.'

'Well, I wasn't managing very well, so I'm grateful to you.'

Her accent, as well as the hair, gave away that she was an Irish immigrant, but Delilah didn't want to say anything too direct in case it looked unwelcoming. 'You're . . . new in town?'

The girl nodded, self-consciously drawing the shawl back up over her hair. 'As you can tell, I'm sure. We've not been here long and I still don't know my way around. I'm supposed to be looking for the railway station, but I got lost.'

'I can take you there – I have to pass it on my way home.'

'Really? That would be so kind. You don't mind walking with me?'

'Of course not,' replied Delilah. 'You're a Liverpool girl now, just like me, and we stick together.'

The smile came again, the hint of a dimple. 'A Liverpool girl. Well, maybe I will be.' She held out her hand. 'My name's Bridget. Bridget O'Malley.'

Delilah took it. 'Delilah Shaw.'

'Oh, what a beautiful name! Is it unusual here?'

They began to walk as they continued the conversation. 'I suppose it is,' said Delilah. 'I've never met anyone else called Delilah, and most other names you hear a lot.' She shrugged. 'I suppose it was just my Ma being all romantic about her firstborn, before she settled down to more regular names.'

'You're the eldest in your family, then?' Bridget let out a sigh. 'I can't imagine what that's like.'

'Do you have family too? You didn't come over from Ireland on your own, surely?'

'Alone? Oh, I've never been alone in my life. My father's dead, God rest him, but I've a mother and eight older brothers.'

Delilah paused mid-stride. '*Eight*? I wonder you ever have trouble on the street with all of them to look out for you.'

'They're not all here – the oldest four are married, and they all went to America before the famine really started to bite. The rest of us held on as long as we could, but we had to give up in the end so we came here. I don't know if we'll all stay for ever, but the boys are out looking for work to support us.'

Delilah couldn't help a brief twinge of jealousy at the thought of a household bringing in four adult male wages, but that was unworthy, she knew. Why, poor Bridget had had to leave *everything* behind her. Never to see her home again, her friends gone, half her brothers on the other side of the world. She'd sailed across the sea to escape what all the newspapers agreed was the deadliest hunger in hundreds of years. Some of those arriving in Liverpool were no more than walking skeletons, and there were tales of men, women and children lying dead of starvation in every village in Ireland.

'It's my brother Frank I'm supposed to be meeting at the station,' continued Bridget. 'He's the youngest apart from me. I think I'm late, so he'll be worried.'

'Worried? Not angry?'

Bridget laughed. 'Frank? Angry? No – any of the others, maybe, but Frank's been laughing since the day he was born.'

Delilah's only answer was a sigh.

'Anyway,' said Bridget, 'here I am talking about myself. What about you? You said you were the oldest? Do you have sisters as well as brothers? Oh, I'd love a sister.'

Suddenly, everything went blurry and started to spin. Delilah put out a hand to the nearest wall to support herself and realised that tears were pouring down her cheeks.

'Oh!' cried Bridget. 'Oh, have I said something wrong? I'm so sorry – I didn't mean to upset you, and you've been so kind.' She put out a concerned hand.

'It's all right,' managed Delilah, after another minute. 'It's just – when you said "sisters" . . .'

'Did you lose one recently?' asked Bridget, in a gentle tone. 'I'm so sorry for your loss.'

'Not exactly.' Delilah knew she'd only just met this girl, but she had no other female friend to talk to, to confide in, and certainly not one of her own age; and Bridget's manner was so mild that Delilah couldn't help sobbing and gulping out the story of how she'd just had to leave two of her little sisters in the workhouse.

Bridget stood thunderstruck. 'You mean – you'd just been through all that, and then you still stopped in the street to help me, a stranger?'

Delilah nodded, trying to stop crying for long enough to breathe. 'I couldn't walk on by and leave you.'

Bridget shook her head in disbelief. 'Why, that's the most . . .' She took Delilah's hand and looked into her eyes. 'That's the kindest thing anyone's ever done for me, and I'll never forget it, I swear.'

'Oh, it was only chasing off a few boys,' Delilah wiped the back of her hand across her face and attempted to stand upright. 'Now, come on, or your brother will worry.'

'Here, hold on to me,' said Bridget, looping Delilah's arm through her own. 'You show me where the railway station is, and then Frank and me, we'll walk you home to make sure you get there safely.'

'Oh, I couldn't . . .' began Delilah, weakly.

'We're Liverpool girls, remember?' was Bridget's firm reply. 'And we stick together.'

It wasn't long before they reached the wide expanse of Lime Street and the entrance to the railway station. Delilah had never been inside it, but she had sometimes heard the hissing, steaming and whistling of the monstrous engines that travelled so miraculously without horses. The railway enabled goods to be brought in and out of Liverpool, and people too; you could get on a train and be in faraway places before sundown of the same day. Manchester, Leeds, even London . . . places she would never see, but which seemed somehow closer thanks to the wonders of the modern world.

A young man was standing still among the throng of moving figures, casting anxious glances about him. Bridget called out as they approached, and he caught sight of her and waved. His hair wasn't quite of the lustrous copper shade of his sister's, and he was thin, but he was handsome – startlingly so, as Delilah could see as he drew nearer, with wiry muscles, a chiselled jaw and bright, intelligent eyes that seemed to laugh at the world around him. She became suddenly aware that her skirt was dusty and her face covered in tracks of tears and no doubt grime from the street as well.

Frank had smiled on first spotting Bridget, but as he took in the two of them and their slow gait his face assumed a concerned expression and he hurried over. 'Bridget? Are you all right? And . . .' He looked at Delilah, who couldn't hold his bright gaze for more than a moment and dropped her eyes to the ground.

'This is my new friend, Frank.' Delilah stood awkwardly while Bridget explained what had happened to her and how Delilah had come to her rescue. Then she stood on tiptoe to whisper a few more words into her brother's ear, of which Delilah caught 'sisters' and 'workhouse'. She felt herself blushing.

Frank waited until Bridget had finished before turning to Delilah. He took off his cap. 'Francis O'Malley, miss, at your service,' he said, with an extravagant flourish. Then, more seriously, 'I can't thank you enough for what you've done today. Your kindness to my sister—'

'Oh, it was nothing, really, just what anyone . . .'

'Good fortune,' he said firmly, 'is not something my sister has known a lot of these past couple of years, but it's come her way today. And for you to show such kind-heartedness to a stranger, at such a time for yourself? You're on the side of the angels.'

Oddly, Delilah couldn't seem to frame a suitable reply. After a moment's awkward silence she wiped at her face. 'Oh, I must look such a mess!'

'It's how you look on the inside that counts, that's what our Mam always says.' He gave her a mischievous look and smiled. 'Besides, you're not too bad on the outside, either – and with those beautiful green eyes you could easily be an Irish girl yourself.'

Delilah was saved from having to make a reply by feeling a tug at her arm. She glanced down to see Jem, who pointed at her face and then ran his fingers down his own to simulate tears. He looked questioningly at her.

'Off with you, boy,' said Frank, but with good humour rather than malice. 'This is a private conversation.'

'Oh,' interrupted Delilah, quickly. 'This is my brother Jem. He works for one of the bootblacks here.'

'Oh, a little brother, is it? Well, I know *all* about being one of those.' Frank grinned down and was a little taken aback to be met by a blank face.

'He can't hear you,' explained Delilah.

The most common reactions, whenever she told people that, were either for them to simply dismiss Jem's presence and talk about him as though he wasn't there, or to step back in surprise as though they could somehow catch his affliction. But Frank did neither of

73

these things. Instead he crouched, so that his face was on a level with Jem's, and mouthed something to him silently. He had his back to Delilah so she couldn't catch what it was, but Jem grinned and nodded in agreement.

'He said, "Your sister's pretty, isn't she?"' came another voice. 'Who is he, anyway?'

Frank looked from Jem to the newly arrived Sam, who was leaning on his broom with a belligerent expression. 'Another brother?' he queried. 'Though not very alike, to be sure.'

'Sam,' said Sam, shortly. 'But you didn't answer my question.' He looked at Delilah. 'You all right?'

'I'm fine,' she replied, wiping her eyes again. 'I just got back from . . . you know.'

Sam's own lip wobbled, and Delilah felt Bridget squeeze her hand in sympathy.

'Well now,' said Frank. 'You probably don't need too much looking after with these fine young men in your family, but if they've got to get back to work then perhaps you'd allow my sister and me to escort you home.' He raised his eyebrows at Sam. 'With your permission.'

Sam's chest expanded. 'If Delilah says it's all right.'

'I'll see you both later,' she said, fondly, kissing her finger and placing it on Jem's cheek.

Bridget took Delilah's arm as they crossed the busy street, and Delilah felt the comfort of her company, even if it was only for a short while. They slowed their pace as they reached St John's market, not going inside the huge building but dawdling a little by the less formal stalls and baskets outside.

'Is it a good way to make a living, do you think?' asked Bridget. 'A lot of the sellers seem to be women.'

'I suppose it depends what you sell, how much demand there is to buy it, and how much you spend on it yourself.'

'Goodness, you've a head for business and no mistake.'

Delilah shrugged. 'It's partly from working with my Ma when she was taking in laundry; if you spend more on soap and starch and coals than you can get for doing the washing, there's not much point.' She hesitated before adding something on a subject close to her heart, again surprised at how much she was opening up, how much she needed another girl to talk to. 'And I'd love to have a stall myself one day, or even work in a shop.'

'What would you sell?'

'Flowers,' said Delilah, without a moment's hesitation.

'Oh, that would be nice, wouldn't it? A fine thing to be surrounded by flowers all day.'

'Yes,' said Delilah, sighing as reality intruded once more. 'But it's just a dream.'

They were silent for a while. As the streets they passed through became gradually shabbier and they neared the entrance to the back alleys, Delilah began to feel reluctant to have Bridget and Frank accompany her all the way home.

'It's fine, really, I can make my own way from here,' she said, at last.

Frank, who had left them to it while they were chatting about markets and flowers, now broke in. 'Delilah – I can call you Delilah, can't I, if you're my little sister's friend? – if the reason you don't want us with you is because you're somehow ashamed of where you live, then don't be.'

'We live in a crowded court off a back alley,' added Bridget. 'It's busy and dirty, nothing like the countryside back home, but that's where we are.'

'Ours is maybe not one of the worst,' said Delilah, 'but it's still not very nice. I haven't come across the sea like you, only across town, but it's all so different from what we're used to.' She thought of their one room, of Meg and of Rosie . . . but, strangely, her despair had started to turn to something else: determination. 'We won't be there for ever.'

'I like your style,' said Frank. 'Good for you. We won't be in ours for ever, either.' He took on a grand tone. 'I intend to make my fortune and to keep my mother and sister in the manner to which they would like to become accustomed.'

'Oh, Frank, you do talk such nonsense,' said Bridget, though Delilah could tell that she said it with affection.

'And so, Delilah,' continued Frank in the same half-playful way. 'Do allow us both to escort you home. It would be an honour.' And then, in a more normal voice. 'Besides, it would be good for us – for Bridget, I mean, to know where you are, in case she wants to pay a social call on you any day.'

Delilah smiled at Bridget. 'That would be lovely. I do get lonely sometimes, despite having so many people around me. It would have to be a Sunday, though – that's the only day I'm not at work.' She made a face. 'I only managed to get half a day off today because I begged and because Mrs Baker knows I'm a good worker who can get the stains out of anything. I have to be back there in a couple of hours for the afternoon.'

'Well, a Sunday it shall be, then,' said Bridget.

They had been continuing on their way as they were speaking, and it wasn't long before they found themselves at the narrow entrance to their court. With a grimace, Delilah led the way in and over to the house in which their room was situated. She hesitated on the threshold, knowing that it would be a new and different experience coming back to find the place empty. Meg was quiet, but she had always been there when Delilah got home from work, ready with a fire going so she could have a cup of tea to warm herself. And little Rosie was normally skipping about somewhere too. But now there was nobody: the boys were out, Annie was with a neighbour for the day, and Meg and Rosie were . . .

Delilah stepped inside the house and opened their door.

The room was certainly cold, with no fire in the grate, but it wasn't empty. Pa was there, and as Delilah came in he struggled up off the broken sofa.

By the time he was upright on his crutches he had noticed the others. 'Who are they?' he slurred at Delilah. Then, in an angrier tone, 'What you doing bringing people back here? And who's he? You got a fancy man?'

He was sweating and shaking, probably because he *hadn't* yet had a drink today; he'd reached the stage where only more alcohol could calm him down. Looking on the positive side, that meant he hadn't found the hidden money – if he had, he'd be out at the gin shop already.

Delilah was both embarrassed and afraid for the safety of her new friends as Pa thrust himself forward, waving one of his crutches at Frank. 'You get out, you hear?'

'I beg your pardon, sir,' said Frank. 'Your daughter helped my sister on the street, and we just wanted to make sure she got home safely.'

He'd been as polite as could be, but Delilah winced, knowing what was going to come next. 'Irish!' thundered Pa. 'You're letting Irish scum here, into my home?' He turned on Delilah.

'Pa, be reasonable,' she attempted.

But it was no use. 'Coming over here. Taking our jobs at the docks! I used to get regular work before all these Paddies came in, and now you're bringing them home?'

He managed to raise one hand to her. She knew he would be off balance, and it would be relatively easy to avoid the blow, but Frank was quicker. He stepped forward and caught Pa's arm. 'Now, sir,' he said in a tone that was calm but firm, 'nobody here has taken your job, and if somebody else has then it's not your daughter's fault, is it?'

Despite the accident – or perhaps because of it, now that he had to use crutches – Pa's arms had remained strong. He wrenched himself free but then collapsed back on to the sofa again, shouting obscenities.

'I . . . I think it would be better if you left,' said Delilah, aware that her face was scarlet. 'I'm so sorry.'

She could have cried with rage and frustration. Just for once, a nice thing had happened – she'd met a couple of people who were friendly and pleasant, a bright comforting spot in a cold, cruel world. Couldn't she even have that? Couldn't she have *one half-hour* of something that had verged on cheer? Pa had ruined it all.

'You'll know best,' was Frank's reply.

'Don't worry about us, not at all,' said Bridget, taking Delilah's hand once more. 'Everyone's father has their off days, and we've all had the same. I'll hope to see you again soon, if you like?'

Delilah could only nod, unable to bring herself to speak further, and they both turned to the door. She was ready to burst with shame that her new friends had been treated so. Bridget's expressed hope of seeing her again was surely just a polite fiction; they would step out of the door now and she'd never see either of them again.

But as they left, brother and sister both paused. Bridget smiled in the sweet, gentle way that already seemed familiar, saying, 'I won't forget your kindness'; and Frank, with an impudent grin that made Delilah's heart flutter, winked at her.

# Chapter Five

Delilah had little time to think of either Frank or Bridget during the next couple of weeks, because earning enough money to enable the family to bring Meg and Rosie home became her overwhelming preoccupation. The days grew shorter; it was dark when she left for work in the morning and dark when she got home. The many hours in between were spent in endless rounds of washing, wringing, pounding, boiling and rinsing interspersed with the additional hard labour of changing and heating the water. In the evenings, after she'd staggered home to a cold, dark room and provided everybody with whatever food she'd managed to find and prepare, she took up her needle and sewed until the day's allocated candle guttered and went out.

Delilah had no time to herself, no energy, no enjoyment in her life. But it didn't matter; nothing did except money, the money that would bring their girls home, in the form of the pitiful stack of coins handed to her by Mrs Baker every Saturday evening. The first challenge was making sure it all actually reached home; everyone knew that Saturday was payday, and there were even more suspicious characters lurking around street corners than usual. If William had finished his own work before Delilah, he would come to meet her at the laundry so they could walk home together past the yawning mouths of the dark alleys and courts.

In order to prevent herself from having too much time to think, Delilah made sure that any spare moments were also filled with work. She kept every surface of their room scrubbed and clean, and then turned her attention to the outside part of the court.

The main problem, of course, was the privies. The two earth closets were shared by the inhabitants of every room in the court's ten houses, which meant that they were perennially filthy and overflowing. They hadn't been emptied in all the weeks that Delilah and her family had lived in the court, and the waste matter was now starting to ooze out across the stone flags. Disgusting as this was, it could get even worse; the stinking slime was getting nearer and nearer to the pump that stood in the middle of the court, and which was their only source of water for drinking and washing. Some of it must even be dripping through the cracks in the flags into the water itself. This did not appear to be bothering most of the court's residents, but Delilah would be damned if she let her younger siblings sink to the level of drinking water that was contaminated with excrement.

She began by knocking on doors and speaking to other women, from whom she learned that a shared responsibility was in effect nobody's responsibility at all: if the privies weren't their own, they saw no reason to clean them, and there was no duty or rota of any kind. Well, Delilah would see about that. If maintaining her own family in a state of decency, respectability and good health meant cleaning up after everyone else, then so be it. But Delilah would use her head as well as her hands. Back at their old house the privy – shared only with three other houses, each of which contained a single family – had been emptied regularly by some kind of office or department run by the city. Surely the city must have a similar responsibility here, where it was more crowded and the situation more urgent?

The laundry workers stopped for a break at midday every day, and Delilah spent her next few dinnertimes on a determined traipse around the city to find out. Her efforts were rewarded when she discovered that she could indeed apply to something called the Nuisance Department, who would arrange for the privies to be emptied and the waste carted away.

Two days after that, Delilah returned home to find the carts just leaving and herself the talk of the court. She looked about her in the dim light: there was still a layer of filth covering everything, but at least now it was a manageable amount. By the time dawn broke the following morning she had scrubbed the water pump and the surrounding flags until they shone. She had to leave it in order to go to work, but she went straight back to it in the dark when she got home, slowly working her way outwards from the pump and towards the privies themselves.

It was another pre-dawn start the following morning, but just as Delilah dropped on to on the stone flags she heard footsteps and the sound of another bucket being put down.

An older woman whose name she didn't know was cautiously lowering herself to her knees. 'Not right for you to do it on your own, love.'

Delilah smiled in the darkness as they worked side by side until it was time for her to leave for the laundry.

\*   \*   \*

The next time Delilah saw the court in daylight was a Sunday morning, and she was pleased with the results of her efforts. The privies would fill up again, of course, but now everyone knew they could call on the Nuisance Department so hopefully the situation wouldn't reach such a dire point, especially if an effort were made to keep them clean in the meantime. And the important thing was that no filth was anywhere near the drinking water; the pump shone brightly and the flags around it were white and clean as the court's horde of small children skipped about.

Delilah was just pausing to take in the air and watch the children play when Bridget and Frank appeared. They waved when they spotted her and strolled over.

Almost without thinking, Delilah appraised her own appearance, happy that she didn't look bedraggled from work. She'd even found time to comb her lustrous black hair that morning; it would never be as light and interesting a colour as Bridget's, but Delilah need not be ashamed to stand next to her, at least.

Frank's bright eyes caught Delilah's, and she felt a little thrill of joy. *Calm down*, she told herself. *He's only smiling at you because you're his little sister's friend.* But she could enjoy the moment anyway, couldn't she? Nobody could take that away from her.

'Are any of these yours?' asked Bridget, as she looked at the playing children.

'Only this one,' replied Delilah, scooping up a giggling bundle in her arms and kissing her. 'This is Annie. She'll be three next February.'

'Well, hello, Annie,' said Bridget. 'Aren't you a little darling? And aren't you lucky to have such a sister?'

'Delighted to make your acquaintance, miss,' said Frank, sweeping into a bow that made Annie laugh and Bridget tell him not to be silly. 'Your brothers that we met before will be too grown-up to be playing here, I expect?'

'They're not as grown-up as all that, but yes, they're used to running around the streets so they don't like to be cooped up here.'

'You've quite a gap between yourself and the others, haven't you? Not like us – Mam squeezing us out regular every year or two until she saw Bridget here and decided to give up.'

'Oh no, there are others – or there were – what I mean is . . .' Delilah tailed off.

Frank looked abashed. 'Of course. I forgot about your two sisters who are on a temporary visit. I'm sorry if . . .'

'It's all right.' Delilah forced herself to meet his eye. 'Temporary, as you say, and then we'll have them back. And I've another brother, William, the next in age after me – he's inside studying.'

'Studying?' Frank sounded surprised, but not in a mocking way.

'Yes. He used to go to school, and he still has some of his books. We've no paper or pens, but he reads as much as he can.'

'Well, good for him. He's a man determined to better himself, I can see.'

There was a slightly awkward pause. Delilah would have liked to introduce William to her friends, but she was aware that Pa was inside the room; he'd been snoring when she came outside, but he might wake at any moment and she certainly didn't want a repeat of the scene of a couple of weeks ago.

Bridget noticed her hesitation. 'Well, now, and shall we not all go for a Sunday walk while the weather is fine?'

Delilah was immediately taken with the idea, but it seemed so frivolous: an hour of nothing but pleasure! But why should she not? The children were all busy for now, the mending she had in hand wasn't much and could be done this afternoon, and her choosing to be miserable wouldn't make one jot of difference to Meg and Rosie. Yes, yes, she would.

She made as if to put Annie down, but little arms were fastened about her neck. 'No, Lilah! Stay here.'

'Well, didn't we say?' interrupted Frank, before Delilah could say anything. 'You're invited too. It will be a treat for me to escort *three* such lovely ladies.'

Annie squeaked in delight and they all set off, Delilah carrying her little sister as they made their way through the alleys and out on to the main road.

'Are we going anywhere in particular?' asked Delilah.

'Ah, there's nowhere green round here, is there?' said Frank. 'That's what I miss most. But we'll go and walk round the finest, widest streets.'

They set off, Delilah enjoying the chill but fresh air on her face after spending most of her week indoors. It was a fine autumn day and she turned her face to the sun as it reached down into the wider streets. The shops were all shut, of course, on a Sunday, but there were a few street sellers about and Frank bought a bag of roasted chestnuts for them all to share, peeling the first one and handing it to Annie.

Delilah would rather have died than admitted how hungry she was, so she selected one from the bag when offered it and tried to pretend it wasn't the only thing she'd be eating until the evening.

'A luxury, my good man,' joked Bridget, in the tone Frank sometimes used.

'Well, there will be more where that came from, dear sister, once I've started my new job.'

'Oh, you've found work?' asked Delilah. 'I'm pleased for you. Where? At the docks?'

'Now, you see,' said Frank, peeling another chestnut for Annie, '*that* is why you are one of the nicest girls in Liverpool. Not everyone likes to see an Irishman taking work. Some get quite angry about it.'

'I'm not one of them,' replied Delilah, firmly, wondering if he was making an allusion to the reception he'd got from Pa. 'Anyone who wants to work should be able to, that's what I say.'

Bridget squeezed her arm. 'He's not going to be at the docks, though. Tell her, Frank.'

'I,' said Frank, drawing himself up to his full height, 'am going to be an employee of the Liverpool and Manchester Railway Company.' He laughed. 'Sounds very fancy, doesn't it? I'm going to be a porter, carrying bags around and no doubt getting shouted at for not being quick enough. But it's work, and it's the start of the upturn in my fortunes, I can feel it.'

'And,' added Bridget, 'it comes with a very smart uniform.'

'Oh yes,' said Frank. 'All the ladies will be coming after me in my uniform, don't you know. I'll be fighting off the duchesses with a stick.'

Delilah joined in their laughter, thinking to herself that he really *would* look handsome in a uniform, but not daring to spoil the atmosphere by saying it. They were obviously only joking, probably in a way they did all the time when they were together. She sighed to herself. What must it be like to have a sibling so close in age and temperament?

By now they were walking down Dale Street, and Delilah paused when they reached the flower shop. It was closed and empty, but she fancied that she could still smell the lingering fragrance of yesterday's flowers. She inhaled deeply and made a wish. *One day . . .*

She changed the subject as they moved on, to take her mind off the yearning. 'And have any of your other brothers found work? I think you said they were all looking?'

Frank's face clouded over for a moment. 'They've found some ways of making money, yes.'

'I'm sure they'll find something better as we go on,' said Bridget, soothingly. Delilah assumed that the others had only been able to get employ in trades they found demeaning, so she didn't ask further, not wanting to upset her friends or spoil what was the most pleasant morning she'd spent in a long while.

'There is a big open park out to the side of town,' said Frank, his good humour returning, 'but it's probably too far to go today, especially for this little lady.' He gave Annie the last chestnut. 'You must be tired, carrying her like that. Will she come to me, to you think?'

Annie was delighted to be placed on Frank's shoulder, and they all walked along side by side, Delilah with a lighter step and arm in arm with Bridget. She kept an eye on Annie, but despite Frank's constant stream of witticisms and light-hearted remarks he was concentrating enough to hold on to the little girl with care.

They wandered past some of Liverpool's great houses, eventually making a circle back towards the centre of the town. They passed the ornate Adelphi Hotel, a place so grand that Delilah didn't even dare to try for a peek inside. Frank loitered for a moment but was happy for the girls to hurry him on once the imposingly-uniformed doorman took a step towards them.

'Not for the likes of us,' said Frank, not sounding as though he regretted it in the least. 'The streets, however, are public property and we may walk along here just like the highest in the land.'

He continued in a similar vein until they passed the railway station, to which he blew a kiss. 'And I'll be back to see you tomorrow morning, my darling – make sure you're there waiting for me.'

The streets became narrower, the shops shabbier, and Delilah was nearly home.

As they neared the entrance that led off Gerard Street and into the maze of alleys, a tall, rough-looking young man detached himself from a group and approached them. Delilah had a moment's apprehension, but his face bore just enough resemblance to Frank's to make it unsurprising when Bridget greeted him.

'My brother Gideon,' she explained to Delilah.

'Very pleased to meet you,' said Delilah. He probably wasn't that much older than Frank, and there was a slight physical similarity, but now she could see him at close quarters she got the feeling they were nothing like each other in character.

He did little more than grunt at first, but when Bridget mentioned Delilah's name he looked at her sharply. 'The one who helped our Bridget in the street when she was lost?' He nodded. 'We owe you.'

Delilah had no time to reply before he turned to Frank. 'Michael sent me to find you. Needs you for this afternoon.'

'I'm not his errand boy any m—' began Frank, in a tone Delilah hadn't heard from him before. Then he stopped, recovered himself, and added more mildly, 'And I'll be along as soon as I can. We have to walk Delilah home first.'

'Oh, I can manage perfectly well,' began Delilah, starting to reach out to take Annie.

'No,' rumbled Gideon, after a short pause. 'Like I said, we owe you, so Frank'll see you home safe. Bridget, come with me now, home to Mam so I know where you are before we set out.'

'I'll see you again soon, I hope,' said Bridget, squeezing Delilah's arm before she dropped it.

'I hope so too,' replied Delilah.

She watched Bridget and Gideon turn before making her way into the alleys with Frank. He seemed much less disposed to talk than he had been earlier, so she didn't bother him with chatter.

They both slowed as they reached the entrance to her court. Delilah had no idea if Pa would be at home or not, but she didn't want to risk it. 'I'll be fine from here.' She took Annie back from him, but now she was home Annie didn't want to be held, and she ran off to play with the other girls in the court.

Frank mustered one last burst of levity. 'Fine from here? What, with no footman or maid, nor pageboy neither?'

She smiled. 'Yes, without any of them. We Liverpool girls are made of strong stuff.'

'Aren't you just,' he said, cryptically, before doffing his cap with a flourish. 'Until next time, my lady.'

'Until then.' She could feel the smile remaining on her lips as she watched his departing back, and it stayed there until long after he'd disappeared from sight.

\* \* \*

When Delilah entered their room it was to find that Pa was inside with Mr Bradley.

'Ah, there she is,' slurred Pa from the middle of a fog of gin fumes. 'Grown into a fine-looking girl, hasn't she?'

'She certainly has,' replied Mr Bradley, observing Delilah from over the top of a glass of his own. His eyes lingered on her, looking her up and down, and he licked his lips.

Delilah wanted very much to ask him to leave, but she couldn't: William's chances of getting work on any given day depended entirely on Mr Bradley's goodwill, so she couldn't risk antagonising him. It was another frustration that made her want to scream, but as there was no avoiding it she would just have to deal with it. So she forced an insincere smile on to her face and made to pass them in order to reach the grate. 'Time to get something on the fire for the children's dinner.'

The room wasn't very large, and Mr Bradley didn't have to move in order to put out an arm to bar her way. 'Oh, no hurry, surely. Why don't you sit down and join us?'

He was, Delilah was sure, acting more drunk than he really was, but that only made the situation more difficult. 'The women in our family don't like to drink,' she managed, diplomatically, while trying to slip away from his grasp.

But he wasn't ready to let the subject drop as easily as all that. 'Now then, no need to be so unwelcoming.' His tone changed, ever so slightly. 'Especially when I've come round to check that your Pa's getting on all right.'

Delilah looked at Pa, who was downing whatever was left in the bottom of a bottle. It hadn't been in the house when she left, so Mr Bradley must have brought it round and let Pa help himself to most of it. He was now roaring drunk and on the way to oblivion, which meant that Delilah and Mr Bradley were effectively alone in the room.

'That's very kind of you,' Delilah replied, still trying to make her attempted move away from him look natural. 'I'm sure he's grateful for your attention.'

'Are *you*, though?' he asked, standing up and moving rather closer to her than she liked.

'I'm grateful to all our old friends. It's nice to know Pa's years of hard work haven't been forgotten.'

'Oh, I don't forget anything,' said Mr Bradley in a low voice. 'I remember who's been kind to me and who hasn't . . . especially when it comes to picking men for work. So many men and boys, and not nearly enough labouring to go round at the moment.'

His implication could hardly be clearer, and Delilah was in an agony of indecision. She wanted nothing more than to push him away from her, to shove him out the door and tell him never to come back, but William's future – their income – the roof over their heads – depended on this man's favour.

She could feel his breath on her face.

Delilah was saved from doing something unfortunate by the door bursting open. Mr Bradley had jumped away from her before either of them realised that it was only Sam and Jem barrelling in, but the moment had been broken and she could think more clearly.

'You must be hungry, boys,' she said. 'And I'm behindhand – I haven't even lit the fire yet!'

Mr Bradley, with what Delilah saw to be some effort, attempted joviality. 'Ah, another couple of Shaws. You'll be looking for work too one day, I suppose.' He paused. 'Well, one of you, anyway.' He gave Jem a look that mingled pity, horror and contempt.

Sam's eyes narrowed. 'I've already got a job.' He folded his arms.

Mr Bradley was so taken aback by being spoken to like that – and by a boy less than half his size – that

Delilah could almost have laughed at his expression. She turned to the fire to hide her face.

'Well, I must be going.' Mr Bradley straightened his coat and stroked the chain of his fob watch. 'A hearty Sunday dinner awaits.' He looked meaningfully at the small dish of unaccompanied potatoes that Delilah had put ready.

She hoped and prayed that he would just walk out, but she was not to have such luck. He leaned in to speak in her ear. 'If your little brother there ever does want proper work at the docks, you'd better train him to improve his attitude.' He moved even closer, his lips brushing her hair. 'And yours.'

She said nothing, standing rigidly until he turned away. He walked out, Sam and Jem looking daggers at him while Delilah tried to stop her hands from shaking.

\* \* \*

The following morning was just like all the others that were starting to blur into each other. Delilah arose shivering in the dark and woke the others. She didn't light the fire; it wasn't worth the coals just for a hot cup of tea. There was some cold in the pot from yesterday, so she drank that and sent William out with the end of a loaf of bread. There was nothing for Sam and Jem, but she managed to find two farthings so they might be able to buy something to sustain them for their long day out of doors.

Once they had also departed, she turned to Annie. What to do with Annie had been one of Delilah's biggest worries after she took Meg and Rosie to the workhouse. Meg was always so quiet that the others barely noticed her, but she'd gone about her daily tasks with a silent efficiency, making sure the room was clean and that everyone had something to eat – and, crucially, she'd been at home to look after the little ones. To add to her burden of guilt, Delilah had rapidly come to the conclusion that she had under-estimated and underappreciated Meg, and now it was too late to say so or to do anything about it.

*No*, she corrected herself, it wasn't too late to act. She could work and earn and bring the girls home, and then she could tell them both how much she had missed them and much they meant to the rest of the family. But in the meantime, there was Annie.

Poor little Annie had been bereft when Meg and Rosie disappeared. She had looked around and hunted for them as though they were hiding, too young to understand where they'd gone. Delilah had tried to explain that they would be coming back, but a tot of Annie's age couldn't grasp any timescale later than 'tomorrow', and she still kept determinedly pulling back the blanket on the mattress or looking behind the sofa in case she might find them there. It almost broke Delilah's heart, but there had been an even worse problem to consider: what to do with Annie while the rest of them were out at work.

To start with Delilah had wondered if it might be possible to take Annie to the laundry with her each day, but the idea was so unworkable that she hadn't even mentioned it. Mrs Baker would never allow it, and it would be far too dangerous to have Annie wandering round where there was so much boiling water. And if Delilah attempted to keep one eye on her sister, she wouldn't be paying sufficient attention to her work, which would result in swift dismissal. No, it couldn't be contemplated.

There was, of course, no possibility that Pa would look after Annie all day. If he was at home he was generally asleep, and if he was awake he was out on the street corners talking to fellow loungers or he was in the gin shop. The humiliation of carting a small girl around with him would be too much to bear, and besides, once he was in his cups he would forget about her and simply leave her somewhere. Who knows what would happen to her then, but Delilah would certainly never see her again.

That left two alternatives. The first, which Delilah knew some other women resorted to, was to leave Annie at home: in the cold, dingy room, on her own, all day. She would have to be tied to a piece of furniture so she couldn't wander off or reach anything that might hurt her, and then left by herself for a minimum of ten hours with nothing to do. Delilah had actually given this serious consideration, as being perhaps the safest physical option, and had even got as far as working out how long a piece of string she could use to enable Annie to walk a little but without reaching the door or the cooking knife near the fireplace. But when it actually came down to it she just couldn't bring herself to condemn the little girl to such a fate.

And so it came to the option of last resort. With so many families living close together there were, of course, many other children around the place, and they were turned out each morning to spend the day playing in the court. Some of the older ones, and particularly the boys, were allowed to range further, but there was a group of girls aged around six or seven who remained in the court all day, some of them looking after younger brothers and sisters.

Delilah had watched them for a while soon after they moved in, seeing which ones Rosie made particular friends with and which were happy to let Annie join in with their games. When she was finally faced with the horrible choice of what to do with Annie during the day Delilah had spoken to them all, but particularly a girl named Clara. Clara had a marginally cleaner face than some of the others, and she had no younger siblings of her own; she was the youngest in what seemed to be a very large family indeed. She was therefore amenable to flattery about being a good girl and a big girl who could look after Annie.

Delilah was fully aware that what she was doing was dangerous. Clara might well be proud to be asked for now, but there was no saying that she might not eventually get bored of having Annie always around, that she might take her eye off her, that she might let her toddle off out of the court . . . but what else could be done? Delilah had to work, and she couldn't bring Annie with her, and that was that. Thank goodness Jemima was somewhere safe – at least Delilah could comfort herself with that thought, however great a hole the loss of her youngest sister continued to tear in her heart. There was no way she could have left a baby, only half a year old, in the care of girls; it was bad enough having to desert Annie.

Delilah was ready to burst with frustration at the way things had turned out. If only life could offer her more choices! But life wasn't like that, was it, so she stamped all the feelings back down inside and did what she did for six days of every week. She bundled Annie up in as many clothes as she still owned, pulled the shawl up over her head and tied it, and put a crust of bread in her apron pocket. She kissed her, took her outside where the other children were already gathering in the pre-dawn light as their parents and siblings went off to work, and left her with Clara. Then she started on her own walk to the laundry, hoping and praying as she went that Annie would still be there when she got home, and that she wouldn't return to find that she'd lost another sister.

# Chapter Six

Something about the laundry was different.

As soon as Delilah arrived she was aware that the buzz of early morning conversation had a different tone to usual. She didn't normally join in too much of the gossip, but she overheard enough snippets, as she was filling her copper with water, to know that a number of women were off sick and that there was something going around. *Marvellous*, she thought, as she started a cold rinse of some of yesterday's sheets while she waited for today's water to heat, *another thing to worry about*.

After that there was the next lot to pound, and Delilah set to work with a will, the exercise warming her. She was concentrating so hard on her task that she didn't notice anything else until a tap on her shoulder made her jump. Mrs Baker was standing beside her.

'Oh! I beg your pardon, ma'am, I didn't see you there.'

'Never mind that.' Mrs Baker sniffed as she looked in the tub. 'You keep your mind on your work, I'll give you that.'

She paused, and Delilah stood in agonised suspense. Surely she wasn't about to be let go? Not with others off and the laundry owner having made a positive comment?

'I'm short-handed in the lace room. You're a good worker,' said Mrs Baker, sounding as though the words were being dragged from her with a hook, 'and you're careful. If you want, you can move there. Same hours, but an extra shilling a week – I'll deduct money, mind, if you ruin anything.'

Delilah could have hugged her. She didn't, of course; she kept her voice level and her jubilation on the inside as she accepted and was pointed in the right direction straight away, a new girl arriving to take over her thankless labour at the big tub.

The room Delilah arrived in was smaller and contained no wash tubs; instead, a series of porcelain bowls were set out on a long table and a number of women were working very delicately indeed. Delilah had never worn lace – it was far too expensive – but she and Ma had occasionally been asked to clean some, and she knew that one careless wash was enough to ruin it permanently. The last thing she needed was to have money deducted from her wages, so she paid great attention to the woman who was set to instruct her and then worked with extreme care, glad that her first piece was not the most delicate of those she could see in the room.

By the end of the day she had become accustomed to the new techniques of wrapping the lace round a bottle to keep it taut, then soaking it in cold soapy water before setting it to boil with the soap still on it. Once boiled it would be put out to dry, still wrapped around the bottle so that the shape of the lace pattern would be retained. After that it passed out of her hands to an ironing room and she could start again with the next piece.

When the bell rang to mark the end of the working day, it took Delilah by surprise. Although the lace room involved much less physical labour than her previous duties, she had been obliged to concentrate much harder, and that had made the time pass more quickly.

She heaved a sigh of relief that she had got through her first day without damaging any lace, and went to fetch her shawl for the walk home. She was one of the last out, but paused when she heard the sound of weeping. It came from a girl of about her own age who was unwinding a dry piece of lace from around its bottle.

'Are you all right?' Delilah couldn't just leave her there.

'It was all going perfectly until just now! But just as I was unwinding it I got my nail caught in it and it's pulled a thread.' She held it up and pointed.

'Don't touch it!' If Delilah did know one thing about lace, it was that pulling a loose thread could be disastrous. She moved closer to examine the damage. 'It's not too bad, I don't think – if that one bit was carefully put back and held with a stitch or two of white thread, you wouldn't notice it at all.'

'But I can't—' began the girl.

They were interrupted by the arrival of Mrs Baker, who had come to extinguish the lamps. 'What are you two still doing here?'

The girl's first instinct was to hide the piece of lace, but Delilah knew that honesty was going to be the best policy – and, besides, Mrs Baker hadn't got to where she was today by being fooled.

'A tiny thread has come loose in this piece of lace, ma'am, but it could be stitched just here and nobody would be the wiser.'

'Stitched? By whom?'

'Well – I could do it, if you'd let me take it home. Mending used to be my work before I turned to helping my Ma with laundry.' Delilah paused, aware that she might have offended the other girl. 'Unless you wanted to do it yourself, of course.'

She received only a terrified shake of the head in reply.

'Very well,' said Mrs Baker. 'Wrap it in a piece of that muslin to keep it safe, and bring it back tomorrow morning. If it's perfect then we'll say no more about it, but if I have to go back to the customer and report damage I'll be taking the cost out of both of your wages, half each.' She addressed the other girl directly. 'And one more mistake from you, Madge, and you're out. The only reason I'm not letting you go right now is that it looks like I'll be short-handed until this sickness, whatever it is, has passed.'

She swept away and began to extinguish the oil lamps around the room. As the place grew gradually darker, Madge whispered to Delilah, 'It's not fair for her to take half the cost out of your wages, when you were only trying to help.'

'Nobody will have anything deducted,' replied Delilah, firmly, wrapping the lace with care in a piece of muslin and putting it in her pocket. 'It'll be as good as new tomorrow, you'll see.'

'Oh, I'd be ever so grateful,' came a relieved voice out of the semi-darkness. 'My Pa would skin me alive if I came home with short wages again this week.'

They left the building together and then hurried off in their separate directions. The walk home allowed Delilah the time for work worries to fade and home worries to take over, and she almost ran the last few yards as she neared the court.

Annie was there, thank goodness. And so were all the others; she was the last home today. William had lit the candle and was inexpertly trying to slice a loaf of bread.

'Did you get work today?' Delilah asked him as she took off her shawl and kissed Annie.

'Yes, all day, so I bought this on the way home.'

She took over the slicing and made sure that everyone had some.

'What's this rubbish, then?' Pa, who was home unusually early, wasn't impressed.

'You know perfectly well what it is, Pa – it's bread.'

'Bread? For a grown man? I need meat, girl.'

Delilah felt her patience wearing thin, but she didn't want to start a fight in front of the children. 'There is no meat, Pa.'

'Well, get some, then! I'm the head of this family and you'll fetch me some decent food.'

'Head of the family?' Delilah couldn't help herself snapping. 'Once, maybe. For now, if you want meat then you get out and earn some money to buy it.'

'Don't you talk back to me, girl!' he roared. He raised a hand but dropped it when he realised she was out of his reach.

He seemed unusually coherent, so maybe now was the time. 'I know you can't go back to labouring, Pa, but there is work that can be done sitting down – making matchboxes or something. Anything that gets a bit of extra money in would help.'

She thought she was making a reasonable suggestion in a reasonable tone, but he was outraged. 'You want to me to do women's work? I might be a cripple, but I've got some pride.'

'Let your pride feed you, then,' she retorted, taking his plate away before he could pick up his bread. 'Or maybe think about being proud enough to provide for your family, if you want to be the head of it.'

He growled and muttered something she didn't catch.

'Why are you home, anyway? You're never normally back this early.'

'Shop's closed, isn't it, and so is the pub on the corner.'

'Why?'

'They're all sick.'

Delilah paused in helping Annie. 'There must be something going about. Lots of women were off work at the laundry today, too.'

'And at the docks,' added William. 'That's probably why I got work all day.'

'I wonder what it could be?'

'Haven't you heard?' asked Pa, in a scornful tone. 'Well, if you haven't then you soon will. It's the cholera.'

\* \* \*

*Cholera*. The word was enough to put fear into even the stoutest heart. Delilah remembered Ma telling her about an outbreak that had occurred in Liverpool when she was a toddler and Jonny a baby, and how it had swept through the most crowded parts of the city. Hundreds – thousands – of people had died. Nobody knew how it spread – except that, like most diseases, it was worse in the poorest areas.

There was nothing she could do, of course, except carry on and trust to luck. So the next morning was the same as ever, except that when she reached the laundry she headed straight for the lace room. Madge was overjoyed to see the mended piece, and even Mrs Baker grudgingly admitted that she couldn't fault it.

The week passed in a blur, but at the end of it Delilah took home a shilling more than she had done previously. Tempting as it was to buy extra food, a treat for the children as Christmas approached and the cold weather really began to bite, she restrained herself. 'That's for you, Meg and Rosie,' she whispered, as she hid the coin behind the loose brick in the corner of the room. 'I said I'd come for you in the spring, and I will.'

Christmas passed almost unnoticed, except for the extra day off – which Delilah could have done without given that it meant a day without pay. But nobody was much in the mood for celebrating as the cholera tightened its grip on the city and the death toll began to rise.

Every day Delilah walked past the entrances to courts and alleys that stank to high heaven as their inhabitants were assailed by bouts of diarrhoea and vomiting; every day she saw people with sunken eyes and shrivelled skin with the telltale bluish tinge. But, miraculously, every day she came home to find that none of this had affected anyone in their own court, where there was not one wake, not one coffin. It was astonishing: nobody could work out why one place should be free of the disease while the surrounding areas were full of it. The mystery was the subject of constant gossip between Delilah and the other women as they cleaned the pump and scrubbed the surrounding flagstones to make sure that no waste or filth got into the drinking water.

The other godsend was that the cholera had not made it as far across the city as the workhouse. Delilah had no way of knowing what was happening to Meg or Rosie, but at least it wouldn't be *that*. She still worried about them, of course, thinking of what they might be enduring and fretting about the workhouse getting more and more full as adults died in their homes and their orphaned children had nowhere else to go. Nor did she think it had reached Brick Street, so Ellen, James and Jemima ought to be safe, although Delilah couldn't help worrying about them constantly, as well as Abraham, mixing with so many men from different parts of the city every day at the docks.

Delilah also thought a great deal about Bridget – and, in the moments when she was honest enough to admit it to herself, about Frank. They had continued to call for her almost every Sunday so they could take a walk, always heading out of the alleys and into the main streets so they could look in the shop windows and pretend they were fine members of the gentry who would be making expensive purchases if only the establishments were open. Delilah always lingered as long as she could outside her favourite flower shop, still dreaming of what it would be like to work there. Remarkably, the shop managed to stock flowers all the year round. At first she couldn't work out how this could be, but Frank – who had known someone who worked as a gardener on a big estate back in Ireland – had explained that they could be grown under glass or in heated sheds, even in the winter. Delilah shook her head in amazement at the wonders of the modern world, but the conversation did plant a seed in her mind. She left it there for now, dormant during the cold winter months, but it would grow.

As she learned during their walks, the O'Malleys had already bettered themselves to the extent of moving – not out of the courts completely, but to a much larger one where they had two rooms instead of one. Delilah had by now met the other brothers, and she didn't wonder that the family was held in respect on the streets and that Bridget hadn't encountered any trouble now that she could be recognised. In ascending order of age and intimidation they were Gideon, Patrick and Michael. Gideon she had encountered previously, feeling a little unsettled, although he was the one who looked most like Frank, resembling him also in being tall and thin. She was more nervous of Patrick, who was slightly shorter but sturdier than his younger brothers, and who hardly ever opened his mouth; and she was downright terrified of Michael, who was shorter still but built like an ox. It might have been worse, she supposed: she'd been introduced with the words 'our Bridget's friend' and received a grunted, 'You're all right,' which helped allay some of her apprehension. Michael didn't seem to have a regular job but he earned money by prizefighting, as could readily be attested by his solid muscles and by the state of his scarred, broken-nosed face.

It was a cold Wednesday in January when Delilah first saw Frank in his porter's uniform. She had left the laundry at dinnertime to run up to the station with a halfpenny for Sam and Jem, and as they were all standing together Frank had emerged, carrying the bags for a prosperous-looking older couple and flagging down a hansom cab for them. When they were safely off he had turned, spotted them and smiled. He looked so incredibly attractive that Delilah's heart fluttered, and she could well believe Bridget's tales of him bringing home extra money in tips.

Frank made his way over. 'Want to come inside?'

'I should say!' Sam's reply had burst forth before Delilah had the chance to open her mouth.

Frank grinned. 'Come on then.' He beckoned to Jem and pointed at the station entrance.

'But won't you get in trouble?' Delilah was worried.

'It'll be fine. Now, see that group of ladies and gents there? Just follow along behind them and I'll bring up the rear.'

Somehow, in the melee of a large group and with the uniformed Frank calling out to people to mind their step and bustling forward just as an older railway employee looked like he might question them, they were inside.

The platform was crowded, and they were able to edge their way through without being too noticeable until they could see the train itself. Delilah gasped, and even Sam was speechless. There was a line of carriages, passengers climbing in and porters passing bags, but that wasn't what caught their attention. No, that was the engine, sleek and shining, standing still but looking as though it might burst into life at any moment; a living, breathing, shuddering dragon.

There was a sudden piercing whistle, and everyone on the platform jumped or exclaimed. Delilah heard herself give a little shriek, and then felt foolish as she smiled at the others.

One person hadn't been startled. Indeed, Jem was moving towards the engine with a dreamy look on his face, so close to it that he could almost . . .

'Jem! Come back!' called Delilah. But he had his back to her and he was too far away to grab. She could only watch as he reached the engine, tentatively laid both his hands on it and then, to her astonishment, laid the side of his face against it and smiled in serene contentment. He closed his eyes for a moment, then opened them again and signed something she didn't catch. 'What did he say?'

Sam's face creased in puzzlement. 'He says it's talking to him.'

'Well, will you look at that,' said Frank, in a tone of wonder and shaking his head.

'Oi! You!' A man in a railway uniform was rushing over, his waxed moustache bristling with outrage. 'You, boy – get away from there!'

'Looks like time's up,' muttered Frank. He stepped forward. 'Mr Carey, sir, I have no idea how that boy got in here, but I'll remove him at once.' He winked at Jem before seizing his arm. 'Come on, you!' He turned back to his superior. 'I'll throw him out bodily, sir, and make sure he gets a good clip round the ear for his impudence.'

Frank continued to call out as he pulled Jem back towards the station entrance, with Jem play-acting just as much and both of them making sure that any attention was on themselves so that Delilah and Sam could follow unnoticed.

Once they were all outside Frank dropped Jem's arm and burst out laughing. 'Oh, my, that did me good! Best thing to happen all week.' And then, to Delilah's surprise, he pointed to Jem, then to himself, and made Jem's sign for 'happy'.

'How in the world did you—' began Delilah, but they were both crying with laughter too much to notice.

'He comes to talk to us sometimes, when he comes outside,' Sam informed Delilah. 'He's sound.'

This was high praise indeed, and Delilah looked at Frank with a new eye.

Eventually Frank calmed down enough to speak. 'Ah, you do me good, you boys. Makes me remember being young.'

'You're hardly old now,' pointed out Delilah.

'Well, you know what I mean. Besides, I was always the smallest, remember, always the butt of the jokes. It does me good to play the big brother for a change.' He realised what he'd said and backtracked. 'What I mean is – well – anyway, I'd better get back to work before Mr Carey wonders where I've got to.' He addressed Jem, wagging his finger theatrically. 'Young man, consider yourself punished!' He mimed slapping the back of Jem's head and that set them both off again.

'Stop it now, or you'll get us all in trouble,' said Delilah, smiling herself and ushering Frank away from them as they began to attract attention. 'But . . . thank you. It was wonderful for the boys to see the train.'

He made a ludicrously formal bow, sweeping off his uniform hat. 'Anything for you and the young gentlemen, ma'am.' And then he was gone.

It was more than time for Delilah to get back to the laundry so she rushed off, hurrying all the way and only just making it in time. But as she worked through the long, dark afternoon, she smiled to herself.

* * *

As January and February passed into March the cholera seemed to be receding, and still their court was not touched. Delilah suffered a heart-stopping shock one morning when she left Annie with the girls and saw that Clara had a black ribbon in her hair, but it was apparently for two much older brothers who lived elsewhere. Delilah, sagging with relief, hugged her and spoke consolingly, but Clara seemed unconcerned; she hardly knew them, having been born long after they had left home.

Delilah continued to earn and put by her extra shillings. It was nowhere near enough to consider bringing Meg and Rosie home just yet, not much more than half, but there was still hope: and if she kept going, if she could somehow be promoted again . . . she didn't want to get too far ahead of herself, but she had to keep one eye on the future, had to believe that things would eventually get better, or she would go mad.

The first hint of spring was in the air and there was still some daylight left as Delilah walked home one Friday evening, one hand gripping the hatpin she had taken to carrying with her when unaccompanied. The number of brothels about the place seemed to have increased in recent months, and the men who frequented them often had difficulty in telling the difference between women who worked in them and women who were simply passing by. Lewd comments she could cope with, but she'd had to fend off groping hands more than once and the sharp steel pin certainly helped. It was not enough to actually wound anyone – she didn't want to end up in court herself – but a sharp scratch with it was enough to make them start back and allow her time to get away.

She felt the usual rush of relief when she saw Annie happily playing in the court. *Count your blessings*, she reminded herself as she went into their room. It was nearly the end of a long working week, so she decided to light the fire so they could have a hot drink of tea to dip their bread into. They'd all become more accustomed to the monotonous diet, though Jem seemed to have stopped growing and she'd had to take in her own and William's clothes more than once.

Delilah was just hanging the kettle over the small blaze when Sam and Jem came in. She could tell immediately that something had happened, though from the way they were looking at each other and grinning it didn't seem to be bad news.

'What is it?'

Jem held out a halfpenny, which she took, but that couldn't explain their glee, surely – he did occasionally bring home a copper or two these days.

Sam said nothing while she smiled and kissed Jem, but then he dug in his pocket and poured a whole stream of coins on to the table. 'There. That's for you, for the savings to get Meg and Rosie back.'

Delilah gaped. 'Where did—'

'Count it,' said Sam, as both boys hopped from one foot to another in excitement. 'How much is it? How much sooner will they be able to come home?'

Delilah sorted through the coins. Sam normally brought home a few pennies a day, but the amount on the table came to a barely believable shilling and fourpence.

She stacked the coins, but made no move to put them away. Instead, she turned to her brother. 'Where did you get this?' She remembered the suggestion he'd made some while back, the one that had made her box his ears. 'Tell me.' She bent to put her hands on his shoulders. 'You look me in the eye, Samuel Shaw, and tell me you didn't steal this.'

His gaze was bold and direct, his tone firm. 'Of course I didn't.'

'Well then, where did you get it?'

'I was outside the station, sweeping like usual, and I saw Patrick O'Malley – he knows me 'cos he's seen me talking to Frank sometimes when he comes outside carrying bags. Anyway, he said he needed a boy to run an errand, and if I did it for him then he'd give me more than I'd earn by sweeping. So I did, and he paid me a whole shilling. And I didn't spend any – I brought it all home to you.'

Delilah wanted to feel relieved, but something wasn't right. 'Why should he pay you so much?' she asked, suspiciously. 'What was this errand?'

Sam immediately clammed up. 'He told me not to say.'

Delilah folded her arms and stared at him.

After a few moments of uncomfortable silence he looked away. 'Can't tell you. Nothing bad, I swear – I just carried something from somewhere to somewhere else.' With a sudden anger, he picked up the coins from the table and shoved them at her. 'Now just *take* it, will you? Pa might be home soon.'

With some reluctance, Delilah let Sam force the money into her hands. He was upset and disappointed, and she realised that she'd wounded his pride by not praising him for his earnings. His intentions had been good, whatever the facts of the case, and she had to remember that he was a ten-year-old boy who missed his sisters.

She relented a little, poking about in the coins and picking out two pennies.

She gave Sam and Jem one each. 'Working men always get some of their wages back to spend on themselves. If you go now you might get to the baker's or the pie shop on Scotland Road before it closes.' She picked out a third penny. 'William must have got work this afternoon or he'd be home by now. Get something for him as well, and that will save him going out again when he's tired.'

She was answered with two matching wide grins as, hardly believing their luck, they clenched their coins and ran out of the door.

William was just entering, caught in the bare-footed whirlwind as it rushed past him. He came further in. 'What was all that about?'

Delilah put the coins down. 'Sam brought all this home.'

His eyes widened. 'How?'

She explained what Sam had told her and added her own worries. 'It must be something underhand, or why pay him so much?'

William thought for a few moments. 'Perhaps,' he said, at last. 'Or . . .' He hesitated.

'What?'

He grimaced. 'Perhaps he thought we were in need of charity, and he didn't want to make it look too obvious. Like Abraham that time.'

Delilah could feel a deep blush of shame spreading over her cheeks. 'Next time I see Frank or Bridget, I'll—'

'What's all this, then?'

Delilah looked up in horror. They'd been talking too long. The door was wide open and Pa was dragging himself inside, his eyes riveted on the money that was still in open view.

'Give me that.' He reached out.

'No!' Delilah managed to get there before him, snatching up the coins and backing away.

William moved to stand in front of her. 'You're not having it, Pa.' But his voice was wavering.

Pa shifted on his crutches, and Delilah initially thought he was going to aim a blow at them, but instead he snatched up Annie, who had toddled over towards William. 'Hand it over!'

A cold hand of fear took hold of Delilah's heart. He was dangerous: yellow-eyed and sweating, just drunk enough to have his wits about him but not so far gone that they'd be able to overpower him. 'Put Annie down, Pa,' she pleaded. 'Please.'

Pa shook his head. Then, to Delilah's horror, he took hold of the little girl's arm and began to twist it. 'The money.'

'No! Pa, stop it!' Delilah felt the tears running down her cheeks as Annie began to cry and then to scream in pain.

'Now, girl!'

There was no holding out – Annie was going to be really hurt in a moment, and Pa just didn't care. He couldn't see past the money and the drink it would buy him. 'Take it!' Delilah heard herself shriek. 'Take it! Just let her go!' She stepped past William and pushed all the coins at Pa, who dropped his daughter like a hot potato to grab at them.

Delilah snatched her up. 'You've got what you wanted – now get out. Get *out*!'

He was long gone by the time Sam and Jem made a triumphant return with three hot pies. Delilah watched them eat, declining all offers to herself by saying she wasn't hungry. Jem broke pieces off his to feed to Annie, who had cried and snuffled into Delilah's shoulder for some time after Pa left but who seemed, mercifully, to be otherwise undamaged. What if Pa had broken her arm? What if—?

Sam's face was rosy, and Delilah simply didn't have the heart to tell him what had happened to his money. After the younger ones had gone to bed, William silently handed over his own earnings, which he fortunately hadn't had a chance to do earlier, and she hid them behind the loose brick, pushing it firmly back into place in case Pa ever noticed it.

Finally, when William was also asleep, Delilah allowed herself to cry, burying her face in her shawl so nobody would hear as she sobbed out her tears of frustration and despair.

\* \* \*

The morning came, as the morning always did.

It was with a kind of numb disengagement that Delilah got up and went about her morning tasks, seeing the boys out and leaving Annie. Pa, of course, hadn't come home; they wouldn't see him until all the money was gone and he sobered up enough to remember where he lived.

The same daze continued as she walked the now familiar route to the laundry, but she was roused from it by the group of shouting, gesticulating women gathered outside the gate, which was oddly still locked.

Delilah spotted Madge among the crowd. 'What's going on?'

'Nobody knows. But if they don't open this gate soon we'll be late starting, and no doubt she'll use it as an excuse for short wages.'

'Wait, someone's coming.' Delilah, who was taller than most of the other women, could see over their heads and shoulders. 'There's a man on the other side of the gate.'

A male voice shouted for them all to be quiet. When the women were all listening, he raised his voice again. 'Mrs Baker has died of the cholera.'

There was a murmur. 'But what about our work?' came a call from the crowd.

The man shrugged. 'The laundry might start up again one day under new ownership, but for now it's closed, so you're all out of a job.'

He walked off in seeming unconcern, leaving the crowd of shocked and desperate women behind him.

# Chapter Seven

Delilah sat at the table, the light from the cracked but now clean windowpane slanting in to warm her folded, idle hands.

She had never been paid very much at the laundry – even with the extra shilling a week, she brought home less than half of what William did. But it was nevertheless valuable income, the money added to everyone else's in their shared endeavour to make sure they had a roof over their head and food to eat. And now it was gone.

She had spent the whole of Saturday traipsing round the city trying to find work, but with no luck. Places were either closing down because their owners had died, or they were overrun with applicants who had lost their jobs elsewhere. Sunday had been a day of panic as she and William tried to calculate how they might eke out their remaining money. Now it was Monday, and she had nowhere to go and nothing to do.

It was quiet, and she was alone in the room. She had tried to keep Annie with her for company, but Annie was so used by now to playing with the other girls all day that she had squirmed and fussed until she was allowed out. So there was silence.

A single shilling piece lay on the table in front of Delilah. She stared at it and past it and *through* it as she let herself sink into her thoughts.

She must bring in money, somehow. If she did not then it was all over: no food, no rent, another eviction . . . and the workhouse for all of them as they were pulled apart and housed in different sections, maybe never to see each other again.

But they had already been pulled apart, hadn't they? The family was scattered across Liverpool, Meg and Rosie in the workhouse, Jemima living with Ellen and James Jenkins, and Ma and Jonny lying cold in the graves that Delilah hadn't had time to visit. This was not an acceptable state of affairs, and simply bringing in a pittance in order to sustain their current lives was not enough. She needed more money and more ambition, so that she could bring all the living members of the family back together.

She needed to think differently.

Delilah picked up the shilling and turned it over in her hands. The picture on the front was of a young woman: the queen. The image was familiar, having been in use for much of Delilah's life, but older people still talked about how odd it was to have a queen rather than a king on their coins. It was strange to think of a woman who had such power, a woman who was so visible in a world filled with men. Of course, she would never suffer the same kind of problems as Delilah: Victoria, in her faraway palaces, would never worry about where her children's next meal was coming from. But she'd still had to fight, hadn't she? The talk on the streets and in the newspapers had been that she should have let one of her uncles take the throne, or that she should have stepped back from her duties once she was married; that she should remain at home like a good wife while her husband or another man took her place on the national stage. But she hadn't.

The face on the shilling grew blurry as Delilah stared right through it once more. She, Delilah Shaw, needed to show some of the queen's courage and take her fate into her own hands. There was no point in sitting here wishing for better; she had to make it happen herself. But there was also no point in looking for another job – nobody would pay a woman anything like a living wage, and she would be forced to rely on men all her life. Much as she loved William, Sam and Jem, and much as she hoped one day to marry, Delilah was not going to spend her life dependent on men or on the goodwill of an employer, male or female. No, she would turn this setback into an opportunity. She would start a new life, carve a new path.

Delilah stood up and put the shilling into her pocket. She knew what she would do.

* * *

The flower shop on Dale Street was still open, still doing brisk business. Well, it would, Delilah supposed; the cholera hadn't really touched the rich parts of town where its customers lived. And that was why the business was a good one to get into. There was no point in selling something that only poor people needed, trading in second-hand clothes or shoes; as soon as hard times came, they stopped buying. But something more high-end, something bought by those who had money to spare and would always have money to spare, that was the thing.

She hovered on the pavement for a while, but there was no point in putting it off. If she left it too much longer then her courage might desert her. She dropped her shawl on to her shoulders, checked her reflection in the window to see that her hair was neat and her face clean, then took a deep breath and walked in the door.

There were two girls inside; the sound of the bell ringing brought one of them forward straight away, but she wrinkled her nose when she saw Delilah. 'What do you want?'

Her evident contempt gave Delilah just the spur she needed. 'Do you always talk to people like that when they come in the shop?'

'Well, you don't look like you're going to buy anything, that's for sure. And if you're looking for work then there isn't any.' She and her companion exchanged glances of superiority.

'I'm not looking for work. I'm here to see the manageress.'

'Mrs Farrell? You want to see Mrs Farrell? You?'

'I do. So kindly inform her that I'm here.'

'I'll do no such thing, you cheeky—'

'What is going on here?' The noise of their altercation had brought the manageress sailing into the front of the shop.

Delilah elbowed her way in front of the shop girl, summoning up her courage and her best accent. 'Mrs Farrell?'

Mrs Farrell held up a pince-nez and peered closely at Delilah. 'Who's asking?'

131

'I've come to speak to you about a business proposition, ma'am.'

'You?' The manageress sniffed and began to turn away.

'Well, if you're not interested in making money . . .' Two could play at that game, and Delilah began to drift towards the door.

'Wait.'

Delilah smiled to herself, then composed her features before she turned to face Mrs Farrell. 'Yes, ma'am?'

'Come into the back parlour and we can discuss your proposition.' She cast a glance at the shop girls. 'We are not to be disturbed.'

Delilah was ushered through the shop and into a room that was part parlour with an armchair and a little table in front of a fire, part kitchen and part storeroom. The scent of the blooms was intoxicating, and Delilah had to suppress her excitement.

Mrs Farrell shut the door firmly, then moved to sit in the armchair. She didn't offer Delilah a seat. 'Well?'

'You have your flowers delivered daily, early in the morning,' began Delilah.

'Yes – what of it?'

'And at the end of each day, when you close the shop, you throw out any of today's flowers that are left over while you wait for your fresh delivery.'

'Is this going somewhere? I don't have all day.'

'I'll buy them.'

'What?'

'Every day. I'll come here at six o'clock every evening when you close, and I'll give you a shilling for whatever you're throwing out.'

Mrs Farrell opened her mouth as if to dismiss the idea, but then she paused, tapping her pince-nez on the arm of her chair. A calculating look came into her eye. 'And what will you be doing with these flowers?'

'With respect, ma'am, I don't think that's any of your business. Once they're mine, they're mine.' Delilah fixed her gaze on the wall above Mrs Farrell's head. 'In the same way that the shilling would be yours, ma'am, and none of my business what you might do with it once I've paid it over.'

'A shilling,' she heard the other woman say, in a considering tone. 'Each day?'

'Six days a week, ma'am, the days you're open yourself. You wouldn't have any to sell on a Sunday.' She risked meeting Mrs Farrell's eye. 'So that's six shillings a week.'

Six shillings a week would surely be a hefty increase on whatever the shop owner was paying Mrs Farrell – why, it was more than Delilah had earned in total at the laundry for a week's hard labour. This was, however, a much more upmarket type of business, so she suffered a few moments of agony while she wondered if the sum would be tempting enough.

'There will be conditions.'

At least that wasn't 'no'. 'What conditions?'

'You are presumably intending to sell off my surplus stock in an attempt to make a profit. If that is the case, you will not sell any flowers within four streets of this shop. You will not give any hint that you know me, or that we do business together. You will never come in the front door of the shop again.'

'Agreed.'

'Very well, than – we have a bargain.'

Delilah tried hard to conceal her jubilation, but she couldn't stop the hint of a smile from appearing. 'Good,' she said, simply, not wanting to shower Mrs Farrell with thanks. This was, after all, a business transaction.

Or, to put it another way, a huge gamble that might end up with her whole family in the workhouse.

'I'll see you at six o'clock this evening, then,' said Mrs Farrell, briskly. 'You'll need to come through the yard to the back door.'

'As agreed, ma'am.'

Satisfied that they understood each other, Delilah left the room. She'd have to go out the front this time, given that she'd come in that way, or it would look odd. She wouldn't be seeing the inside of the shop again any time soon, though, so as she passed through it she looked surreptitiously about her to try to gauge what she might be buying this evening, while not hesitating long enough to give the supercilious shop girls any kind of satisfaction. Then she stepped out the front door with her head held high.

She made sure she had put some distance between herself and the shop before she finally let her knees give way.

It was a momentary weakness, however, and she soon overcame it; she had work to do. On the way home she visited St John's market and haggled a stallholder into selling her two wicker baskets for a knockdown price. One was deep, with a curving handle over the top; the other was almost flat and could be worn like a tray suspended from her neck. She also invested some precious coppers in a ball of string. That would have to do for now, but it was a start.

At six o'clock precisely Delilah knocked on the back gate of the flower shop. Mrs Farrell opened it to admit her and then pointed to a heap of mixed flowers on the ground. 'There. I'll have your shilling first, and then you can take them. Take them all, mind, then I've not to pay anyone to cart them away.'

Delilah handed over the money and then knelt down to inspect the first goods that her business had bought. She had been half-afraid that she would be faced with flowers that were rotting, or that had been stamped on or otherwise destroyed in retaliation for what Mrs Farrell had thought was her impudence. But the lure of the additional income had evidently been stronger than any irritation: although there were a few crushed blooms that were unusable, the majority were simply a little wilted and would easily last until she could sell them tomorrow.

She collected them all into her baskets and stood. 'Thank you. I'll see you at the same time tomorrow.'

Mrs Farrell nodded and hurried her out through the gate; Delilah heard it latched and bolted behind her.

She began to hum to herself as she set off, surrounded by a cloud of fragrance.

\* \* \*

There had been daylight enough for Delilah to see her way home, but none of it penetrated the little window on the ground floor of the court, surrounded as it was by the tall, closely packed buildings. She knew the room's dimensions by now, however, so she walked confidently to the table to set the baskets down and then over to the grate. She'd placed kindling before going out and was able to put her hand on the tinder box without looking.

Soon the comforting glow of the coal fire illuminated the room, softening the bleakness, and the kettle was boiling.

William came in. 'What's that lovely smell?'

Delilah nodded to the flowers on the table and then smiled at his confusion. 'That,' she said, 'is the start of my new enterprise.'

Once everyone had eaten – dry bread dipped in tea – Delilah lit that evening's candle and set to work.

The others crowded round. 'Tell me more about it,' said William. 'Can I help at all?'

'I spent a shilling on these flowers,' explained Delilah. 'Now I'm going to split up the pile and make them into lots of separate little posies. I'll put them in water overnight – that doesn't cost us anything – and then tomorrow I'm going to take them out round the streets and sell them. If I can sell more than twelve at a penny each then I'll have made money, and then I go and spend another shilling on more flowers and we keep the difference.'

'Flowers?' said Sam, with just a hint of scorn in his voice. 'Who's going to buy flowers?'

'People with spare money,' replied Delilah with composure. 'Don't worry, I'm not going to try and sell them round here in the courts and alleys. There's plenty of better places in town.' She paused. 'Annie, darling, it's lovely that you want to help, but could you put those down please?'

Sam lost interest and wandered off to throw himself down on the mattress. Annie followed him and was soon asleep in his arms.

William made an attempt to pick out some individual flowers and form them into a bunch, but the result was so mismatched and lopsided that he grimaced and untied it again. 'I think I might be just hindering.'

'Not to worry.' Delilah looked at his exhausted face. 'You've already done a day's work – you're allowed to sit and do nothing. Or read one of your books if you don't mind sharing the light.'

He nodded and fetched one of his remaining volumes.

'Latin?' asked Delilah, glancing at it.

'Latin. Like Pa always said, it'll never get me a job, but if I want to read it in my own time then why shouldn't I?'

'Exactly.'

They sat in companionable silence for a while, he reading and she selecting and tying flowers. Of course, she was an absolute beginner at this. She had no idea what most of the flowers were called, or if there was a particular way they were supposed to go together, so she would just have to rely on instinct. These purple ones would go nicely with the pink, wouldn't they? A pale, soft, gentle sort of effect. While those orange ones would form a dazzling, vibrant combination with the yellow.

Jem, who had been standing by the table the whole time, tentatively picked up a bloom and handed it to her.

'Oh, Jem, I'm not sure that one will go with these. Look at the colours.'

He shook his head, sniffing at the flower he'd picked and then leaning to bury his nose in the ones in her hand. Then he gave it to her again.

To humour him she put it with the others and sniffed the whole bunch. She paused. She inhaled again. Actually . . . 'Do you know, I think you might have something there.'

He grinned, and then made one of his rare attempts to speak. 'Can't hear,' he managed in a rusty voice, probably the phrase he'd had to say out loud most often during his life when people questioned him. But now he tapped his nose and followed up with an intelligible, 'But can smell.'

'Oh, of course you can, darling!' Delilah dropped the flowers to hug him, and William put his book down long enough to pat their little brother on the back.

Delilah had already learned her first lesson: group the blooms by fragrance as well as colour. Jem remained by the table, helping her to pick out and match flowers. By the time she'd tied a couple of dozen posies her ball of string was looking alarmingly smaller, and she realised she'd have to factor that in as an additional cost.

'I'll have to try to tie them with less string,' she said to Jem, making sure her face was lit by the candle flame.

He nodded and then paused, biting his lip in thought. Then he scrabbled through the pile of discarded flowers – those that were too crushed to be of any use – and picked out one with a long stalk. Carefully, he pushed his thumbnails into it and then peeled it into two long halves. He did the same again with each half, ending with four very thin, flexible fibres. As Delilah watched, he took up a posy and used one of his new ties to wrap around it. It held the flowers in place perfectly.

Delilah kissed him. 'Jem, you're a genius. And my first farthing of profit is going to buy you a currant bun.'

They worked on until all the usable blooms had been tied, and then Delilah sent Jem to bed. She took their bucket outside to fill with water and returned to place all her precious stock in it. The safest place to store it, given that Pa would probably be home later and not too careful in his movements, was under the table, so she tucked it in place before she settled to sleep herself.

An additional advantage of her new business was that the scent of the flowers drowned out the aroma of damp and mould; she inhaled deeply as she drifted off.

The next morning Delilah woke everyone as usual and sent the boys out. Pa, as expected, had staggered in at a very late hour; he was now snoring on the broken sofa, but thankfully he hadn't upset the bucket of flowers under the table. She dragged it out and arranged all the tied posies in her baskets. There were twenty-four, so if she sold them all she would have two shillings; one to take to Mrs Farrell to buy tomorrow's flowers, and one to keep. If she could do that every day she'd have six shillings a week profit – more than she'd earned at the laundry. And who could say that she might not even get more flowers for her money some days? She began to feel the first stirrings of hope for the future.

She looked down at Annie, who was trying unsuccessfully to tie her own apron strings. Smiling,

Delilah crouched to do it for her, then wrapped the shawl about her as well. 'It might be spring, but it's still chilly out there, so keep this on while you play.' She had considered taking Annie with her so that she could keep an eye on her, but after some thought she'd decided against it. She would no doubt need to cover many miles across the city in order to make sales, and Annie would get so tired that Delilah would have to carry her – no easy task when she had the two baskets already. So, just for now, Annie would have to continue spending her days in the court with the other girls. As the months had gone by Delilah had become a little less anxious on this point; Clara, as the youngest and least important in her own family, had been so taken with the idea of being the 'big girl' who was in charge of another that she'd stuck at it. Delilah decided that if she made a whole shilling profit today, she'd buy Clara a bun too.

Once Annie had happily run off outside to play, Delilah checked her looks in the window's reflection. Much as she wanted her flowers to sell themselves, she was aware that a pretty yet respectable appearance and a smile would help, so she made sure her hair was smoothed and her skirt straight. She risked extracting one bloom from a particularly generous bunch and tucked it in her bodice for luck.

'Today,' she said to her reflection, 'is the first day of the rest of your life, Delilah Shaw. So go out and seize it.'

She settled one basket round her neck, picked up the other and walked out of the room.

# Chapter Eight

By the time Delilah made it home that evening she was almost in tears.

She didn't know how many miles she'd covered as she'd tramped round the city, but she'd been walking almost without cease for nine hours, so it must be quite a few. Every time she'd tried to stop to sell her flowers from one location, she'd attracted the attention of a constable who had moved her on. Her boots were old and worn, rubbing her feet into painful blisters, but of course there was no possibility of getting any others so she'd just had to put up with it. The only alternative was going barefoot, which she hadn't done since she was a child and which would undoubtedly be worse.

It wasn't the pain that was concerning her most, though – it was the fact that she'd made a loss. Despite all her best efforts, her smiles, her cajoling of potential customers, she'd sold just eight posies all day.

This was a disaster. How could she have gone so wrong, wasted those precious pennies that could have been spent on food? And what was she to do now? Never mind a profit, or any celebratory currant buns for the children – if she was going to continue with the idea she would have to take another fourpence out of the kitty simply in order to buy tomorrow's flowers.

William was already in the room when Delilah arrived back, at around five o'clock, which was more bad news as it could only mean that he'd had no work for the afternoon. This was confirmed by him putting down only a shilling and – she counted the coins – ninepence with an embarrassed expression. 'Sorry.'

He was fourteen; he shouldn't be expected to carry a whole family, to be the breadwinner. He was also not physically suited to being a manual labourer, but what other choice was there? If only they could somehow find him what she thought of as a collar-and-tie job – one where he could sit at a desk and use his brains rather than his back. There were plenty of clerks around at the docks, and he was easily clever enough to do the work, but the way into such positions was hidden from the likes of them.

'It's not your fault,' she reassured William. 'You can't expect to catch Mr Bradley's eye every day, not morning and afternoon. Especially if it's heavy work and there's big men around.'

'That's just it,' he replied in a mournful tone. 'I did see him this afternoon, and there was plenty of work as two ships had arrived early from America as well as the others that we were expecting. There was more than enough to go round, but he picked everyone except me – I ended up there by myself on the stand, looking like a fool.' He met her eye. 'I know I'm a joke, and I wish I was big and strong like Jonny and Pa, but I'm not, so what can I do about it?' He rubbed the back of his hand across his eyes.

She took his hand. 'You're not a fool, or a joke. You're a smart boy and you're going to grow into a clever man, a good man, a man who's worth knowing.'

'Chance would be a fine thing.' His tone was hopeless.

'You listen to me, will you? Things are going to get better. We'll *make* them better.'

He sniffed back the tears that were threatening to fall and sat up straight. 'If you say so. Now, enough about me – how was your first day? I'm sorry, that should have been the first thing I said when you got in.'

For a moment she couldn't speak.

'Ah.' She still had hold of William's hand, and he shifted position so now he was pressing hers. 'My turn to tell *you* that things will get better?'

Delilah didn't have the energy to wipe away the tears that began to roll down her cheeks. She told him, through her gasps and sobs, all about what had happened. How so many people had wanted to stop and chat, had admired the flowers, but how difficult it had been to turn that into actual sales. She finished by pulling the seven pennies and two halfpennies from her pocket and putting them on the table next to his earnings.

'And now I don't know what to do.'

'What do you mean?'

'Well . . . I was supposed to go back at six today to buy more flowers for tomorrow.'

'And so you shall.'

'Really?'

'Delilah,' said William, with a firmness that surprised her, 'you can't give up after one day. There are so many examples of where an idea has been successful, but only after it's been given time to grow.'

'Did you read that in one of your books?'

'Yes, but you can see the same sort of thing in newspapers and pamphlets, can't you? Every business, every fortune, started from somewhere.'

Delilah rather suspected that some people made a great deal of money because they were rich to start with, but she didn't say anything out loud. 'So, you think I should go back there again?'

'I do.' William pushed the silver shilling across to her. 'You take this, and I'll put the rest away along with whatever Sam comes home with.' Delilah saw him glance across to where the clock would have been, before catching himself. 'It can't be far off six o'clock now – you'd better get going. Do you want me to come with you?'

She shook her head. 'You wait here so the boys don't come home to an empty room. And call Annie in once the sun goes down and it gets chilly.' She wiped away her tears and stood up, forcing her aching muscles to obey her so she could walk steadily.

Within an hour Delilah was back with more flowers. She was still unsure about what she'd done – the scent was lovely, but they couldn't eat it, could they?

She went to put the baskets down by the table and was surprised to see a new loaf of bread on it. She looked round enquiringly to be met by Sam's grin. 'Bought it on the way home, didn't I?'

'He brought home more than we were expecting,' added William, meeting Delilah's eye over the heads of the others.

She desperately wanted to question Sam, to make sure he'd come by it honestly, but her exhaustion was just too much, especially when coupled with the relief of knowing that her gnawing hunger might unexpectedly be satisfied – it had been a long day and she'd eaten nothing. She sank into a chair.

Sam, who had obviously been bracing himself for an argument, came to stand before her. 'I didn't do anything wrong, Lilah, honest to God I didn't.'

She nodded and summoned up a smile. 'Well, let's slice it then. And maybe by the end of the week we'll have jam as well.'

The evening passed in much the same way as yesterday, with Delilah and Jem making up little posies that were beautifully balanced in terms of colour and fragrance, before she went out to fetch the water to store them in. There were only twenty this time, but that hardly mattered given how few she'd sold today – it would just mean fewer leftovers tomorrow.

She looked critically at today's remaining bunches, wilted now after being carried around in a dry basket all day.

William saw what she was thinking. 'Will you keep those ones as well?'

'No,' she replied, after some hesitation. 'No, I won't. If I'm to sell to people who have money to spare, I need to get a reputation for quality goods. I might be able to sell a couple of those, but when people saw how bad they were they wouldn't buy from me again.'

He nodded approvingly. 'That sounds like a good business decision. I'll go and put them in the ash can, shall I, along with those other bits you're throwing out?'

'Yes. No – wait.' Delilah had an idea. She untied all yesterday's posies, keeping the string, and then used some of Jem's home-made stalk-twine to make them up into six larger bunches.

'What are those for?' asked William, sweeping up the rest of the discards.

'For spreading a little happiness.'

He looked puzzled but, seeing he was to get no other reply, finished clearing up and went outside.

The following morning, when it was time to leave Annie in the court, Delilah went outside with her. As Clara and the other little girls started to congregate, Delilah handed round the bunches of flowers.

'What, to keep?' Clara's eyes were the size of saucers.

'Yes, to keep. To say thank you from me for looking after Annie.'

The squeals of absolute delight, the joy on their faces as a small piece of colour and beauty entered their lives, made Delilah turn away and wipe her eyes.

*   *   *

William had been right. Giving up after one day would have been a mistake; it would have been weak, and that was one thing Delilah was determined never to be. She would learn from yesterday and make a better showing today, and she would do it for her family.

Now, where had she enjoyed success? Best to go there and avoid those areas where she'd had a lot of talk and no sales. And where else in Liverpool might the middle classes or the more well-off workers be found on a weekday morning? Where hadn't she been yesterday that she might try?

Even as she considered these matters Delilah's feet took her in the direction of the railway station – this would provide rich pickings, surely, with many smartly dressed men coming into the city for their day's business. As she approached she could see that the bootblacks who lined part of the street were doing a good trade, so she wandered up and down their stands while the gentlemen were to all intents and purposes being held captive, one foot on a box while their shoes were polished to a gleaming shine.

Unfortunately it wasn't as effective a strategy as Delilah hoped. These men were on their way to offices; they had no female companions and they didn't want to buy posies for themselves. The experience was disappointing, but it did give Delilah a couple of ideas. Firstly, that she would come back to the station in the evening when these same gents were on their way home, to persuade them that what they needed was to take a nice bunch of flowers home to their wives or mothers. And secondly, tonight when she made up the posies, she would leave some flowers to one side to sell singly. Some of the smartly dressed men had a small bloom in the buttonhole of their suits, so attempting to sell those first thing in the morning would be a good strategy.

She left the row of bootblacks, smiling at Jem as she passed him industriously clearing up after the old fellow he helped out. She had sold nothing, but she wasn't downhearted – she would use this as an opportunity to learn. Once again she was grateful to William for not letting her give up.

Sam was busy in the middle of the road, sweeping, but there was so much traffic about that she didn't dare try to attract his attention in case she caused an accident. She wouldn't be allowed to trade inside the station itself, she knew, so she was on her way past the entrance when Frank suddenly appeared.

He didn't see her at first. He was carrying a suitcase in each hand and another bag under his arm, presumably for the couple who were emerging from the station just behind him. When he did spot her, his face broadened into the smile that made her heart melt – she had to remind herself once again that it meant nothing. He winked and turned to the gentleman of the couple, a very young man with a shiny scrubbed face and a collar that was slightly too tight. 'Ah, sir, you're in luck, if I may say so. Here you are newly arrived in Liverpool with your beautiful bride, and you've an opportunity to buy her some flowers before you even reach your hotel.'

Delilah smiled at them as they stopped to inspect the contents of her tray basket. The lady touched her husband on the arm. 'They are nice, and it would be lovely to have the fragrance as we walk these busy streets, to remind me of the countryside.' She looked around almost fearfully at the traffic, as though she'd never seen anything like it before.

'Anything for you, my dear,' said the blushing young man. 'You choose one for yourself.'

A little gloved hand hovered over the basket. Delilah picked up the posy she thought was the most scented – the blooms individually chosen by Jem yesterday evening. 'Might I suggest this one, madam? I'm sure you'll like it.'

The purchase was made; Delilah put the day's first penny in her pocket and bestowed her most grateful smile on Frank as he led the young couple up the road, talking all the while of the wonders of Liverpool. 'St George's Hall, there – won't it be a grand sight when it's finished? And over there you'll see . . .'

Delilah spent much of the morning wandering around the environs of St John's market. Everyone said it was the largest such market in the whole kingdom, and she could well believe they were right when she looked at the huge brick building, with its fancy stone entrances and the dozens – hundreds? – of windows. She couldn't sell her wares inside it, of course, because that was only for people who paid to rent a space there, but the bustling crowd outside gave her a few sales. It also gave her a few more ideas, and the beautiful daydream that she might one day have a fixed stall where people would come from miles around just to buy her flowers. The owner of the establishment in which Mrs Farrell worked must have started from somewhere – why shouldn't she?

As noon approached she began to make her way down to the docks. As he was on his way out this morning, William had mentioned that he'd seen Abraham yesterday and that he'd wished Delilah luck with her new venture. She hadn't seen Abraham for some while but knew that he'd been helpful in getting William work, so she thought she might try to catch him while he was on his dinner break. Besides, she had another very good reason for wanting to visit the docks.

The tall masts of the ships could be seen long before anything else, of course, as could the dome of the huge new Custom House. Next came the noise: the shouts of the sailors, dockers, hauliers and warehousemen, the rumble of carts, the slapping and creaking of ropes, and high above it all the shrieks of gulls as they whirled and swooped. And finally the smell, a heady mix of tar and smoke, coffee, pepper, spices, rum, tobacco . . . anything that could be imagined. Delilah inhaled deeply as she walked towards it all.

Delilah passed the Custom House, feeling very small and insignificant next to it, and then she could see the water. She was in Canning Dock, which meant she had to head a little further south in order to reach Queen's Dock, where Pa and Jonny used to work and where Abraham's warehouse was situated. All the world seemed to be here today, men of every conceivable skin colour hurrying about their work as goods from across the globe were unloaded. Delilah did often wish that life had been a little kinder to her, but at times like this she was proud of her home city, proud to live in a place that was at the centre of global commerce. Why, people all over the world from the East Indies to America must know of Liverpool.

As she neared his warehouse she spotted Abraham, sunning himself outside with a chunk of bread in one hand and a piece of cheese in the other. He saw her just as he took a large bite out of the bread, his eyes smiling at her over the top of it. As Delilah reached him he moved up, so she could join him in the patch of sunlight, and they stood for a moment without speaking. He finished his mouthful, looked at her more keenly, and silently offered her the cheese. After a moment's hesitation she took it, biting into it gratefully and hoping that her stomach wouldn't react too loudly and give away her hunger.

'William told me about the new venture,' said Abraham when they'd both finished eating. 'How's business?'

'Better,' was her reply. 'I haven't quite broken even yet, but I've already sold more today than yesterday, and it's not much past noon.'

He dug in his pocket and fished out two pennies. 'How many flowers will that buy me?'

'Oh, really, you don't need to . . .'

'I can if I want to,' he insisted, taking her hand and pushing the coins into her palm. 'Thanks be to God,

156

I earn a steady wage here, enough to have something over once I've eaten.'

'What about your rent, though? Ours has gone up twice recently and I'm sure it's probably the same everywhere.'

'Ah, I sleep in a little cubby in the warehouse, so I can keep watch over it at nights. So no rent, but it's not very pretty and a bunch of flowers will cheer it up nicely.'

'Well, if you're going to put it like that . . . all right. But you get two bunches for your twopence, the same as anyone else would.' A thought struck her and she counted the remaining posies. 'And that,' she said with a smile, 'is one penny to break even and another that is my very first profit.'

Abraham held out his hand to shake hers. 'I can't tell you how honoured I am, Miss Delilah, to be the man who is responsible for that.' He seemed strangely overcome.

'Still a long way to go before I can fetch Meg and Rosie home, but it's a start at least.'

'And a fine one too.' He made an effort to pull himself together. 'Now, what are these ones called? These purple ones?'

Delilah had to admit that she didn't know. 'I know which ones look nice together, and what each one smells like, but I've got no idea of their names.

I should probably learn, though I don't know how. I don't think the woman I buy them off would take kindly to being asked for a lesson.'

Abraham thought for a moment. 'Perhaps it's the sort of thing you might learn from a book. I'll ask James Jenkins next time I see him.'

'James Jenkins?' Delilah was astonished, thinking of the large, taciturn man who had been their Brick Street neighbour all those years. 'What would he know about flowers?'

'Oh, not flowers, child – books. He's very keen on all this, what-do-you-call-it, "self-improvement". He goes up to those public lectures and such, and I've seen books in his house the couple of times I've been there.'

'Well, I never knew that.' Delilah's reply was vague, because the sound of the name had taken her thoughts in an entirely different direction. 'Do you know,' she began, not quite knowing how to continue, 'little Jemima, the baby . . .'

'Your sister,' he said, gently. 'I've heard nothing bad, but the next time I see James I'll ask after her particular, and then send word with William.'

'That's so kind of you.' Delilah took in a deep breath to try to stop herself from crying. 'I'm sorry,' she managed, eventually. 'Our problems must seem very tiny compared with what you've suffered during your life. I know you were once . . . you were once a . . .' She tailed off.

'It's all right, you can say it out loud,' he replied. 'Keeping silent about it won't make it go away. I was a slave. My mother was a slave, and my *father*' – he spat out the word with more contempt than she had ever heard him express – 'was her owner.'

'In America.'

'Yes. I stayed there until she died, and then I ran away and got myself on a ship heading for England and Liverpool.'

'And you've been here ever since.'

'Your government abolished slavery, so here I'm a free man, I get paid for my work and I could walk out and leave any time I wanted.' He exhaled. 'You can't know what that means to me.'

She laid a hand on his arm. 'I'm glad you're here.'

He patted it. 'Me too, Miss Delilah. I've been here, oh, twenty years now – I knew your Pa and your Ma before they were married – and here I'll stay, at least while slavery is still alive and legal in America. Earning my money, and spending it on flowers if I choose. I can *choose*.'

There was a brief silence, and then he took a deep breath and changed the subject. 'Now, speaking of work, I'd better get back to it.' He nodded at the groups of men who were beginning to assemble at the stand in the hope of being picked for the afternoon's labour.

William would be in among them somewhere, which reminded her. 'Yes, yes, I should go too,' said Delilah, picking up her handbasket. 'I'm glad I came to talk to you, and I nearly forgot – I wanted to thank you for your kindness to William.'

'It's no charity,' he said, straightening his cap. 'He's a keen lad, for all he's not strong, and deserves work. If I can ever put a word in for him then I will.'

'Thank you.'

'Now, where are you off to?' he asked, as they made their way across the front of his warehouse.

'I thought I might go up to the northern docks, where the pleasure boats set off from.'

'Those paddle steamers that go up and down the Mersey or across to north Wales?'

'Yes. Have you ever been on one?'

'Oh no.' He laughed, but then his voice took on a harder edge. 'I won't ever go aboard a ship, in case I "accidentally" find myself on the way across the Atlantic. Not even a paddle steamer on the Mersey. That's why I stay up here, waiting for the fruit to be unloaded and brought to me before I organise storing it and moving it out.'

They had reached the door. Abraham paused, looking like he was about to say something. He eventually came out with, 'Well, good luck for your afternoon's business, Miss Delilah, and remember you're in profit now. I'm going to put these beautiful blooms – whatever they're called – away safely.' He disappeared inside the cavernous building.

'Goodbye!' she called after him. She was sure that he'd been on the verge of saying something completely different, but she had no idea what it was.

Delilah was puzzling over the question as she turned away, hardly aware that she was about to walk into somebody until the shadow fell over her.

She looked up; it was Mr Bradley.

'Well, well,' he said, blocking her path. 'Fancy seeing you here.'

Delilah greeted him politely, glancing around surreptitiously to make sure they were not alone. Fortunately there were plenty of people about the place, a few women as well as all the male workers.

'Selling flowers, eh?'

'Yes, Mr Bradley.'

'Well, you surely won't make many sales around here among these lads.' He indicated the lines of men waiting for work.

'No, I was just on my way up to the pleasure boats.'

161

'The pleasure boats. Now there's a thought.' He licked his lips in the way that Delilah didn't like. It made her feel as though he was eyeing her up like a mutton chop.

'So, if you'll excuse me . . .' She made as if to continue on her way.

'Oh, not so fast! It's not often we get a sight like you down in these parts. Let me make the most of it.'

'It's half past twelve, Mr Bradley.' Delilah looked pointedly at the clock on the warehouse wall.

'So it is,' he said, consulting his pocket watch with no particular hint of urgency.

'I won't keep you, sir – I'll be on my way.'

'Selling flowers.'

She was getting irritated now, though still wary of seeming to appear rude. 'As I said.'

'Well, I'll buy a bunch from you, then. How much?'

Delilah couldn't resist the temptation to double the price, but he made no objection. Indeed, he handed over a threepenny bit. 'Keep the change, my dear.' He leaned in. 'And just remember, there are other ways a pretty girl like you could make a bit of money. Much easier than carrying all this round the streets.'

She took his meaning but pretended not to understand, pocketing the money as she tried not to shudder. Then she walked away. She'd hardly gone a few steps when she heard the men in the labour queue sniggering; she turned just in time to see Mr Bradley toss his flowers away before he went to address them.

*     *     *

Delilah's afternoon, once she'd managed to push the uncomfortable scene with Mr Bradley to the back of her mind, was profitable. Anyone boarding a paddle steamer at the northern docks was there because they had money to spend on a ticket for an afternoon's pleasure, and many of them were couples or families in a holiday mood. She was able to persuade a number of husbands and fathers to part with their pennies, and by the time five o'clock came she had sold her entire stock.

It was time to go home, time to put away her gains and then head out to buy tomorrow's flowers. She wasn't familiar with this end of the docks, but she could orient herself by the dome of the Custom House over to her right. She turned up a street that she didn't know, but which she was confident headed in the right direction.

The first sense of uneasiness started to nudge Delilah as she left the crowded docks behind. By the time she was out of hearing as well as sight the nudge had turned into a full-blown stab, her senses screaming at her that she was in danger. She tried to remain calm as she made her way past various doorstep loungers and their predatory stares, but the way was getting narrower. Her instinct was to turn and run back the way she'd come, but her street sense told her that was absolutely the last thing she should do – any hint of weakness would invite attack. So she continued on her way, keeping her head high and trying to work out where she was. *Think*. She'd left the docks further north than usual, so this road must be running parallel to . . .

It was when she saw the canal bridge ahead of her and the public house next to it that Delilah realised where she was. She was in Chisenhale Street, known far and wide as the most notorious in Liverpool. The bridge was a particular danger point, but her only choices were to keep going and cross it, or to turn back. And she could hear footsteps behind her.

Delilah's heart was in her mouth as she walked past the rough-looking men congregating outside the public house, hearing their catcalls. To stop would be dangerous, but to ignore them completely would be just as bad. She settled for a nod and a tight smile and stepped on to the bridge.

Ahead of her, just at the highest point over the canal, the way was blocked. A couple who looked like new arrivals, maybe even fresh off the boat today, were being held up by three Liverpool men who were telling them that there was a toll to cross the bridge.

There was still enough light for Delilah to see the consternation and fear on the faces of the immigrants. 'A toll?' said the man. 'I'm sorry, sir, I had no idea. We'll go back and find another way.' He put out a skeletal hand to take the woman's arm.

'Oh no,' said the heavy-set man who had first spoken. 'You're on the bridge now, so you have to pay whichever way you go.' He looked over the parapet. 'And it's not a good day for a swim.'

His associates moved to surround the now terrified couple, but then one of them noticed Delilah and pointed. 'Well, well,' said the heavy-set man. 'Even better.' He eyed her up and down.

Delilah couldn't breathe. She stood paralysed, ice running through her veins, knowing that the worst was about to happen and that there was nothing she could do to prevent it. She wouldn't be able to fight off three men. Why, *why* had she come this way?

With a grin that showed off his blackened teeth, one of the Liverpool men stepped towards her.

'Stop.'

The voice had come from behind Delilah, and it held a note of command. She turned to see Patrick and Gideon O'Malley looming towards them all, and she wasn't sure if she now felt weak at the knees from relief or from additional fear.

The men on the bridge were not backing down; they now stood side by side, facing up to Patrick and Gideon, and Delilah thought she caught the gleam of a knife blade. The brothers wouldn't retreat either, she was sure, so she and the Irish couple were trapped in the middle of what was soon to be a violent confrontation. How could she get away? And help them get away too? She couldn't swim, so jumping over the side of the bridge wasn't an option, which meant that escape could only come from slipping past one or other of the parties.

All of Delilah's senses seemed heightened as she tried to prepare herself for the next few minutes, hoping they wouldn't be her last.

'I said stop.'

It was the same voice as before, calm, not even raised; and it hadn't come from either Patrick or Gideon. Delilah hadn't noticed that Michael O'Malley was behind them, and now he pushed his way forward, his brothers closing up behind him.

One look at the terrifying scarred face and distinctive physique was enough to inform the Liverpool toughs of whom they were now dealing with. They began to whisper among themselves.

Michael came close enough to Delilah to look in her face. 'Thought it was you.' He turned to the three Liverpool men. 'Go.'

The group's leader opened his mouth to argue, but his two friends were already backing away. He tried to tough it out, and Delilah had a sudden vivid memory of the boys who'd been bullying Bridget on the day they'd first met: this man knew he couldn't stand against Michael, but he was trying to save face in front of his friends. 'You can have her,' he blustered, waving at Delilah, 'but we saw these other two first.'

'You don't bargain with me.' Michael's voice was still calm, and he made no further move forward. He didn't need to. Within moments all three of the men were gone.

The terrified young couple on the bridge hadn't stirred an inch. The man put his arm round the woman, who Delilah could now see was pregnant, and spoke in a wavering voice. 'I'm much obliged to you, sir . . .' His eyes were wide and panicked, and with good reason; as far as he was concerned they'd just swapped one danger for another.

Something about his accent, however, made Michael look at him more sharply. 'Where you from? Where exactly?'

'Thomastown, sir, in County Kilkenny.'

Michael grunted. 'Thought so.' He took a coin from his pocket and held it out. 'Get some food.' Then he turned to Patrick. 'Find them somewhere to lodge for the night.'

Tentatively, the man sidled forward and took the silver with a hand that shook. 'You're on the side of the angels, sir.' He nodded at Delilah and then he and the woman followed Patrick over the bridge and out of sight.

Michael turned to Delilah. 'You shouldn't be walking this street. Gideon here will see you back to the main road, but don't come this way again.'

'I won't,' said Delilah, fervently. 'Thank you.'

Michael made no reply, simply jerking his head at Gideon before turning to stump his way back to the public house.

Delilah followed her escort over the bridge and to the far end of the street. He didn't open his mouth the whole way, and she didn't dare try to start a conversation. A few men loomed out of doorways and alleys as they passed, but they melted away again as soon as they saw Gideon.

They came to a wide thoroughfare. 'Vauxhall Road,' he said, shortly. 'Follow the main road round and don't take any more shortcuts.' He was gone before she could thank him.

By now Delilah was trembling from the narrowness of her escape. But she couldn't burst into tears here, and neither could she go home to hide away. She had no way of telling the exact time, but surely it must be nearly six o'clock by now? If she were not to lose her evening's purchase of flowers she'd better hurry up – she didn't think that Mrs Farrell would wait more than a minute past the hour before giving up on her and locking the gate.

She reached Dale Street just as the church clocks were striking six, and handed over her money – twelve individual pennies, which didn't please Mrs Farrell, although she didn't refuse it – before scooping the flowers up into her baskets.

She was breathing more easily by the time she set off home, but her peace was not to last: a tall, thin figure limping towards her proved to be William.

'What is it? What's happened?'

His expression was grim. 'I came out to find you – thought this might be where you'd be at this hour.' He stumbled.

'William – tell me! Who's hurt you? Were you attacked on the street?'

'Not on the street, no.' His hollow eyes met hers. 'But Pa has found the loose brick and the money we were saving up.'

# Chapter Nine

It was just as bad as she'd feared.

Delilah burst through the door on her own, because she'd shoved the baskets at William and left him to catch up as best he could while she picked up her skirts and ran. The three younger children were all on the mattress and she went straight to them. Annie was howling, tears and snot covering her face as Jem held her. A trickle of blood ran down from the corner of his mouth but he seemed otherwise unharmed. He had his arms tight round Annie and was making 'shush' noises as best he could. Over her head he looked solemnly at Delilah and then down at Sam, who was lying quite still with his face to the wall.

Delilah put out a hand. 'Sam?'

He turned over and she gasped. His poor little face was black and blue, bleeding and swollen. As she tried to support him into a sitting position he whimpered and clutched at his ribs. 'Sam, did Pa do this to you?'

He nodded, very slowly. 'He . . .' There was a pause as Sam tried to breathe in through his bloody nose and swollen lips. 'He found the money,' he croaked. 'I tried to stop him, Lilah, we all did! But he took it all.' He crawled into her embrace in a way he hadn't done in years. 'He took it all, and now how will we get Meg and Rosie back?' He dissolved into tears and she rocked him back and forth, whispering over and over again that it wasn't his fault.

A shadow darkened the entrance, but to Delilah's relief it was William. He put the flower baskets down and shut the door. 'How is he?' He limped over to join them all.

'What happened, William? What happened?'

'He was already here when we all got in. He was unsteady and with all of us in here he tripped over something and went flying. He landed near the loose brick and saw straight away what we'd done. He was furious – I've never seen him so angry. Yelling about how we'd tried to trick him, how he was entitled to our money. He pulled it all out while he was lying there. I tried to stop him, of course, but I had to make sure Annie was out of his reach first – you remember what happened last time.'

Delilah nodded. She was still holding Sam on her lap and rocking him. 'And then?'

'By the time I'd done that he'd got hold of one of his crutches. He swung it round and it hit me on my knee. That knocked me back, and by the time I'd got close again, Sam was on him.'

Delilah hugged Sam tighter, and William put out a hand to stroke his hair. 'You know what he's like, our little firebrand. He was just as angry as Pa was, and he flew at him, yelling and punching and trying to get the money back. Problem was, he ended up on the floor too, and then Pa had him.' William swallowed. 'He held him with one hand and kept punching and beating him with the other. I tried to stop him, to pull him off, and so did Jem, but you know how strong his arms are.'

'Oh, my poor Sam,' said Delilah, kissing the top of his head as he clutched at her. 'My poor, brave boy.'

'Anyway, by that time we were all making so much noise that a couple of lads came in from over the court – you know, Clara's brothers. They're friends of Sam's so between all of us we managed to pull him and Jem out of Pa's reach, but nothing on earth was going to get that money away from him, and he still had it when he went out.' William hung his head. 'I'm so sorry about the money, I really am, but I thought

172

Sam might be dead, and . . .' He too dissolved into tears.

'It's all right,' said Delilah, becoming the fifth and final person in the room to cry. 'You had no choice – and *of course* Sam is more important than the money.'

Sam looked up, the sight of his battered face making Delilah weep all the more. 'But the money was for Meg and Rosie,' he whispered. 'I want them back, I told Meg I would always look out for her. And now what are we going to do?'

Delilah gathered them all in her arms. 'We're going to do what we always do. We'll stick together, and we'll start again.'

They all sat entwined on their dirty mattress in their cold, empty room until long after it was dark.

\* \* \*

The next morning heralded a beautiful, fresh day, which somehow just made it all worse. Delilah was tempted – so tempted – to throw Pa out and tell him to fend for himself, but there was no point: he knew where they lived and the door had no lock. And they couldn't move anywhere else without him because they couldn't afford it and nobody would rent a room to a single woman and a group of children anyway.

No, they were better off, she thought bitterly, staying where they were. At least they had some friends in the court who would help them through the worst, a community of people who knew that life was hard and who supported each other however they could. Delilah gave Clara a grateful hug when she left Annie, holding on so long that Clara began to squirm, unused to such gestures of affection.

Delilah set off, flowers piled high and their worsened financial situation and the word *spring* competing for attention at the forefront of her mind. When she had taken Meg and Rosie to the workhouse back in October she had told them she would be back to collect them 'in the spring'. But when was that? Now? April, May, June? The thought that they might be incarcerated there, thinking she had abandoned them, ate away at her insides. If only she'd been allowed to visit, she could have explained things to them, asked for their forgiveness and a little more patience. As it was she'd have to rely on them believing that she was doing her best.

She forced an artificial smile on to her face as she approached Lime Street. She had a number of buttonhole flowers ready and would attempt to sell them to the gentlemen as they exited the station or stopped to have their shoes polished. An individual bloom was, of course, less than a quarter of a normal bunch, so she shouldn't really charge more than a farthing, but as she saw the well-fed, well-dressed, self-satisfied men she thought to herself that they would probably see very little distinction between a farthing and a halfpenny, whereas the difference to her would be great, especially if she sold quite a few. And it was all in a good cause, so she decided to be bold.

Her daring was rewarded: she sold every buttonhole and had made a good portion of her shilling outlay back before the sun was much higher. And she still had all the other bunches left.

Any glimmering of optimism she might have been feeling was soon quenched by the sight of Sam, who was leaning on his broom in an attitude of pain. Delilah had told him, begged him, to stay at home today, but he had dragged himself out of bed with a doggedness that would have earned him a medal if he'd been a soldier. 'We need the money,' had been his short explanation. After a few sips of tea he'd added, 'and I don't want to lose my place.' Then he'd stood up straight, winced, and taken a few steps. 'See? Come on, Jem.' And that had been that.

As Delilah was looking at Sam and wondering if it would harm his standing among the other boys if she were to go and ask him how he was, Frank emerged from the station. He was carrying no bags and he cast a hurried glance over his shoulder as he came. 'Wondered if you might be here round about this time, like you were yesterday. I heard what happened last night – are you all right?'

Delilah was wondering how he could possibly know about what had happened at home when she realised he was speaking of her experience in Chisenhale Street. So much had happened since then that she'd honestly almost forgotten about it.

'I'm fine, thank you. I hadn't realised where I was walking – it was stupid of me.'

Frank took her hand, and for one shocking, delightful moment she thought he was about to raise it to his lips. He recovered himself, however, as a group of people passed by. 'When I heard, I was . . . anyway, I beg you not to go there again. The boys might not be there another time.'

'I won't, I promise. And please . . . do thank your brother Michael for me. I don't think I did so properly.'

'Michael won't mind that.'

'But still. Promise?'

'I promise. Now, I'd better get back before anyone – Jesus, Mary and Joseph!' She could see that he'd spotted Sam. 'What in the name of all the saints has happened to him?'

'It was . . . a family matter.'

Frank's mouth set in a line. 'If you mean that your Pa beat him, say so.'

Delilah looked at the ground.

'But why – no, that's none of my business. All I'll say is . . .' He waited to continue until she was looking at him again. 'If he ever touches you, I won't answer for my actions.' He hesitated. 'In the meantime, if you want me to have a word with Michael . . .'

'No!' she cried, before realising that probably sounded ungrateful. He was only trying to help. 'I mean – no, thank you, Frank. It's a family matter and we'll deal with it.' He looked unconvinced. 'You wouldn't want anyone interfering in your family affairs, now, would you?'

'No,' he conceded. 'But beating women and children is a different matter.'

'Really, it will be fine,' she said, firmly. 'Pa is my Pa and I have to respect that, however much I might wish things to be different.' She tried to bring her tone back to normal. 'Anyway, you'd better get back inside before you're missed.'

'I had.' He looked torn. 'All right – if you're sure . . .'

'I am.' She managed a smile. 'I'll see you soon, Frank.'

'I hope so.' He summoned up a hint of his usual flippancy. 'Until then, my lady, farewell.'

Delilah watched him go, then stood for a few moments watching Sam. He was now surrounded by some of the other boys who were looking at his black-and-blue face with awe and asking him questions. She saw him beginning to brag, and decided to move on; the admiration of his peers would hardly increase if a sister came over to make a fuss of him.

She felt the coins jingling in her pocket as she began to move off. 'Work to do, Delilah,' she said to herself. 'Work to do.'

\* \* \*

As the weeks went by, business improved. There were setbacks, of course; mainly wet days when the bucketing rain meant that not so many people were about in the streets, and those who did venture out through necessity were markedly less likely to want to stand around and buy flowers. But in general sales were very good, and Delilah had become adept at knowing the best times and places for business. Buttonholes for gentlemen in the morning, followed by a circuit round the markets; the pleasure-boat docks in the afternoon. As the days grew longer she also ventured out in the evenings, doing a brisk trade outside the theatres as the ladies and gentlemen arrived for their evening's entertainment.

And all now in a better knowledge of how to avoid the constables. Not that she was doing anything illegal; far from it. But some of them couldn't see a woman out on the street on her own without accusing her of soliciting – or, worse, themselves soliciting for 'favours' in return for not making up an excuse to drag her to the police station.

It also helped business that the variety of flowers available to her had increased as the seasons changed. Perhaps it was because they could be grown outside at this time of year, rather than under glass, as Frank had once explained? Delilah was still frustrated that she didn't know what most of the flowers were called; maybe she would head down to Queen's Dock again sometime soon to see if Abraham had managed to talk to James Jenkins about finding a book. Every time she thought of it, though, she ended up postponing, wary of running into Mr Bradley again. Since that day in March William had had steady work and she didn't want to jinx it by having to fend off the overseer's advances again.

Yes, business was good and earnings were good, but was it yet enough to enable them to fetch the girls home? That was the only thing that mattered.

\* \* \*

Delilah looked at William across the table. 'We haven't got enough, have we?'

He shook his head.

She banged her hand down in frustration, making the coins jump. 'Why is this all so difficult?' She wanted to scream.

William spoke gently. 'We're in a better position than we were before, even if we're not quite there yet. Just a little longer . . .'

'But I don't want to wait longer! I want our girls back!'

'So do I.' That wasn't William, it was Sam, who had appeared beside her. 'I'm not doing enough. I'm getting too big to do this street-sweeping now, like a nipper. I should go out and get a proper job.'

Delilah looked at him through her tears. 'Sam, you're ten years old. All right –' she forestalled him – 'nearly eleven. But nobody would give you a man's job, or a man's wage, no matter how keen you are.' She hugged him, despite his protestations. 'We all want to have Meg and Rosie back, but it's up to the adults to find a way to make that happen.'

Jem, Sam's shadow as ever, had also materialised and was gesturing to his brother. 'He says, William's not an adult, and neither are you, really.'

'Well, no, but I'm the oldest, so it's my responsibility.'

'It's not,' said Sam, fiercely but quietly, as he looked at the prone figure on the sofa. 'That's what parents are s'posed to be for, isn't it?'

This was, of course, very close to Delilah's own opinion on the subject, but she couldn't say that. As she sought to come up with an answer that would satisfy both Sam and her own conscience, William put a calming hand on Sam's arm. 'Yes, yes it is. But nobody can help that Ma's dead, and, well, lots of families have useless fathers. Families come in all shapes and sizes, and this is ours, so we have to make the best of it. Look how well Delilah's done, these last few months, working for all of us.'

'I know,' said Sam, 'and I'm proud, I am. But the last thing I said to Meg was I'm her brother and I'll be here for her, and look at me.'

Delilah gazed into his fierce little face and had a sudden glimpse of the adult he would become, but he wasn't that adult yet, and she had to take care of him just like all the others. 'You're not going out to get a man's job, not just yet. Give it another year and maybe we can find you some work as an errand boy down at the docks or something. But you're too small for labouring, and running yourself into an early grave won't help anyone.'

'All right,' he replied, with evident reluctance. 'But when? When can we get Meg and Rosie back?' He

181

picked up a halfpenny that had rolled off the table when she'd thumped it, and held it out.

William had been writing figures down on a scrap of paper he'd found somewhere. 'If we continue as we are at the moment – that is, earning the same and spending no more – I reckon another four months will see us with enough put by to feed everyone properly, even if money tails off a bit during next winter. And by this time next year I'll be not far off sixteen, and Sam nearly twelve.'

Delilah began counting on her fingers. 'It's the first of May today. So four months would be . . . the beginning of September.' She swept the coins off the table and wrapped them in a scrap of cloth. 'Best hide this before he wakes up again.'

Jem took it from her and tiptoed over to the mattress, which he lifted in order to scrabble around and find the broken floorboard under it. Pa would probably find it, eventually, but Delilah made sure that at least one of the children was sitting on the mattress at all times whenever Pa was at home and conscious. It would be nice, she thought, if the inside of their home was safer than the streets outside, but here they were.

She stood up and moved to the door.

'Where are you going?' asked William.

'To the workhouse.'

'What, now?'

'Yes. It's a shame we're not allowed to visit them regularly, to let them know that we're working for them and we haven't forgotten them, but I have to go this once, at least. It's Sunday afternoon so maybe they might let me see Meg for a little while to explain.'

'Do you want me to come with you?'

'Me too.' That was Sam.

She hesitated. 'No – if it's still the same matron as before, she was a bit brusque, so it probably won't help if we turn up in a pack. I'll go on my own. You stay here and mind Annie, and make sure someone is sitting over there if Pa wakes up.'

She shut the door behind her and made her way out of the court. The little girls were chasing each other round, giggling, and it made Delilah feel even more sad and useless. What sort of life had she condemned Meg and Rosie to in the workhouse? Yes, they would be fed, but as to the rest . . . who knew? Were they making them work? Would anybody actually *care* for them?

As she walked, she tried to be practical with herself. If they were at home, Meg and Rosie would be among people who loved them. But love didn't put the roof over their head or the food in their bellies: money did that, and they didn't have enough of it. Life in the workhouse might be hard, but they were fed three meals a day and had been sheltered from the worst of the weather. *And they would be kept apart from men*, she added to herself as she passed the entrance to the court that held the local brothel. It was noticeably busier here than in the surrounding lanes, despite it being broad daylight, and she tried to hurry past. That didn't stop her getting more than one lewd offer, which she ignored; and any hand that reached out towards her was soon withdrawn after a sharp scratch from her hatpin.

Then she was past the immediate danger and out into the wider main streets. The shops were closed, of course, but there were enough respectable-looking people strolling about and taking in the spring air to make her feel easier. She allowed herself a few moments to gaze into some of the display windows, admiring the clothes and goods, but she didn't let the envy get to her. Those things weren't for the likes of her and her family, and that was that. A toyshop filled with model soldiers, dolls and a magnificent rocking horse gave her pause and drew out a sigh, but she forced herself to walk on.

It wasn't long before she reached the workhouse and found her way to the door by which she'd entered before, so many months ago. She took a deep breath and stepped inside.

\* \* \*

As ever, Delilah was destined to be disappointed – and in more ways than one. She rang the bell of the Receiving Room, but the matron told her it was strictly against the regulations and that she wouldn't have Meg and Rosie brought down unless Delilah was going to take them away. The temptation was huge but Delilah just about managed to resist it, reminding herself again and again that the workhouse wasn't the happiest of places but that the girls were at least being fed, clothed and sheltered.

It was the second disappointment, however, that really broke her heart. Desperate for any crumb of detail about their lives, she asked the matron if Meg and Rosie were happy. The matron probably meant to be kind, probably meant to reassure Delilah about her sisters, but when she said, 'Why, I heard Meg saying, only the other day, that she liked it here much more than she did at home,' Delilah could have sunk through the floor.

The matron's words haunted her as she left the building and started to make her way down Brownlow Hill. *They liked it better in the workhouse.* How could she possibly have failed her family to such an extent that Meg would feel that way?

As Delilah reached the place where she had first met Bridget, she found that Frank was waiting for her.

'William said you were up this way,' he said, falling into step beside her. 'I'd called at yours to see if you wanted to come for our afternoon walk.'

'Isn't Bridget with you?' Delilah couldn't see her anywhere.

'She's at home. She's fine, don't worry,' he added, as he saw Delilah's worried expression. 'Our Mam's a bit off-colour today, and funnily enough she preferred to have her beautiful soft-spoken daughter by her side rather than any of her great lumbering sons.' He paused, looking more awkward than Delilah had ever seen him. 'Of course, if you don't want to come for a walk just with me, that would be understandable and not a problem . . .'

Delilah was touched by his concern, but given that she walked the streets all day talking to strangers and selling them flowers, she didn't think a stroll with a young man who was a family friend could do much harm. Besides, she rather liked the idea of having him all to herself for an hour or two.

'I can tell from your face,' said Frank, 'that you've not had good news from your visit to the workhouse.

Let's walk now, out to the green space of the park, and you can tell me as much or as little as you want.'

He indicated the direction that lay out of town rather than back towards the centre. They walked for some time, past larger and larger houses that were spaced further and further apart, until Delilah was beyond her knowledge. Only then did she see ahead of her the gates, with a great open space beyond.

She stopped. 'Surely we're not allowed in there?'

'Ah, but we are. Prince's Park, open to the general public – and that includes you and me, last time I checked.'

As they passed through the grand entrance Delilah could hardly believe that nobody attempted to stop them, but they were soon through.

'A bit of green is what you need,' said Frank, waving an arm. 'And it's all here. Trees, grass, paths, a lake and a carriage drive.' He regained some of his old confidence. 'I'm sorry to be escorting you on foot, my lady – next time we'll come in your carriage, and drive round waving at the commoners.'

Delilah took a few steps along the path. Still nobody leapt out to tell them that the park wasn't for the likes of them.

'Ah, it's a wonderful city you have here,' Frank continued, in a more serious tone. 'In Ireland, the rich keep their beautiful grounds to themselves – no admittance to the ordinary man, nor no food when he's starving, neither. But here, your rich men build town halls and parks and schools. Imagine having a place as nice as this and letting Francis O'Malley into it!' He took a few more steps before adding, 'My brothers – the older boys, that is – they all said that America was the place to be, but I reckon I'll stay right here in Liverpool.' He looked at her sideways.

'It is lovely, isn't it? I'll have to bring Annie here one day.'

'You must. But for today we've only really time for a quick turn round the circular path and then back home, otherwise your brothers will worry about where you've got to.'

'All right.'

Frank stopped walking. He started to say something, stopped, then pulled at his collar. To Delilah's astonishment, he was actually blushing. Finally he spoke again. 'I wonder, while we're strolling . . . would you consider taking my arm?' He held it out, elbow first, in an unmistakeable gesture.

Delilah didn't think that anything could have made her happy on such a bleak day, but she felt her heart skip as she slid her arm through his.

They began to walk again. 'Now,' said Frank, 'if only I had someone to buy flowers from, I'd be laughing. Though I'd better not try picking any, I suppose – there must be limits to Liverpool's welcome.'

'I wouldn't advise trying it,' replied Delilah, glancing over at a man in uniform who was raking gravel on another path. 'Let's not ruin our afternoon by being thrown out.'

They continued in silence for a few minutes, Delilah suddenly shy even though she was holding Frank's arm, and he seemingly the same. After a while he gently opened the subject of the workhouse and she was able to pour out the tale of her trip there, and the pain she had felt at hearing Meg's words.

He listened to it all without interrupting. Even after she'd finished he waited a few moments before attempting to speak, thinking carefully about his words. 'Nobody,' he began, 'who was lucky enough to have you for a sister could possibly be happier away from you than with you. That matron has made some kind of mistake.'

'I did wonder if she thought she was comforting me by saying how happy the girls were, but she didn't really seem the comforting type.'

'I haven't seen her, but I'd be willing to believe you're right. I don't think they employ people in those places to be kind and comforting.'

Delilah bowed her head in sorrow at the thought of what Meg and Rosie must be enduring.

'I'm sorry,' said Frank. 'I've upset you by saying the wrong thing. I didn't mean to . . .'

'It's fine, really – I know what you mean and I'm sure you're right.' Delilah raised her head but didn't dare look him in the eye. 'It's just . . . I've failed everyone in my family. The girls stuck in the workhouse and Jemima apart from us too, although she's well cared for. Annie running wild all day, every day, and getting into who knows what kind of danger. William so tired and sick-looking all the time, trying to be a man at his age. And even the boys—' She stopped herself just in time from saying something about Sam falling into 'bad company', which might sound like an insult to Frank's family. 'And Jem,' she continued, hoping he hadn't noticed the slip, 'he's all right for now, but what's going to happen to him when he's older?'

She was still holding Frank's arm, and now he used his other hand to cover hers, a touch at once so comforting and so thrilling that she didn't know how to feel about it. 'They will all be all right,' he said, firmly, 'because they have you. And you've got . . . friends.'

'Yes, yes I have.' Delilah tried to focus on that. She had Frank and Bridget, Ellen and James Jenkins, and Abraham. Their support would see her through for now, and eventually the boys would get older and grow into men. And, she realised, what was most important of all was that she had herself to rely on. She had made her own way so far, and she would continue to do so.

As they came out of the park and set off back towards the city Delilah slipped her arm away from Frank's, walking on her own through the streets that were her home.

*  *  *

Mondays were now Delilah's day of least work. The flower shop was closed on Sundays so she couldn't buy anything to sell; she therefore tended to spend the day cleaning their room, taking her turn at scrubbing the flagstones of the court, planning meals and buying food.

Today was different. After yesterday's visit to the workhouse and her walk with Frank, Delilah decided to visit Ellen Jenkins. She felt guilty – another thing to feel guilty about! – that she hadn't been able to pay any attention to Ma's oldest friend, who must surely miss Ma almost as much as Delilah did. Besides, Delilah ached to see little Jemima, who was now almost a year old.

Returning to Brick Street didn't feel as much like 'coming home' as she'd thought it would. The bricks and the cobbles of the place she'd lived for most of her life now seemed strange, and there were many faces she didn't recognise among the children playing on the street as they enjoyed the fresh May air.

The door to the Jenkins' house stood wide open, as did most of the others. A year ago Delilah would simply have walked in, because that was what neighbours did, but now she felt oddly hesitant about doing so. To knock, though, would be far too formal; only the rent man did that. Instead she settled for calling out, 'Ellen, are you there? It's me, Delilah,' before stepping over the threshold.

The sight that met her eyes was at once beautiful and a dagger to her heart.

Ellen was sitting on a chair, a piece of knitting discarded on her lap as she leaned forward. She held her hands out in front of her, forefingers extended, and grasping those fingers was a pair of plump baby hands. Jemima was standing up, balancing herself on unsteady little legs as she held on for dear life and chuckled with joy. The delight was reflected on Ellen's face as she laughed. 'Who's Mama's clever girl, then?'

Her attention was so fixed on Jemima that she hadn't either seen or heard Delilah. Delilah stood for one moment, watching the two of them completely wrapped up in each other, and *happy*, and then she turned on her heel and left the house, the once-familiar street blurred and strange as she stumbled away.

\* \* \*

There was nothing to do but keep working, so that was what Delilah did. Every day from Tuesday to Saturday she trod her familiar route, and on Sundays she forced her aching and ill-shod feet to take her out to Prince's Park, where she sold enough flowers to strolling and courting couples to make half her weekly takings again.

The docks were busy over the summer, and William had work. Delilah, to her secret shame, asked fewer questions when Sam came home with unexpectedly large amounts of money, simply doling some of it back to him and hiding the rest. The coins piled up under the broken floorboard, untouched by Pa.

And now, at the end of a very hot Friday, it was the last day of August. Pa was out, everyone else was home, the money had been counted several times and it was enough. Tomorrow Delilah would keep her promise and bring Meg and Rosie home.

They all spent the evening excitedly talking about how wonderful it was going to be, how much of a change they might expect to see in each other, and what they would all do to celebrate. Delilah planned out her route to the workhouse and fell asleep thinking of the two beautiful, smiling faces she was going to see in the morning.

She set off early, her heart singing as she walked.

# Chapter Ten

'I'm afraid that both of your sisters are dead.'

Delilah's mind refused to believe that she'd heard that correctly.

'Did you not hear me, Miss . . .' the matron leafed ostentatiously through some papers — 'Miss Shaw?'

'I've come to pick Meg and Rosie up,' whispered Delilah, although whether the words were addressed to the matron or to herself she couldn't tell.

The woman sniffed. 'I suppose that it's only natural that the news should come as a shock. But . . .' She looked meaningfully at the door.

'But,' said Delilah, as the room span around her, 'I came here in May and the cholera was over by then. And it hadn't reached this far anyway.'

This time the sound from the matron was more definitely one of irritation. 'That's correct. But the workhouse became much more crowded as a result of the cholera – orphans and so on – so it was more difficult to cope when a summer fever swept through both the girls' sections where your sisters were housed.'

Something about that caught in Delilah's mind, but at first she couldn't work out what it was. She let the matron's words run through her head again, and then she had it. 'Sections? You said, "both the sections" where Meg and Rosie lived?'

'Yes. Really, girl, do you know nothing or are you just not paying attention? The girls are divided into sections by age, so on the day they arrived your sisters were separated so that one could go to the under-tens house and the other to the over-tens. Now, if there's nothing else . . .' She made an actual move towards the door this time, as well as looking at it.

'Separated?' Delilah couldn't move. All this time she'd been thinking and worrying about what was happening to Meg and Rosie in the workhouse, but her one tiny consolation had been that at least they'd been together. But they'd been apart, apart from each other as well as the rest of the family, for nearly a year . . .

Delilah buried her face in her hands.

'Miss Shaw, I really do have many matters to attend to. I'm sorry for your loss, of course, but you have no

196

further business here.' The matron was holding the door open. 'I don't want to have to summon assistance.'

Somehow, Delilah found herself in the street outside the workhouse. Is that where she was? Where was she? She was dizzy.

Unable to walk, Delilah sank to the ground. With her back to the wall and her knees drawn up, she buried her face in her folded arms and tried not to be sick.

That hadn't just happened, had it? No, no, she must be dreaming. In reality she was still at home, and in a few moments she would wake up, walk to the workhouse and collect Meg and Rosie. Then they would all go home together and plan their joint future.

Their dear faces swam before Delilah's tightly closed eyes. But they wouldn't look like that now, would they? They were a year older than when she'd last seen them. Meg would be nearly fourteen by now, and Rosie almost seven. Meg would be old enough to get a job once she came home, and Rosie could look after Annie, getting to know and love once again the little sister who had long since stopped looking for her.

Delilah had no idea how long she remained there, fists curled and face buried. If she didn't get up, didn't walk home alone, then it wasn't real. And if it *was* real then she didn't want to go home anyway. Far better just to sit here and never move until she died.

'Delilah?'

She didn't move.

'Delilah? Is it yourself?' Delilah felt someone crouching down next to her. Hands touched her own and the soft voice spoke again. 'Look at me, darling girl. Come on, now.'

Delilah managed to raise her heavy head. The eyes that were staring, full of compassion, into her own were Bridget's.

'I knew you were coming here this morning, and I just wanted to see that everything was all right.'

Delilah could form no words, no words at all. She was so tired. It was an effort just to hold up her head.

The soothing tones continued. 'I saw you come out on your own, and then collapse here. Is . . . is everything . . . ?'

A voice said, 'They're dead,' but Delilah didn't realise it was her own.

Bridget's arms were around her. 'Oh, my poor darling girl.'

'What's all this, then?' interrupted a male voice. Delilah looked up to see a workhouse porter looming over them. 'You can't stay here. Off with you – either inside or away, I don't mind which.'

Bridget was saying something to him, something that made him speak again in a slightly less belligerent manner, but she couldn't hear the words. All she could hear thumping in her head over and over were the words *both of your sisters are dead*. She knew she would hear them again and again, every day and every night, until the end of her life. And it was all her fault.

Bridget was trying to lift her. 'Come, now, the best place for you is at home.'

Delilah allowed herself to be helped to her feet, and then felt Bridget's arm through her own. 'Now, can you walk? I'll stay with you the whole way, I promise.' Delilah still didn't quite know where she was, or why her hands and feet should be so cold on such a hot day, but Bridget was her friend, wasn't she? So she should go along with her. She should go home.

Without Delilah having the slightest idea how it happened, she found herself back in the court, back in their room, sitting on a chair.

'Stay there a moment while I light your fire, and before you know it you'll have a hot cup of tea.'

Bridget began to bustle round while Delilah stared at the wall. *Both of your sisters are dead.*

Some people were coming in. Vaguely, Delilah heard the sound of female voices whispering. 'Poor girl . . . sisters . . . she was so excited . . . wait, my kettle's already boiling, it'll be quicker . . . might have a bit of sugar somewhere . . . such a shame for her . . .' Figures flitted in and out of the light, and Delilah found a hot cup put into her hand. She had no idea what to do with it.

Bridget helped to lift it to her lips. 'Some hot, sweet tea – it will do you a bit of good.'

Delilah felt some of the sugary, scalding hot liquid slip down her throat. She coughed, drank some more, and the room came into focus. She was surrounded by kind, concerned faces; not just Bridget's but those of a number of the court's women, the ones whose daughters played together and who now shared the toil of cleaning the outside court and the privies so that everything was clean and healthy. They also, when needed, formed a formidable barrier to any local husband who got too drunk and decided to work it off by coming home to punch and kick his wife.

'You're one of us,' said Bet, Clara's mother, when she saw Delilah's questioning look. 'You work hard for your family, and my daughter's never forgotten you giving her those flowers that time.'

It was just at that moment that Pa came in. He looked like he'd spent much of the night in a gutter after getting so drunk that he couldn't make it home, which was in all probability exactly what had happened.

He looked bemusedly at the cluster of women, then growled and tried to push them out of the way so he could claim the sofa. 'What's going on?'

Delilah didn't have the energy to tell him. Bridget opened her mouth, but she was forestalled by Bet, who had witnessed Pa's tirades against the Irish several times. 'John, there's been some bad news.'

'Eh?' He stood still, leaning on his crutches, unable to push his way through the crowd.

'Delilah here has just been to the workhouse to collect your two younger daughters, and I'm afraid they've both passed away.'

Delilah felt several comforting, supportive hands on her shoulders.

Pa snorted. 'Good riddance to 'em. Fewer mouths to feed, and useless female ones at that.'

That did it.

For months and months Delilah had been working until she dropped, trying everything she possibly could to keep her family alive, the anxiety at times threatening to overwhelm her. And Pa had done nothing – no, worse than that, he had actively hindered her. He had stolen their hard-earned wages and beaten and threatened his children. Delilah had made every excuse under the sun for him: that the accident hadn't been his fault, that the drinking was understandable, that he hadn't been all that bad a father before . . . but all she had been doing was fooling herself. Pa had not one single shred of family feeling, not one ounce of compassion for his children. His family were nothing but an encumbrance. He could hear that his two little girls had died, and *this* was his reaction.

Energy and rage suddenly surging through her, Delilah leapt from her chair and threw herself at him. The group of women scattered out of her way as she thumped into him, screeching and pummelling him on the chest until he fell over. She stood over him, screaming that she wished he wasn't her father, that she wished she'd never set eyes on him, and plenty of other things she couldn't even remember, until she found herself ending with 'and you can either sober up and find yourself some work or you can *get out*!'

At that, he pushed himself up on his arms so he was in a semi-sitting position. 'You can't say that to me, girl – you'll have some respect for your father.'

'*Respect?*' Delilah almost spat the word. 'I used to think I owed you respect, and that's the only reason you've stayed here this long. But you're nothing to this family except a danger, so we'd be better off without you.'

'And how are you going to stop me coming back?' he asked in a sneering tone. 'There's no lock on the door.'

'We'll move.' Delilah surprised herself with the words. 'One day you'll come home from one of your drinking sessions and we'll have gone, gone somewhere where you'll never find us.'

Even Pa's drink-addled brain could understand that, and he started to look a little less sure of himself.

'And,' added Bet, 'as long as they live here you'll have all of us to get past if you want to hurt Delilah and those poor children.'

Pa looked up at them. They were strong Liverpool matrons, united in solidarity, and he was lying on the floor as they surrounded him with their arms folded. He shut his mouth in a line and said nothing, but the lack of argument was enough for Delilah for now.

Once Pa was safely asleep most of the women began to drift away; they did, after all, have their own concerns to attend to. Bridget remained with Delilah the whole afternoon, either listening to Delilah tell her all about Meg and Rosie or sitting with her in a supportive silence.

It was a little earlier than usual when Sam and Jem burst in through the door, excited to see their sisters for the first time in almost a year.

Sam skidded to a halt when he saw the scene before him. 'Where's Meg? And Rosie?'

Delilah couldn't leave it to anyone else to tell them, so she squeezed Bridget's hand and stood up. 'I'll be all right now.'

'Are you sure?'

'Yes. And you'd better go or your mother and your brothers will be worried.'

'All right then. I'll call back tomorrow.'

'If you've time. I've got so turned around today I can't even remember what day it is.'

'Saturday today, Sunday tomorrow. So it's selling flowers in the park if you've still the heart for it.'

'What other choice to I have? And . . . thank you. For everything.'

Bridget hugged her. 'We Liverpool girls stick together,' she whispered in Delilah's ear, and then she was gone.

Delilah turned to the boys, making sure that her face was fully visible. She didn't have to crouch as much as she used to. 'Sam, Jem, I'm afraid I have some very sad news.'

Jem reacted as she might have expected; he dissolved into tears and wanted Delilah to cuddle him. But Sam refused to believe it. He shouted 'It's not true! It's not!' at her repeatedly, getting angrier and angrier each time, and then he lost control of himself completely, howling and screaming and punching his fists on the door, the wall, anything he could reach.

William came in, carrying Annie. 'What's all the . . . ?' He took in the room at a glance, put Annie down gently and moved to enfold Delilah and Jem in his arms. 'Oh, our poor babies.'

It took a long, long time to calm Sam down, his furious rage aimed at himself as much as the uncaring, unfair world, but eventually William managed to stop him before he'd hurt himself too badly, taking the pounding from Sam's weakening fists on to his own chest while tears ran freely down both their faces. Delilah sat with the sobbing Jem and Annie on her lap, so numb by now that she didn't think she could cry any more.

Later, once the younger children had fallen into an exhausted sleep, Delilah told William everything about her day. He listened in silence until she got to the part about Pa, and then cast a surprised look over at the now empty sofa; Pa had gone out again to 'drown his sorrows', a phrase that had made Delilah snort with derision.

'Really? You said that to him?'

'Yes. And he's going to start work next week, or else.'

\* \* \*

On Monday, when there were no flowers to sell, Delilah made her way down to Queen's Dock. Thankfully eluding Mr Bradley – for she did not know how her nerves or her temper would stand another conversation like the last one – she found Abraham and told him what had happened before explaining her plan.

He made a move as though he would take her hand, and then drew back. 'Miss Delilah, I am truly sorry for your loss. I remember little Meg used to come down here sometimes to bring your Pa's dinner, and she'd look about her in that quiet, solemn way she had, taking it all in, and I used to wonder what she was thinking. I didn't know young Rosie, of course, but if she was your Ma's daughter then I'm sure she was a lovely little girl.'

'Thank you.' After that there was a silence that stretched out so long that Delilah was afraid she'd start crying again. 'So,' she said, with an effort, 'you think the oakum idea is a good one?'

'If you want to get your Pa to work it's as good as any. He can do it sitting down and you do need tough hands to be able to pick apart those fibres. It's what they make the men do in the workh— but anyway, yes, it's a fine idea.'

'Where will I get the bits of old rope from?'

'Plenty of those around the docks.' He scratched his head. 'If you head down a way towards Brunswick Dock there's a yard where people queue up for piecework. Tell

Sol I sent you, and come back to me if you have any trouble.'

Delilah thanked him and made her way to Brunswick Dock. The yard in question had its gate open so she could see the piles of old bits of broken or frayed rope. They were no good as they were, but the fibres could be picked apart and then used to make matting, she knew, or mixed with tar to seal the linings of wooden boats.

The yard was under the charge of a man with even blacker skin than Abraham, to whom Delilah addressed herself.

He looked at her face with something of a startled expression. 'I didn't know he had any relatives.'

Of course, Delilah supposed it was natural for him to assume that anyone doing a favour for anyone else would be kin. 'Oh, no, nothing like that. He's an old family friend and he knows that Pa's accident wasn't his fault, so he's just trying to set him up with a bit of work.'

'Aye, well, could happen to anyone,' replied Sol, crossing himself for luck. 'It was your Pa, then, was it, and your brother? That accident last year?'

'I'm afraid it was.'

'Well, you'll have plenty on your plate then.' He began to fill a sack with pieces of rope. 'You pay me a shilling for this. Then you take it home, get your Pa to pick it, bring the loose bits back in the same bag when he's finished, and I'll check it and weigh it. It's paid by the pound of fibre, to be sure that people aren't trying to send their sacks back half-empty or filling them with rocks to make the weight.'

When the bag was full he hefted it and pursed his lips. 'You'd probably get two shillings back for this lot, if it's all there.' Then he twisted the top and held it out to her.

Delilah handed over a shilling and took the sack. It was much heavier than a basket of flowers but she thought she could manage to get it back home. 'Is there any time limit?'

'No, just bring it back when it's done. Of course, quicker work means you get your money sooner.'

'Thank you, sir.'

He grinned. 'You can come back any time, miss, and welcome.'

Delilah was puffing by the time she got home. It was a hot day, and she idly wondered how men would manage at their labour if they had to do it wearing a corset and a full skirt that reached the ground.

Pa was in, though he looked very groggy. She fetched a cup of water, resisted the temptation to throw it in his face and handed it to him. 'Drink this.'

He did, making a face when he realised what it was.

She didn't give him the chance to speak. 'Right. This here is a sack of old bits of rope. You're going to sit down and you're going to pull them all apart into fibres, and then I'm going to take it back to the docks. Whatever money they give me for it, I'm going to keep half towards your rent and food, and you can have the rest to spend on . . . whatever you like.'

He stared at her, probably trying to work out whether it was worth arguing or not. But surely a regular supply of money would be tempting to him?

'There's no time limit,' she continued, 'but we won't get paid until it's done. It's man's work so you don't need to be ashamed if you want to do it outside. Or if you're too embarrassed you can do it in here. Just . . . get it done.'

He didn't make any move to open the sack; but then again he didn't attempt to throw it at her, either. She reckoned that the best way to get him to consider it, to let the idea sink into his befuddled mind, was just to leave him to it.

* * *

Two weeks later, Pa was on to his third sack. It was too good to last, surely, but just for now Delilah would take the break from having to deal with his temper and his violence.

She still cried every evening, but she kept going, because what other choice was there? Her remaining family needed her. They cried too, she knew they did, but only Jem and Annie would let her see it; William tried to hide his red eyes from her, and Sam kept coming home with more and more bruises from all the fights he was picking.

Today was even more of a trial. The fifteenth of September had always been a day of note in the house because it was, by coincidence, both William's birthday and Meg's. Ma had always managed to find a good meal to put on the table that day and she served it up with a hearty kiss for both of them.

Today William was fifteen; Meg, if she'd lived, would have been fourteen. Delilah wasn't sure if any of the younger ones realised the significance of the date, but she could tell that William did, and the two of them had carefully avoided mentioning it. Once the evening came, however, and the children were asleep, she moved to where he was sitting and dropped a kiss on to the top of his head. 'Many happy returns.'

He sighed. 'To me and to . . .'

Delilah sat down in the other chair. 'I know.' She raised an imaginary glass. 'Here's to you on your birthday, Meg darling, gone but not forgotten.' She paused for a moment to collect herself before toasting William, too. 'And here's to you, dearest brother. Let's hope that by next year we've got some real glasses.'

William raised his own. 'To a better future.'

# Chapter Eleven

*September 1850*

A year later, the glasses were still imaginary.

Twelve months had passed in a blur of repetition, the days and weeks blending into each other without anything of note occurring. They all did the same things every day, spread out across the city, and they ate together in the evening, trying not to mention the little ghosts who should have been there with them at the table. Delilah's head was empty, and her heart was empty, but despite her anguish she found that life somehow went on. That it had to go on.

She had continued to sell flowers, making enough of a profit to contribute her share of the family income. It was hard, hard work, on her feet all day every day and outside in all weathers, but it was much better than any realistic alternative she could think of. She had, in fact, expanded a little, buying discarded flowers from a second shop as well as from Mrs Farrell so she had more stock available, though there was very little respect in either transaction. The new shopkeeper, a man, looked down on Delilah, curling his lip every time he was obliged to speak to her, and she was still forced to creep in the back gate of the Dale Street shop every evening, as though she was doing something underhand rather than engaging in proper business. How she longed to be able to walk in the front door with her head held high!

But now was not the time to worry about that – the money was what counted. The additional income had enabled her, after a wrestle with her conscience about the cost, to buy herself a new pair of boots to replace the ones that had worn right through. Well, not actually 'new', of course – nobody in their part of Liverpool enjoyed the luxury of buying brand-new clothes or footwear – but still with plenty of wear in them. She also managed to get a thick shawl for the winter for a knockdown price, one that would keep her warmer now that she spent all day out of doors rather than just a short journey to work. The winter weather could be vicious. Some days she slipped and slithered over frozen cobbles and her hands turned blue with the cold as she tried to sell the few flowers that could cope with being out of doors in her basket at this time of year; on other days the sky hardly got light at all and the rain bucketed down, forcing her to take shelter in any doorway or corner that she could before she was moved on and forced to brave the deluge once more. Winter was the time that she most wished she could provide more for her family – a warm home, a roaring fire, plenty of good, hearty meals. But, as she could vaguely remember Ma saying to her once, 'if wishes were horses, beggars would ride'. Wishing was no good: determination and hard work was what brought results.

Bridget had sometimes come out with her, though she had much less opportunity of late. Back in the awful, dark days after she'd learned of Meg and Rosie's deaths Delilah had been obliged to struggle against feelings of extreme lowness, feelings that everything was meaningless, that there was no point getting up and going out. She had forced herself to, of course, because of the children, but that was almost a negative way to go about things – she only existed to look after them and her life was just duty and never any pleasure. It was Bridget who had helped her to see past that, who had visited her, spoken to her, sympathised with her and accompanied her when she had to go out into the world. Bridget's company had, in a very real sense, saved Delilah. Truly, she had been repaid a hundred-fold for her act of kindness on the day they had first met, and their two distinctive but contrasting heads, copper red and raven black, had become a familiar sight as they walked the streets and charmed the customers together.

The reason that Bridget had time to help Delilah was that she didn't need to work – or, at least, she hadn't needed to a year ago. Since then there had been a painful rift in her family. Delilah could not help but be aware, as everyone in this part of town was, that the name O'Malley was by now enough to strike terror into even the hardest Liverpool tough. The prizefighting that Michael had engaged in following his arrival in the city had at least been semi-legal, but he'd only been using it as a cover to get to know Liverpool and its ways before branching out into more creative and violent ways to make money. She'd seen a hint of the terror he inspired on the bridge that evening; now, with Patrick and Gideon backing him up, he ran an empire that stretched from his base in Chisenhale Street, where even the police feared to tread, out through all the nearby wards. Delilah didn't know the exact details of what the brothers did, but she'd been personally affected by it on the day that Sam had arrived home white-faced and staring with horror, stammering out that he didn't want to run errands for them any longer no matter how much they paid him. He didn't say any more and Delilah didn't ask, but for once she'd been content with a drop in their income – some things were more important.

Mrs O'Malley had never been happy with the career choice of her three sons, and Frank and Bridget, Delilah knew, shared her opinion although they hadn't dared say it out loud. But shortly after Sam's incident Frank had apparently been brave or foolhardy enough to have a stand-up row with Michael, and the result was that the two halves of the family were now estranged and living entirely separately. Frank had to support his mother and sister on his own, and Bridget had found herself a job. With so many advertisements carrying the phrase 'No Irish need apply' there was not much choice, so she now spent six days a week sewing in an airless sweatshop. If she got the chance she still came out with Delilah on a Sunday, as she considered selling flowers in the park with her friend as a treat after spending so much time indoors.

Frank had taken on a second job, working in a hotel in the evenings after he'd finished at the railway station, but he'd been sacked from it as soon as it had come to the attention of the management that he was one of the notorious O'Malley brothers. It was deeply unfair, but what could anyone do? Delilah could only sympathise with both of them and help where she could, making sure Bridget got some rest as well as air on Sundays, and spending part of each Monday visiting the increasingly lonely Mrs O'Malley. If their rooms were cleaner when she left than they had been when she arrived . . . well, that was just coincidence.

Delilah also managed the occasional visit to Ellen Jenkins, taking her any spare flowers as a gift and concealing her sadness as she watched Jemima play. But it was such a treat to be able to talk about Ma, and Delilah learned more about her mother's earlier life than she'd ever known before. She could now picture the two of them, Ma and Ellen, laughing their youthful way round town just like her and Bridget, living life to the full before marriage had curtailed their freedom and – in Ma's case, anyway – constant childbearing had worn her down.

On a couple of occasions Delilah had been there when James had come home for his dinner in between shifts at the docks, and he'd recalled that Abraham had mentioned Delilah to him – something about a book, and flowers? She explained, and the next time she came there was a volume waiting for her, borrowed from the friend of a friend. Delilah took it home and treated it like the treasure it was until she knew the names of every flower in her baskets, then returned it in pristine condition.

The book had contained the Latin names of flowers as well as the English ones – words Delilah couldn't read but which William had found fascinating. He was standing in front of her now, raising his imaginary glass in what she suspected would become a yearly ritual between the two of them.

Today was the day that would have been Meg's fifteenth birthday and that was William's sixteenth. Delilah had to look up at him quite steeply; although he was by no means muscular he had gained a great deal of height and now towered over both her and Pa – probably one of the reasons why Pa was a little calmer these days, afraid that if he tried anything he'd get a proper wallop in return. Not that William would strike anyone, unless seriously provoked; he hadn't been that kind of boy and he wasn't going to be that kind of man. He remained Delilah's main worry, pushing himself to engage in the heavy manual labour that was all that was available, working through and beyond his strength as he tried to move from a boy's wages to a man's. If he carried on, Delilah was worried he'd end up in an early grave.

They were gathered in the room: William, Sam, Jem, Annie and herself, all that remained of the family except Pa, who had done his day's oakum picking and taken his allowance to the gin shop. Delilah had arranged a treat for them all – one consequence of their tragedy was that she had a little more money to spend as they weren't trying to save up enough to bring their sisters home, a bleak irony that never failed to stab her in the heart whenever she bought anything. But those who were left needed her, and it was something to be able to provide them with more and better food.

'There's hot pie for everyone, and when we've eaten it there's gifts.'

*What, for everyone?* Some months ago Jem had shined the shoes of a gentleman who was interested in education for the deaf, and who was now teaching him – for free, as an experiment – a new and quite detailed form of sign language, twice a week at a special school for children who couldn't hear. Jem, in turn, was teaching the others at home, and Delilah was finally discovering how much he had to say for himself now that he had the means to express it.

She replied in sign language herself instead of speaking, her movements not quite as smooth as his. *Yes, for everyone. But eat first.*

They all tucked in, and soon the room was full of the happy sound of a family enjoying a good meal.

Once the pies had been demolished, all eyes turned to Delilah expectantly. She left them in suspense just for a few seconds and then laughed. 'All right. Now, William first, because it's his birthday.' She produced a white cotton shirt for him that she'd made especially for his long, thin frame by cutting up a much larger one she'd bought second-hand and sewing it anew. As he began to thank her she held up a hand. 'Ah!' Then she handed over the main part of the present – a starched collar to go with the shirt. 'If you want to look for the sort of job that needs a collar, best have it ready to start with.'

He turned it over and over in his hands, then leaned over to kiss her cheek. 'It'll be my lucky collar, I'm sure. And I'm even luckier to have you for a sister.'

'What about us?' Annie was unable to contain her excitement, fidgeting in her seat.

'Well, this is for you.' Delilah took from her pocket a bright blue hair ribbon.

Annie clapped with joy. 'Tie it in, tie it in!' Once Delilah had fastened it, the little girl ran over to look at her reflection in the window. 'Oh, wait till I show Clara!'

Delilah looked at her, enjoying her delight. Annie was four and a half now, almost big enough to start coming out with Delilah on her rounds. Delilah had let the question lie for a while, but as Bet was now making noises about her youngest daughter finding a job, it would need to be faced soon. But today was not the day to worry about it.

She turned to Sam and Jem. Sam was twelve, almost twelve and a half, just on the verge of starting adolescence and promising to turn into a burly young man like Jonny had been. He was impatient to move on from being a crossing sweeper, anxious to play his part in the family and earn a proper income.

Delilah reached under the table. 'Now that you're growing up, I thought you'd need these.' She flourished a pair of boots. 'And, I know Jem is younger, but I also know you share everything. I couldn't risk you ending up with one boot each, so . . .' She produced a second pair.

They whooped with delight: neither had ever worn shoes, and getting a pair was a sure sign of growing up.

Jem signed, *Thank you*, and then added, *But what about you?*

'Oh,' said Delilah out loud, 'my best present is seeing you all happy, warm and fed.' And she meant it: the past was the past, but the future looked better, even if they didn't have glasses to drink a birthday toast.

\* \* \*

William decided to start his quest for a clerking job the very next day, setting off extra early in the hope of catching Mr Bradley before anyone else arrived. But he was back not long afterwards with the surprising news that the overseer wouldn't talk to him about it until he'd spoken to Delilah first.

'What can he possibly mean?' It was a Monday, so Delilah was still at home. 'Nobody needs to talk to a man's sister before giving him work. Surely he should be checking that you can read and write and add up.'

William shrugged. 'I can't work it out either, but it's what he said.'

Delilah was as irritated as ever at how much power Mr Bradley had over their lives. 'I'd better come, then.'

They made their way to Queen's Dock together. By now it was time for the morning's work to be allocated, so Delilah stood by while Mr Bradley attended to that, pleased to see that he picked William but aware that it would be yet another morning of backbreaking labour for him, unloading sacks of coffee beans from a newly docked ship. Hopefully William would soon have work much better suited to his capabilities, recording and tallying up the sacks instead of carrying them. She had a very uneasy feeling about her forthcoming discussion with Mr Bradley, but she would have to be as polite as possible while trying to tell him how clever William was and how he'd be an asset to any office.

As soon as all the men had dispersed to their work, Mr Bradley beckoned to Delilah. He held the door of his office open for her politely and then followed her in, shutting it behind him. He sat in the chair behind his desk and gestured to the one opposite it. 'Please, my dear, take a seat.'

Delilah still had the feeling of unease, and was glad to have the solid wooden desk separating them. 'It's about William, Mr Bradley.'

He nodded and sat with his fingers steepled as she launched into the speech she'd been preparing in her head all the way there. William was extremely bright, not to mention hard-working, he'd been to school and had received many good reports from the schoolmaster, he could read, write a neat hand, reckon figures at speed. She emphasised what the benefits would be to Mr Bradley and the company he worked for, sensing that this would be a better tactic than simply saying she was desperate to find William a better job.

He kept his eyes on her through it all, but she got the impression that he wasn't really listening.

When she'd finished he leaned back. 'You do amuse me.'

'I beg your pardon?'

'You, sitting there and giving me chapter and verse about your brother's education, when you must know why you're here.'

Delilah began to experience the same heightened awareness of danger that she had felt on the evening she'd accidentally walked down Chisenhale Street. 'I'm here because you wanted to speak to me before you would employ William as one of your clerks.'

'You're here because you need to persuade me if you want me to employ him.'

'That's what I'm doing, isn't it?'

His demeanour changed. 'Oh, don't play the innocent with me, girl. You know exactly what you're here for.'

She was becoming increasingly aware of that, but, with panic rising, she wondered if she could still extricate herself from the situation by pretending not to know what he was talking about. 'Mr Bradley, I—'

He got round the desk quicker that she would have thought possible, and stood over her. She could see the bulge in his trousers.

'Come, now, let's be sensible about this,' he said, reaching out to toy with a strand of her hair.

He was standing so close that it was difficult for Delilah to get out of the chair, but she managed to push it back so she could stand up. Maybe the tough-Liverpool-matron act would be better than the pretence of innocence. 'Please don't touch me.'

'Don't touch you?' he laughed. 'What, like this?' He ran his hand down her arm.

She slapped it away and stepped back.

He sighed. 'It's going to be like that, is it?'

'I'm leaving now, Mr Bradley.' Delilah moved towards the door.

'If you do, your brother will never work again.'

That gave her just enough pause to enable him to cover the ground between them and seize her. She just about managed, 'How dare—' before his hand clamped over her mouth.

He put his lips close to her ear. 'Let's be clear about the bargain. I know what you want, and you know what I want. So be nice, and we'll both be happy.' Revoltingly, he licked the side of her face.

Really panicking now, Delilah struggled to free herself, but without success.

'What are you making such a fuss about?' continued Mr Bradley, shifting the arm that was pinioning her so he could put his sweaty hand on her breast. 'A girl like you, poor, walking the streets every day? I'm sure you sell more than flowers. And I'm sure that fancy Irishman of yours knows the inside of your skirts as well as the outside.' He began to push her towards the desk.

For one moment, Delilah made herself stop. Her struggle against his restraining arm ceased and she went limp.

He felt it. 'That's better. Now, be a good girl and do as you're told. I flatter myself you might even enjoy it enough to come back for more.'

Delilah had lived in the court and walked through the nearby alleys every day for the last two years, and there was a reason she'd come through the experience unmolested. She'd gone limp in order for him to drop his guard, which he duly did, loosening his arms from around her so he could use them to lift her skirts. As soon as her arms were free she spun on her heel, drew back her fist and punched his face as hard as she could. Not an open-handed slap, as he might have expected from a woman, but a proper punch. *You put all your weight into it*, Sam had said, and she did; the force of years of hard labour at the laundry tub was behind her knuckles as they smacked into his jowly face.

The pain she felt in her hand was incredible, but it had worked; he staggered back with blood spurting from his nose. She took advantage of his surprise and discomfort to shove him back against the wall, and then her hatpin was in her hand.

She held the sharp point of the four-inch-long steel pin close to his eyes as they widened in terror. 'I've only ever used this on men's hands,' she said, 'but I'm sure there are other places it could be used to good effect.'

She backed away, still holding it out in front of her as she moved towards the door.

He spat, a mixture of blood and saliva landing on the floor. 'You'll regret this.'

'I doubt it.'

'I'll break you all. Your precious William will be home at noon and he'll be there for some time – they'll be no work for him, nor your other brothers, not ever. Not until you come crawling back and *begging* me for my attentions.'

Delilah left the office without replying and slammed the door behind her.

Once she was outside her knees gave way and she staggered. But she couldn't collapse yet, not here, not so close to where he still was. Besides, she thought she was going to be sick.

The dock was, as ever, busy. The nearest men were queueing up to deposit heavy sacks of coal on a wagon, and some cast a curious glance at her as they waited.

The tallest among them heaved his burden up and over the tailgate, then turned. 'Delilah?'

It was James Jenkins. He strode over. 'I thought that was you. What . . .' He took in her face and the office door behind her, and his mouth set in a grim line. 'Let's get you out of here.' She felt herself being ushered away from the office, then he stood by her until she stopped shaking and was relatively confident that she wasn't about to lose the contents of her stomach.

'No need to say.' James was never a man to waste words, for which Delilah was thankful. 'I have to get back to work, but if you want to go up and see Ellen . . .' He left the rest unsaid.

'Thank you, James, I'm grateful. But I'll be all right to get myself home.'

'Sure?'

'Yes.'

Delilah straightened herself and moved away, feeling his eyes on her as he made sure she was capable of walking before he left.

The further she got from the docks, the steadier her gait became. What had just happened – and what had nearly happened – was dreadful, but it was over. It was all over. Yes, William had lost the best chance of work that any Liverpool man had, for more were employed at the docks than everywhere else put together; but on the other hand, they were finally free of Mr Bradley's malign influence, of the power he wielded over them. She had left him behind, and there was surely no reason she should ever have to see him again.

\* \* \*

Delilah was busy scrubbing around the court's water pump when William returned, as she knew he would, in the middle of the day.

To her surprise he was accompanied by Abraham. Delilah stood to welcome him, and he stepped forward with his hands outstretched. 'Miss Delilah, are you all right? James told me and I had to come.' His face was full of concern for her, but under it she could see that he was absolutely furious, more angry than she'd ever seen him. He was actually shaking.

The court's little girls stopped their skipping game to cluster about Delilah and stare. Clara in particular was looking from Abraham to Delilah with a puzzled expression.

'I'm sorry,' said Abraham, noticing. 'I didn't mean to scare any of the children.'

'It's probably just because you're a stranger – I don't think I've ever seen you so far from the docks before.'

'No, I don't venture too far from my place of employment, just in case. Specialist fruit porters are few and far between, and I'm the best, so they're keen to hold on to me. Otherwise, as you know, I'm afraid I might end up on a ship. Anyway,' he continued. 'I came here to see you were all right.' The anger returned. 'That Mr Bradley wants teaching a lesson.'

While Delilah was grateful that anyone should care so much, his expression alarmed her. 'Abraham, please! Please don't do anything, or even say anything to him. I've already lost William any chance of more work – I don't want to be responsible for losing your job too.'

His face was a picture of reluctance, but eventually he nodded. 'If you say so. You're the injured party here, so you get to choose.'

She took his hand and looked into those green eyes. 'Not injured.' She couldn't resist a tiny smirk. 'It wasn't me who ended up with a bloody nose.'

His face creased into a smile. 'Really? Well, I might not say anything to him directly, but if word should happen to get round the place that a woman beat him – mentioning no names, of course – while he was doing something he shouldn't, it might take him down a peg or two.'

'I wouldn't be sad to see that happen,' she replied, with a straight face. 'Now, Pa's inside just finishing up the last bits of oakum picking in the load he's got at the moment. Would you like to step in and see him?'

That was odd, she thought, as she heard herself speak the words. Normally she wouldn't invite anyone inside as she didn't want them to witness their poor standard of living, but she knew Abraham wouldn't look down on them for it, wouldn't *pity* them.

He shuffled his feet awkwardly. 'Best not. He might not want to see me, in case it reminds him of times past. Of how he used to work at the docks, I mean, and now he can't while I still do.'

'You might be right.' Delilah sighed.

'But if he's just finished a sack I'll be happy to carry it back now, to save you the trouble. Then I can bring the money and a new one up here tonight after work, or William can come and fetch it after Mr Bradley's gone home. I don't think – if you'll excuse me advising you, Miss Delilah – that you should go near Queen's Dock for a while.'

'That's very kind, thank you.' Delilah shivered, then pulled herself together to fetch the bag from inside.

'I'll come and get the new one from you later,' said William, who had stood silently by during all this time. Delilah wasn't entirely sure if he knew the full story of this morning's events or not, or if she even wanted him to know. The shame should be Mr Bradley's, not hers, but she couldn't help feeling it anyway.

'Yes, please don't put yourself at any risk coming up here again, especially after dark,' she said to Abraham. 'I couldn't stand it if anything bad happened to you.'

Abraham seemed almost overcome. 'Really?'

'Of course.' Delilah remembered that he had no living family at all, nobody to care whether he lived or died. How awful to be so alone. She paused, trying to form her thoughts into something that wouldn't sound too foolish. 'However bad life gets, it's bearable with good friends and family, and we need to treasure them.'

'Yes,' said Abraham, swinging the sack on to his shoulder. 'Friends and family should always be treasured.'

# Chapter Twelve

That evening Delilah contemplated their financial situation as, with Jem's help, she made up tomorrow's bunches of flowers. William's income would be nothing at all until he found something else, and the loss of any possibility of dock labouring was a huge blow. However much she had wanted to get him out of it, at least it had brought in some money while they searched for something better. Pa was still, surprisingly – Delilah might almost say *suspiciously* – continuing with his oakum picking, but it was slow and it didn't pay very much; about three shillings of profit for the three sacks he got through a week. Delilah or William would carry it down, see it weighed, take the coins and then give back a shilling for the next sack. Delilah kept strictly to her promise of giving Pa back half of his earnings to spend on gin. She didn't like it, but it was unrealistic to expect him to give it up entirely, and this way at least they could keep some control of his drinking and she could put the other half towards rent and food.

William had been bringing in about fifteen shillings a week while he had regular work, and that was now all gone. Until he found something else, or until they could get Sam some waged labour, she would have to be the family breadwinner. So be it.

William came in just as she was trying to work out how much they would have to cut down on food in order to keep up with the rent payments. He put down the sack. 'Abraham had it ready for me – he picked it up earlier when he dropped the other one off.' He pulled some coins out of his pocket. 'Funny, I didn't think it was much heavier than usual, but he said we got two shillings for it, even after paying out for the new lot.'

Delilah took the money, perfectly aware of how that had come about but too tired and worried about the future to think about finding Abraham and chiding him. Instead she gave thanks for good friends.

She hesitated as she came to put it away. 'I did promise Pa half of everything he earned, but he'd only be expecting sixpence . . .'

'You also promised to feed the children,' said William, firmly, taking the coins from her again and dropping them in the drawstring bag that lived under the broken floorboard. 'And given that I've been stupid enough to end up out of work, I'll take responsibility for underpaying him so we can use the difference to buy bread.' He pulled a sixpence from the bag and placed it on the table.

'But you didn't . . . I mean, it was me who . . .' Delilah couldn't find the right words.

William took her hand. 'I might be younger than you, but I'm not a complete innocent. I should never, ever have put you in that position this morning; I just wasn't thinking straight. I *do* want to get a better job, better so that I can earn more – and have a working life that lasts a bit longer – so that I can start to pay you back for all you've done.'

She began to demur but he continued. 'You've been mother and father to me and the others, as well as the best sister anyone could wish for, but, well, now I'm a man and it's up to me to take some responsibility. Mr Bradley doesn't hold sway everywhere – there are other docks, so tomorrow morning I'll go and queue up at one of those and take my chances.'

The following morning Delilah went out on her now familiar rounds with an added feeling of urgency. All the work, all the heartache of the past two years, and now they might end up right back where they started – in danger of losing the roof over their heads. But perhaps all was not lost; by now she had a number of regular customers, so the buttonhole flowers were all gone before she'd been at the station for half an hour, and business was brisk outside the market.

She reached the pleasure-boat docks – still safe to visit, as Mr Bradley was half a mile away – a little early, before any passengers had started to arrive. Seeing that there were no constables nearby, she gratefully took a few moments to sit down, rearranging the display in the baskets so the blooms would appear to best effect.

A few people began to trickle past, and a couple paused by her.

'Delilah?'

Delilah looked up into a face she recognised from somewhere, but couldn't quite place.

'It's Madge, from the laundry. Remember me? You helped me by sewing that torn bit of lace that time.'

'Of course.' Delilah stood up. 'How nice to see you again.'

'Is this what you've been doing, then, since the laundry shut?'

'Yes. I decided I liked it better than being stood over a hot tub all day.'

'Ain't that the truth. Well, one good turn deserves another.' Madge elbowed the young man who was with her. 'You buy me one of those bunches of flowers. Whichever is the most expensive.'

Delilah looked at them both more closely as he stammered and fumbled with some coins. He was young and semi-respectable in a suit that hadn't been mended too many times. The contrast between his appearance and that of Madge, in her gaudy low-cut dress and with her face slathered in far too much rouge, made the nature of their relationship obvious.

Madge took her flowers from the young man. 'Now you just wait over there while we have a little chat, and I'll be with you in a minute.' His face took on a sulky expression and she squeezed his hand. 'Don't you worry, love, just one minute, and then you'll have me for *all* the rest of the day.' She fluttered her eyelashes and he took a few paces back, mollified, turning to look at the boats.

'He's not bad, considering,' said Madge. 'There's plenty worse, and I'll get a few treats and some food out of today's work as well as the cash.'

Delilah shuddered at the thought of how easy it would have been for her to fall into a similar line of work, and she wanted to tell Madge that she was sorry it had happened to her, but would that be insulting? 'I'm glad to see you looking well,' she managed, eventually, thinking that was safely neutral.

'Oh, you know, the occasional bruise and some of these fellas aren't too nice in their habits, but it's a living, isn't it? And I make more than I ever did at the laundry.'

'They're starting to board,' interrupted the young man from his position a few yards away. 'We'd better get going.'

'Well, it's been good to see you, Delilah,' said Madge. She sniffed the flowers. 'And these really are lovely.'

'Freesias,' replied Delilah. 'Probably the last ones for this year.'

But Madge was already turning away, taking the young man's hand and pressing herself close to him as they made for the boats.

Delilah watched her for a few moments, and then forced a smile to her face as she began to move among the crowds, persuading the happy holidaymakers that their day would be made complete by the purchase of her flowers.

William was already home when she got back, which wasn't a good sign. 'No luck?'

He shook his head. 'I tried Canning Dock today. Nobody knew who I was, so I was right that Mr Bradley couldn't blacklist me there, but of course the overseer there had his own regular men and he was bound to pick them first, over and above a stranger. I'll go further up and try George's or Prince's tomorrow.'

But the following day it was the same story, as it was on the next and the one after that. All the overseers had their favourites, men who got regular work – as Pa had been used to under Mr Bradley – and they were picked first. And if more men were needed on any particular day, there were plenty to choose from who were big and burly; who was going to hire a thin, gawky boy ahead of them?

It was with some surprise, then, that Delilah heard the words, 'I've got a new job,' as William came in one evening towards the end of September with a sack of rope pieces for Pa.

'What?'

'Oh, don't get too excited, it's a pittance, but it'll be better than nothing until I can find something else.'

'Doing what?'

William pointed to the sack. 'Sol, at the yard, is getting overrun with so many people wanting to pick oakum because they can't find other work. So he wants someone to help with the weighing and measuring and so on.'

'Well, that's kind of a clerking job, isn't it?'

'I suppose you could put it like that, yes. Only ninepence a day, but I can pick the stuff myself whenever there's time, and I'll get paid extra for that by weight, same as everybody else.'

Ninepence a day. For six days a week that was . . . four and six? A far cry from what a man could earn labouring, but it would buy a loaf of bread each day if she could keep up with the rent and everything else.

She congratulated him and went back to tying flowers.

\* \* \*

The following Sunday Bridget and Frank both joined Delilah for her round of the park. It was a beautiful sunny day, no hint of autumnal chill in the air yet, and Delilah had a wide selection of posies in her baskets. She was hopeful of good sales, and so it proved: there were many couples and families taking advantage of the fine weather and the green open spaces.

Delilah was standing by a bench and busy chatting to a solitary and very serious young man about which flowers would be best for him to buy for the girl he was walking out with – a kitchenmaid, apparently, and one who didn't see the outside world very often – when she became aware of a whispered conversation taking place between Frank and Bridget. She completed the sale and watched the youth hurry off in the direction of the far side of the park to meet his beloved before she turned to the others.

Immediately they both assumed straight faces. 'How about if I stay here with your baskets for a while,' suggested Bridget, with a sideways look at her brother, 'while the two of you go for a walk? It would be nice for you to have a stroll without having to carry them. And don't worry, I know the prices of everything if anyone should want to buy.'

Delilah shook her head. 'That's not allowed. I've tried it a couple of times before and always got moved on by a constable or a park keeper. They can't stop me selling as long as I move round, because it's a public place, but as soon as I sit still it means I'm setting up a shop, or something, and they don't permit that.'

'Oh.' Bridget's face fell, and she looked uncertainly at Frank. He rolled his eyes at her and jerked his head, clearly trying to tell her something.

'Well,' continued Bridget to Delilah. 'Then how about the other way round? I'll take the baskets and walk, and the two of you can have a sit down. That will be a nice rest for you.'

Bridget quite obviously had something in mind – did she maybe want to have a try at selling by herself, to see if it was the sort of thing she could do instead of working in the sweatshop? – so Delilah thought that the best thing to do was agree. 'Of course. We'll wait here until you come back, won't we, Frank?'

'Oh yes,' he said, picking the baskets up and shoving them at his sister in his haste for her to be gone.

Bridget whispered something in his ear that Delilah didn't catch, and then set off. Frank indicated the bench and waited for her to take a seat before he joined her.

There was a silence.

Delilah was very comfortable sitting quietly; it was a change from the constant obligation to chat and be charming so that she could make more sales. And she was by now very easy in his company, having long ago accepted that he saw her only as his little sister's friend.

But Frank seemed unusually fidgety.

'Delilah,' he said, at last.

'Yes?'

'We've known each other quite a while now.'

'Yes.' She did a quick calculation. 'Almost exactly two years.'

'Is it really? How time flies.'

There was another silence.

'And . . . ?' Delilah was curious as to what he was going to say. She hoped it wasn't going to be any kind of indication that they should all see less of each other.

'What I mean is, we've had time now to get to know each other.'

'We have.'

'Bridget's never had such a good friend, and I know my Mam thinks the world of you too.'

Delilah was touched. 'That's very kind of you to say, Frank. I think the world of both of them too.' There were other words that she really, really wanted to add, but she didn't dare.

'That's good. And . . . what I mean is, *I* . . .' He stopped again and swallowed.

This really wasn't like Frank at all. Delilah stared at him in puzzlement.

He stuttered a couple of times, then broke out with, 'Oh, for the love of God, Francis!' in a tone of frustration, loudly enough to cause some nearby walkers to turn round. 'Will you just spit it out!' he told himself.

He stood up, strode away a few paces, came back and stood before her. 'Right.' He took a deep breath. 'Delilah, I admire you more than any girl I've ever met. More than that, I love you. So what I'm saying is . . .' He dropped to one knee, reached towards her, stopped, remembered to take off his cap and tucked it under one arm, then took her hand. 'Will you make me the happiest man in all of England and Ireland, and marry me?'

Delilah could hardly believe what she was hearing. A surge of joy, of absolute exhilaration and delight, ran through her. He loved her! He really did see her in the way that she saw him, as someone to share his life with. Every single fibre of her being wanted to say yes – *yes* I will marry you, *yes* we can leave it all behind, *yes* we can be happy.

But that was impossible.

Delilah closed her eyes and allowed herself to bask in the joy just for a few short, blissful moments. They were moments she knew she would remember for the rest of her life, but for now she had to come back to earth.

Frank was still on one knee, and the two of them were beginning to attract attention from passers-by. Not in a bad way; they were all smiling and no doubt ready to applaud or congratulate the happy, handsome young couple once the girl did what she was supposed to and said yes. But none of them knew anything about Delilah's life, and she wished they would just go away. 'Frank,' she said, in an urgent whisper. 'People are looking at us. Please, get up and sit on the bench with me.'

His face fell as he scrambled up to sit beside her. 'That's not precisely the answer I was hoping for.'

She took his hand. 'I have never been as happy as I was just then, not once in my whole life.'

'As you were just then? Not now?'

'I just . . . before we decide on anything, we need to be practical.'

He brightened a little; after all, she hadn't actually said 'no'. 'All right, practical it is, then.' He waited for her to elaborate.

'What I mean is – it's not just us, is it? It's the children and Bridget and your mother.'

He looked at the floor. He knew it too, but he wasn't ready to face it.

'If you and I moved somewhere together, just the two of us, what would happen to all of them? Can you possibly imagine the lives that my brothers and sisters – *sister* – would have if I upped and left? If they only had Pa?'

Frank mumbled something that she didn't catch because he was still hanging his head.

'And your family, too. Bridget could never earn enough to support your mother on her own.'

Now he looked up, his face red. 'I've got three brothers all living in Liverpool.'

'And your mother disapproves of what they're doing. If she doesn't want to live on the proceeds of—' Delilah brought herself up short; she had nearly said 'crime', but she didn't want to make the accusation quite so bald. 'On money that they might not have earned through honest labour,' she went on, carefully, 'then that's up to her, isn't it? And Bridget – if she was reliant on Michael and the others, do you think it would be long before she was dragged into their kind of life? Doesn't she deserve better?'

Frank said nothing.

'I'm sorry,' continued Delilah, gently, squeezing the hand that she still held, 'but it's no use pretending that our families don't exist. We have responsibilities, both of us.'

He had tears in his eyes now. 'But it's not *fair*!'

Delilah knew as well as anyone that life wasn't fair, and she wished she had the luxury of sitting complaining about it while someone else thought of the practical details.

They sat in silence for a few minutes before Delilah began again. 'What if . . .'

He looked at her with hope dawning in his eyes. 'What if what?'

'I was just wondering if . . . oh, I wish I was better at arithmetic.'

'Just tell me what you're thinking.'

'Well, what if we were all to move in together somewhere? You and me, your mother and Bridget, the children and . . .' She tailed off. 'And we'd have to talk about whether Pa came too or not.'

He stared at her.

'What I mean is, if I keep bringing in the same as I do now – maybe more, even – and you keep earning, maybe we could swap our two separate places for one bigger one? We'd need at least three rooms, a whole house, even, because we couldn't ask your mother to share with the children, but if you and I and Bridget and William were all bringing in money, maybe . . . ? And you must be earning a decent wage to be able to afford where you live now, paying for it all yourself.'

Frank's hand had been gripping hers ever more tightly, but now it slackened and he sighed. 'There's something I have to tell you.'

'What?'

'Michael still pays our rent.'

'What!'

'Ma said she wanted nothing to do with him, with any of them, unless they took to honest work, but Michael came to me and said he knew I wasn't earning much and he wasn't about to see his Mam and his sister starve even if they didn't want to see him. So he told me he'd pay the rent directly to the landlord and I was to keep my mouth shut about it.' Frank hunched his shoulders. 'And you don't argue with Michael.'

'So you wouldn't be able to keep that place with two rooms without him?'

'No. Nor earn enough to rent a big place for all of us, neither.'

'I see.'

Frank shook his head. 'I've been saving what I can out of my own pay, though, saving just enough for the two of us so I could ask you to marry me.' He swallowed. 'And you still haven't given me an answer.'

Delilah turned away, her eyes full of tears.

'But don't you love me?' His voice was desperate.

She let her tears fall. 'Yes, Frank. Yes, I do love you.' She turned back towards him, taking both of his hands in an urgent grip now and looking him in the eye. 'I've loved you since the day we first met. But getting married isn't all about love – it's about being able to live, and it's about family. You've got yours and I've got mine – and once we were married we'd no doubt start having children of our own as well. If getting married ends up with someone starving or with more children going to the workhouse to die, then it's not worth it. I'm sorry.'

'So that's a no, then?'

'It's a no until we can find a way to make it work for everyone. Just to give us some time to think. Until—'

He shook his head and jerked his hands away. 'No, it's a no because you don't love me enough to even try.

It's because you think more of those children than you do of me.' His tone was bitter as he stood. 'I'm sorry to have ruined your afternoon.'

He stalked off without another word, leaving Delilah staring after him.

She'd had to, hadn't she? She'd had to answer as she did. The idea of the two of them marrying and running away to live somewhere by themselves – the idea of having Frank all to herself – might have seemed beautiful for just a few seconds, but how could it be? It would be monstrously selfish, and anyway she wouldn't have been able to enjoy her new life amid all the guilt and worry about those she'd left behind. Yes, William was nearly an adult, but he couldn't keep the others and he certainly couldn't control Pa. The life they would all lead without her didn't bear thinking about. But she'd only meant to say 'not yet', not the definite 'no' that Frank seemed to have understood. And now it was too late to call him back; his wounded pride had increased his pace and he was already out of sight.

Delilah still hadn't collected her thoughts when she saw Bridget coming towards her, from the direction in which Frank had headed. She approached very warily. 'Delilah?'

Delilah stood up. 'Yes, yes I'm here.'

Bridget put the baskets down and pulled a few coins from her pocket. 'Probably didn't sell as many as you would have, but . . .' She pushed the money into Delilah's unresponsive hand, then cleared her throat. 'Can I ask . . . ?'

'You probably know some of it already,' said Delilah, dully. 'Frank asked me to marry him, and I said no.'

Bridget gasped. 'But . . .' she said, after a moment, 'I know that you like him. So if you turned him down then you must have had a good reason for it.'

'Frank didn't think so.'

Bridget was looking at Delilah in concern, but she was also turning her head back the way Frank had gone, evidently torn.

'It's all right,' said Delilah, realising that her loss was about to be doubled. 'You have to follow him. Don't worry about me, I'll be fine.' She took a deep breath. 'You go – family has to come first.'

# Chapter Thirteen

Delilah couldn't stay sitting on the bench, not now she had her flower baskets back – a park keeper would inevitably appear out of nowhere to move her along. So she gathered everything up and made her way towards the gate on the town side of the park.

Her conversation with Frank replayed itself over and over again in her head. With each retelling she thought of different things she might have said, different ways she could have approached the subject, but it didn't matter because each time the result was the same: she couldn't marry the man she loved if it meant abandoning the family who depended on her. Something had to be lost, and better her happiness than the children's lives.

On one point she was determined: they would never know of the sacrifice she had made for their sakes. If she mentioned anything about what had happened today then William, and probably Sam as well, would say that she had been wrong, that she should put her own life first and that they would be fine by themselves if she married Frank. But once that decision was made there was no going back on it: marriage was for life and she wouldn't be able to change things if she saw the children suffering without her. Even a man as nice as Frank would expect his wife to stay under his own roof.

This resolution gave Delilah enough courage to make it all the way home. Somehow – for she couldn't remember any of the transactions – she had made a few more sales on the way home and there was now just a single posy left in one basket. She took it up and pressed her face into it, inhaling the scent, as she came to the narrow entrance way.

The last few shards of sunlight were slanting into the court as she stepped into it. There was still plenty of the afternoon left, but once the sun dipped below the level of the tall houses it could not reach into the narrow space so it always seemed that evening came more quickly here, the darkness swallowing the court before it turned its attention to the wider streets. The usual crowd of small children were playing, the girls calling out to Delilah and one or two of them hovering around her when they saw the leftover flowers, a rarity these days. Delilah presented the posy to Clara and told her to share it, and they all squealed in delight and ran off to the far corner with their prize.

Pa was sitting on the outside step of the house that contained their room, but he wasn't picking oakum there, as he sometimes did; he was drinking from a bottle. Despite only getting the odd sixpence back from his earnings and not having stolen anything from his children for a while, he still seemed to have plenty to spend on drink and Delilah often wondered how he managed it. She hoped he wasn't getting bottles from the gin shop on credit, which would result in a threatening visit at some point when he couldn't pay it back – but no, they wouldn't do that, would they? There were far too many drunks around the place, and they'd be out of business if they offered credit. He must be getting it from somewhere else.

Delilah was not in the mood to question him about it just now, so she merely said, 'Hello, Pa,' and made as if to walk past him.

'Where you been, then?' he slurred.

'Out selling flowers in the park, Pa, like I do every Sunday.'

'Got money?'

She took a pace back, out of his reach. 'Yes, but it's not for you. You have to earn your own.'

He waved the bottle. 'Bloody woman, thinking you can tell a man what to do, and your own father, too.'

'If I hadn't told you what to do, Pa, you'd have been dead in a gutter a long time ago.'

'Well, you won't do it much longer.'

'Won't I?'

'No.'

He didn't explain further, but he was still blocking the doorway and she didn't want to get too close now he knew that she had money on her. So she simply stood, her arms folded.

After a while he finished the bottle and heaved himself upright on his crutches. He struggled and swayed but she made no move to get closer or to support him, in case it was a trick.

'Think you got one over on me,' he mumbled. 'Making me pick oakum and do work that's beneath my dignity.' He leaned forward and she could smell the gin fumes even from several paces back. 'I'm your father and I say what goes, and I've got the law on my side.'

He was evidently even drunker than he looked; Delilah had no idea what he could be talking about. 'Pa, I'd like to go inside. Can you get out of the way, please?'

A sly smile came over his face and he lurched away from the door. 'That's right, you go in.'

Delilah took a step and then hesitated. Something wasn't right. 'Why?' she asked, suspiciously. 'What's going on?'

'I've made a good bargain.' He sniggered. 'Sorted out your future for you, I have.'

'Pa, what's this all about?'

'You can thank me, girl, 'cos I've done you a favour.' He waved at the door to their room.

Delilah sighed. She was going to have to face whatever it was at some point, so it might as well be now. She put out a hand towards the latch.

'I've arranged for you to get married,' said Pa, just as the door swung open to reveal the smirking face of Mr Bradley.

# Chapter Fourteen

Delilah immediately tried to back out of the door, but Pa was blocking her way.

'Now, now,' said Mr Bradley, coming forward. 'Is that any way to greet your future husband?'

'Future nothing,' spat Delilah. 'I'm not going to marry you!'

'Ah, but you will,' he continued, unabashed. 'Your father says you will, and legally you're his property so you'll do as you're told.' His eye roved over her in a way that might have made her turn away in disgust if she hadn't been so angry. 'And once we're married, you'll be mine.' He licked his lips.

Realisation dawned, cutting through the rage. 'Oh, so it's you who's been putting ideas in Pa's head, is it? He would never have quoted the law to me outside if someone hadn't put him up to it. And I suppose it's you who's been buying him all that drink recently, too.'

'Just to show him how much of a friend I am to him, in his time of trouble.'

'You're no friend to any of us.'

'I am, and I will be. Just think what I could do for you all.'

Delilah was about to let rip another furious retort when Pa belatedly joined the conversation. 'You keep your mouth shut, girl. Mr Bradley's offered me good money for you so you'll marry him and like it.'

'You *sold* me?' Delilah couldn't keep the incredulity out of her voice. Then she turned back to Mr Bradley with a look of utter contempt. 'And you thought you could buy me?'

He looked amused. 'Of course I can buy you! I'm a man with money and you're a girl with none, so I can do what I like and you have to go along with it.'

Delilah had been aware, all her life, that this was the way of the world, but to have it spelled out so plainly still cut deep. Oh, why hadn't she said yes to Frank's proposal, only an hour ago and yet now half a world away? At least then she'd have had someone on her side, someone to stand with her. Someone who *cared*. But now it was too late.

Mr Bradley couldn't have any idea of what she was thinking, but he noticed her momentary hesitation. 'Let's be sensible. As your father says, you'll end up as my wife anyway, and it would be so much nicer if we could come to a voluntary arrangement.'

'There is nothing you could possibly offer that would make me marry you.'

'No? You haven't heard my terms yet.'

'Terms? What is this, a business agreement?'

'That's exactly what it is. Marriage isn't all about romance, you know, it's about family.'

These were so close to her own words in the park that Delilah gasped. How much more was she going to be made to regret the events of this afternoon?

Mr Bradley sat down at the table as though it were his desk. He motioned to the other chair but Delilah remained standing, unwilling to be caught the same way she had been in his office. If she stayed on her toes she might be able to make a swift exit if necessary, if she caught Pa by surprise and knocked him off balance before he could catch her.

'Option one,' began Mr Bradley, who still seemed completely at his ease. 'You marry me of your own free will. Your father gets a cash payment for his . . . support. William gets a job as a clerk with promotion prospects if he does well. Young Sam gets steady labouring work. And I dare say we can even find something for the little simpleton if we look hard enough.'

'He's not—' began Delilah, furiously, but Mr Bradley held up a hand. 'Result: respectability all round, not to mention adequate food and housing. I'm well aware that you've been managing on less and less since . . .' he cast a glance at Pa – 'since William found himself unable to secure regular work.'

'And you think I should sell myself for this?'

'You might find it an attractive option when you consider the alternative.'

Delilah snorted. 'The alternative is that we carry on as we are without having anything to do with you, which is just fine.'

He wagged his finger, shaking his head with an assumed expression of sadness. 'Oh, my child. So naïve. No, my dear, that's not the option at all.'

She said nothing, though a feeling of dread began to creep over her.

'Let me spell it out for you, seeing as you don't seem to understand.' Mr Bradley began to enumerate on his pudgy fingers. 'If you don't marry me you will starve and be forced to sell yourself on the street anyway, and I assure you that you won't like it. William will lose even that pathetic little job he's doing at the moment, and neither he nor your brothers will work at any of the docks again once I've spread the word. And, let me see. That James Jenkins has been heaving coal for ten years now – he's bound to start slowing down soon and he won't be able to hold on to that well-paid position that supports his wife and that delightful little girl of theirs.'

Delilah gasped. Surely he couldn't . . .

But there was worse to come.

'And finally,' said Mr Bradley, his smile becoming nastier, 'it would be a dreadful shame if your friend Abraham should accidentally find himself on a ship bound for America. Something he's been keen to avoid for years, of course, but such accidents do happen when sailors are drunk or ships short-handed.'

He fell silent and folded his hands in front of him on the table. 'Now choose. You'll marry me either way, but the longer you take to say yes, the fewer privileges come along with it, and the more the . . . alternative options come into play.'

Delilah found that she couldn't breathe properly. For some reason there wasn't enough air in the room. Her head felt fuzzy, she was dizzy . . .

'That's the job for your youngest brother gone,' she heard Mr Bradley say from a great distance. 'Not that he'd have been much use anyway.'

Delilah opened her mouth, but no sound came out. Was there nobody here to help her?

'Are you *sure* you don't want young Sam to get some good, honest labouring work? By the look of him he'll be well suited to it as he grows.'

The panic was threatening to explode, to shatter Delilah into a thousand pieces. She collapsed on to the second chair in an attempt to avoid falling to the floor.

'Oh dear,' he began again. 'It seems—'

'I'll do it!'

Mr Bradley leaned back with a satisfied smile, and Delilah realised with a sinking heart that the words had been her own. She was just conscious enough to attempt some damage limitation, adding 'in the spring' before he could open his mouth.

He looked less pleased. 'What?'

Delilah tried to pull herself together. 'I said, I will marry you in the spring. You can't expect me to be ready straight away, and the spring is a much nicer time for a wedding.'

'How like a woman,' he sneered. 'But you and your family don't get any of the benefits until the wedding is over and the certificate signed. I'm not *that* lovesick.'

'Agreed.'

'Very well.' Mr Bradley stood. 'Now, if my soon-to-be father-in-law would leave the room – or not, it makes no difference to me – perhaps we could arrange an advance on our connubial bliss.'

Delilah didn't quite understand his words, but there was no mistaking his intention as he moved towards her with his arms outstretched and horrible look of hunger in his eyes. 'Absolutely not!' she cried, somehow finding the energy to spring from her chair and move away.

'Don't be silly. Now we're engaged, certain liberties are permitted.'

Delilah backed into Pa, and for one awful, terrible moment she thought he was going to grab her, to force her to submit to Mr Bradley's demands. But he'd been watching their exchange with what seemed like amusement, and now he took the opportunity to use the tiny bit of power he had gained over the man who had ruled his working life for so long. 'Now then,' he slurred, putting out a hand to stop Mr Bradley's advance. 'We're respectable people, don't you know. If my daughter wants to stay clean until she's properly wedded and bedded then she can. Besides,' he added, as the main point worked its way into his addled brain, 'you don't get her on her back until I've had my money.'

'And you won't get that until the wedding is over,' snapped Mr Bradley, angry and frustrated but thankfully looking like he was preparing to back down, on this point at least. But he couldn't resist a final dig. 'I'll leave you both for now to your *happy* family discussion about your future.' He straightened his waistcoat and waited for Pa to move away from the door so he could pass unimpeded. As he did so, he managed to get close enough to Delilah to whisper in her ear. 'And you'd better start thinking about exactly what you're storing up for yourself once you're under my roof.'

He left.

Delilah wanted to scream at Pa, wanted to hit him and shake him until he was aware of how he'd just ruined her life, but the events of the afternoon were just too much and she collapsed back on to the chair.

He looked like he'd been preparing a victory speech, and he'd even got as far as 'And that's what you get for—' when he saw the weeping overtake her. He left her to it for a while, but when it went on and on, Delilah scaring herself with her inability to stop, she felt the unusual sensation of a hand on her shoulder.

She looked up into a face that almost resembled the Pa she'd known when she was younger. 'Stop that now,' he said. 'You girls all want to get married, and he's as good a catch as any, better than most. You won't have to worry about food or a roof over your head.'

She pushed his hand away. 'It's a bit late for that now, Pa. You *sold* me, remember? Like an old pair of boots.' Didn't she have a right to feel bitter? 'I've given up everything for this family over the last few years, everything except my own dignity. And now you've stolen that from me as well.'

The memory of the old Pa disappeared again, and the uncaring drunkard returned. 'Have it your own way, then. I'm off out, so you can get something on the fire.' He pushed open the door. 'It's getting dark so the others'll be home soon.'

And then Delilah was alone. Alone with her thoughts and the impossibly large wave of everything that had happened today, crashing over and over and threatening to drown her if she wasn't careful.

Feeling the need to punish herself, she told herself that as she'd already thrown away her chance of happiness with Frank, and would be miserable about it for ever, then what did it matter if she married Mr Bradley? If she was going to be miserable her whole life she might as well be miserable with a full belly. But the thought of a 'full belly' only reminded her that she'd have to comply with all Mr Bradley's demands, would have to bear his children, and that made her feel sick. Losing Frank was one thing, but this really was infinitely worse. How could she possibly face it?

Just then the others all came in together. They looked hungry, which was no surprise given how little food had been in the room for the last couple of weeks. She had only lit the fire now to boil water for tea; the meal itself would be bread and jam. And next week there would be no jam.

And that, she knew, was the reason why she had to go through with the arrangement. Her family needed her, and she had to do whatever it took to protect them even if the prospect made her shudder in horror.

Delilah knew she wasn't fit to look at, so she turned away from them to poke the fire. As she stared into the red coals, she began to pray for a miracle.

\* \* \*

Miracles failed to happen over the autumn.

Delilah could feel the walls beginning to close in on her. She was actually earning more money than ever before, pacing the streets from dawn to dusk and beyond, but she just couldn't support the whole family on her own. She tried to avoid thinking about the fact that if it *had* been just her and Frank, with no other dependants to think of, they would have been able to manage very nicely on their joint income. But whenever she allowed herself to fly off into a little pleasant daydream, even just for a moment, the cold, hard reality of the situation hit her. She *did* have to support everyone, she was losing ground while she did it, and she was going to have to marry Mr Bradley if she wanted the boys to have any chance of decent work in the future. She was doing it for them, and that must serve as her reward.

One of the worst things about her situation was that she had nobody to talk to, nobody to share the burden with or to ask for advice. There was no point in talking to Pa, the only other person who knew; and besides, she was still so furious with him that she could barely stand the sight of his face. She couldn't talk to William, as she had decided she didn't want him or the younger children to know what she'd done. She didn't want to talk to Ellen or to Abraham, partly out of shame and partly in case she let slip what Mr Bradley had threatened against them, which would just complicate matters. And she couldn't talk to Bridget because she didn't see Bridget any more, and that was almost the worst blow of all.

Bridget had called once, early in the morning of the Sunday a week after the terrible day. She wanted to check on Delilah, but her concerns were only with what had happened in the park, for she had no idea about what had occurred afterwards and Delilah didn't tell her. Delilah half-wondered if Bridget might bring a message from Frank, perhaps a request for her to reconsider, but she didn't. Instead she brought the news that Frank had left Liverpool, giving his family no idea of where he was going or how long he might be away.

Although Bridget didn't know it, she was hammering the final nail into the coffin of Delilah's dreams. Any tiny sliver of hope she might have had about escaping Mr Bradley had relied on Frank. She didn't know how, exactly, but even the thought that he was near, that she might soon see him and speak to him, had been a comfort. And now that was gone too, and she had been responsible for great changes in Bridget's life as well as her own.

With Frank and his income gone, Bridget could not hope to support herself and her mother, and this had thrown them back into a reliance on Michael and the others. Michael had been angry about everything that had happened without his knowledge; he'd immediately banned Bridget from working in the sweatshop and told her to stay at home and look after her mother like a good girl should. He'd also had some words – which Bridget wouldn't repeat – to say about Frank, his situation and his suddenly disappearing, and Delilah got the impression that she herself wouldn't get quite such a friendly reaction if she were to encounter the remaining O'Malley brothers again. Michael's orders were also, explained Bridget finally, that she wasn't to see Delilah again. 'He said he thought you were different, but he always knew we couldn't trust anyone except other Irish, so I'm only to stay near home and talk to other women that have come over on the boats.' She raised her eyes to Delilah's. 'I'm so sorry.'

'Oh, how you must hate me for doing all this to your family!'

'No! No – not at all.' Bridget took Delilah's hand and held it to her cheek. 'None of this is your fault, darling girl. I don't know exactly what you said to Frank, because he wouldn't tell me, but I know it was something about money and having to care for us all – Mam and me as well as your younger ones. And how could I possibly hate you for wanting the best for all of us?'

'But still – look what's happened.'

'And that's not your fault, either. We live in a world built for men, and all we can do is make the best of it.' Bridget closed her eyes and pressed her lips together in an effort not to cry. 'I wish I could stand up to Michael, could tell him I was going to see you whether he liked it or not, but . . .' She broke into half a sob. 'When I marry, I want a man who's gentle and kind – is that too much to ask? But I can see the road in front of me.' Her tears began to fall.

Delilah embraced her. 'There now. You mustn't go against what Michael says, do you hear me? You're the best friend I ever had and I'll miss you—' She had to stop for a moment to compose herself before continuing. 'And I'll miss you, but I can't risk putting you in danger. I'd rather not see you if it means I know you're safe.'

'Oh, Delilah!'

After a few moments Delilah moved back and wiped her eyes. 'You'd better go, get back before you're missed.'

Bridget nodded, stood up and left.

Delilah hadn't seen her since that day, more than two months ago now. Every so often, on her way around the city, she thought she caught sight of a head of bright hair, but either she lost it, or it was too far away to see if it really was Bridget, or it turned out to be someone else; there were so many Irish in Liverpool now that red hair was not as unusual as it had been.

Mr Bradley called round to see them with a distressing frequency. To start with he had made one or two half-hearted attempts on her person, but she'd rebuffed him and he didn't argue. This was not, she suspected, out of any sense of decency but rather that he enjoyed making her uncomfortable about it and reminding her of what was to come: once they were married she would have no choice other than to do what he wanted. The thought made her shudder and whenever it occurred she tried to suppress it, but it remained lying in wait, ready to leap out at any unexpected moment when she might feel a twinge of happiness about something and need taking down.

He was here now, the evening before Christmas Eve. Delilah would be physically safe from him, she knew, for everyone was at home, it being too cold and dark for running around outside after their meal. Today he'd decided to play Lord Bountiful and had turned up with hot food, watching the conflicting emotions on Delilah's face as she simultaneously despised him while watching the children eat a good meal.

'Nice to see them enjoying themselves,' he said to her in a knowing, mocking way. 'And nearly Christmas, meaning the year's almost over. It won't be long until spring.' Delilah understood the emphasis on the final word, even if nobody else did.

She tried to ignore him, concentrating on tying her flowers by the light of the single candle.

Jem was next to her, and he stopped working for a moment to gaze into her illuminated face. Then he looked carefully to make sure that he had his back to Mr Bradley before signing, *You don't like him, do you?*

Mr Bradley was busy talking to Pa, so Delilah signed back, *No, I don't.*

*Neither do I.*

*But . . .* began Delilah, before stopping. The complexities of the situation were far too great for her command of sign language. *It's difficult,* she managed.

Jem looked at her, at Mr Bradley, and back at her again, but he said nothing further.

'What's that you're doing over there?'

Delilah jumped, but it appeared that Mr Bradley was referring to the flowers, not her unseen conversation with Jem. He came to stand over them, and Delilah felt Jem's hackles rise even as she shifted position herself so she wasn't touching Mr Bradley as he moved uncomfortably close.

'Ah, your little flower business,' he said, still maintaining the jovial tone he'd been using since he handed out the food. 'How charming.'

'It's not charming.' Delilah mentally scolded herself for rising to the bait, but she couldn't help it. 'It's hard work and it brings in an income.'

He sensed that she knew she should have kept her mouth shut. 'Well, you won't need to keep it up much longer, will you?'

She stared at him, shaking her head and hoping he'd understand that he'd said too much, but it was the wrong reaction; it gave him the advantage.

'What I mean is,' he said, loudly and to the room in general, 'once we're married I shall insist that you give it up. I'm perfectly able to keep a wife in comfort, and it would be embarrassing in the extreme to have Mrs Bradley walking around selling flowers – or anything else – like a common street girl.'

There was silence. He smirked triumphantly as he tucked his thumbs into his waistcoat.

Delilah could feel William staring at her in astonishment and, she thought, horror. Sam had understood too and was now signing to Jem, so rapidly that Delilah couldn't catch it while she was only half-looking at them.

'Oh, didn't you all know?' continued Mr Bradley, addressing them all but aiming his venomous smile at Delilah. 'Your beautiful sister and I are to be married in the spring. She's obviously been so overcome with joy that she's forgotten to mention it.'

The atmosphere was tense for the rest of the evening. Everybody felt it except Pa, who was oblivious because Mr Bradley had brought a couple of bottles round. Annie didn't understand, of course, but she picked up on how unhappy everyone else had become and she started to whinge and asking to be picked up. As it happened, this did Delilah a favour as Mr Bradley, becoming increasingly irritated with the noise, announced that he was leaving. If he was expecting a hearty farewell then he was to be disappointed; a roomful of hostile faces watched him in silence as he put on his coat and left.

Once he had gone, all eyes turned to Delilah. She couldn't do it – she couldn't face their questions, their disbelief, their accusation. Before any of them could open their mouths she ran outside.

The court was empty, though she could hear plenty of noise from inside the houses and from the alleyway that ran past the entrance to this and the many other nearby courts. That was probably, she realised, because it was absolutely freezing out here. Nobody in their right mind would be standing around in the chill air – especially when they'd left in such a hurry that they hadn't put their shawl on – when they could be sitting by a fireside. But then, she wasn't in her right mind, was she? Otherwise she would never have agreed to marry Mr Bradley.

Delilah hugged herself and bounced up and down in a futile effort to keep out the cold. But she couldn't go back in, not just yet. She looked up at the narrow band of sky that was visible between the tall buildings and tried to count the stars, so far away and so oblivious to everything that was going on down here. *Wish upon a star*. But there were no answers to be found there – the only answers to anything would come from inside herself.

She was shivering now, but she stood stubbornly outside for a good while longer. Eventually the cold started to seep into her bones, and she reluctantly conceded that making herself sick with a chill wasn't going to help anyone.

At least she had only one person to face. By the time she got back in everyone was asleep except William, who was at the table staring into the last guttering remnants of the candle. Delilah sat down and glared at him defiantly without speaking.

'Is it true?' he asked, eventually, dragging his gaze away from the flame. 'You're going to marry *him*?'

'Yes.'

'I don't understand.'

'No, of course you don't.'

'You don't like him – in fact you actively dislike him. And after what happened that time – how *could* you, Lilah? How could you?'

She felt the first stirrings of anger. 'I did it because there was no other choice.'

'Of course there was a choice! All you had to do was say no, and he'd leave us alone.'

The laugh that escaped her came out like a bark. 'Leave us alone? William, you don't know anything about it.'

'Tell me, then.'

She was irked enough to let some of it slip. 'William, he stopped you getting a job at his dock, and he can stop you working anywhere else down there too. And not just you – Sam and Jem will never work either, and then where will we be?'

'But we could have worked something out! You know none of us would ever want you to marry him, not for us. We could have managed, somehow!'

Delilah slammed her fist down on the table. 'William, you earn ninepence a day, and the others about sixpence between them. How are we supposed to "manage" on that?'

His face was agonised. 'But for you to . . . you can't, Lilah, you just *can't*.'

'DON'T TELL ME WHAT I CAN AND CAN'T DO!' In her anger and frustration she had raised her voice too far and the children were stirring, so she dropped it to a furious whisper. 'I will happily tell Mr Bradley that I won't marry him, that I never want to see him again, as soon as you show me *another choice*.'

His face fell and she knew she'd upset him. He would think that she was blaming him, which she wasn't, not really, but it was unfair of him to tell her she'd made the wrong choice when he knew very well there wasn't another one.

Delilah was desperate to get away, desperate for some time to herself, a space to be alone, but that was the one thing she never had. So she settled for turning her back, wrapping her shawl about her and hunching down into it. He got the message, and there was silence as the candle flared and then went out.

# Chapter Fifteen

As she went outside to attempt to get some water out of the frozen pump on Christmas Eve, Delilah blew on her hands and wondered if it was even worth going out today. Who was going to buy flowers in this weather? And what was the point anyway if she was soon to have to give it all up? Might as well surrender now, marry Mr Bradley right away and get it over and done with. But she'd spent money on those flowers and time arranging and tying them, so it went against everything she stood for to just waste them. She was still her own woman, and she would go out if she wanted to.

When Delilah got back inside William was fixing the starched white collar on to his shirt. He looked at her shamefacedly. 'Yard's closed today, but offices in the town will still be open. I'm going to visit as many as I can to see if they have any positions.' He picked up his coat and made a face at it. 'Not as smart as the shirt, but I can't really go without it or I'll look even worse.'

She took it from him and made an attempt to dust it down. 'No holes in it, at least.'

'No, because you've mended it. Taking care of me, like you take care of all of us. Like you always have done.' He risked meeting her eye.

Her heart went out to him. She reached up on her tiptoes and kissed him on the cheek. 'Good luck. Maybe you'll find a Christmas miracle.'

'Maybe we all will.'

After he'd gone Delilah woke the others. The railway station would be busy today so the boys were preparing for a long day; she wrapped them up in as many layers as she could find.

Once she'd done the same with Annie and left her out to play, Delilah picked up her baskets and made her way out to the main streets. The buttonholes went quickly outside the station, as usual, and Delilah was beginning to wander in the direction of the markets when a bustle of activity outside a church caught her eye.

It was a wedding, a rich-looking one. The groom and his best man had just arrived, both resplendent in scarlet regimental coats as they were greeted by the small crowd of friends who had gathered. Three girls of about Delilah's own age, all dressed in lavender gowns, giggled and blushed and turned their heads away as the best man addressed them with a jovial expression. None of them, Delilah noted with a professional eye, were carrying flowers even though they must surely be the bridesmaids.

The men lingered on the pavement for a while, but then someone pointed to an approaching carriage and they both strode up the steps so as to be inside the church before the new arrivals could see them.

Delilah was in no particular hurry to get to the markets so she drifted over to join the crowd – not mingling with the guests, of course, but loitering at the back with the curious passers-by. Everybody loved to see a bride, and with everything that was going on in her own life the subject was of particular interest, painful as it might be.

The carriage came to a halt, and a middle-aged man whom Delilah assumed was the bride's father climbed out. He looked prosperous; a merchant, perhaps, smart in a well-cut suit that was straining slightly across his stomach as he turned back to hold out a steadying hand, the bridesmaids standing ready behind him to assist.

A sigh went up from the onlookers as the bride stepped out of the carriage. She had followed the new trend of choosing a white dress. This had been unusual up until a few years before, but the queen herself had broken with tradition for her own wedding; Delilah vaguely remembered a picture from a penny paper being passed around all the women on Brick Street at the time. And, of course, whatever the queen did was sure to be picked up in refined circles, so the bride emerged in a cloud of white silk and lace. She was a beautiful girl, pale and delicate, but that wasn't what fixed Delilah's attention. No, what Delilah noticed most of all was that the bride looked radiantly happy. This, her wedding day, was evidently the happiest of her life. She had beatific smiles for all and sundry as she paused for a moment on the carriage step to survey them.

Her eye caught Delilah's for a moment and Delilah, without really thinking about it, curtseyed to her. Then the bride stepped down and Delilah lost sight of her, but she soon became aware of the word 'flowers' being bandied about, and then the bride's father was pushing his way through the crowd. 'Flower girl! Was there a flower girl here?'

Delilah found the crowd opening up before her and hoped she wasn't about to be embarrassed or humiliated in some way. She had a perfect right to be here, didn't she, on a public street?

But the man was smiling so broadly that he couldn't be about to reprimand her. Instead he beckoned. 'Come! Come here, miss.'

Delilah made her way forward and soon found herself surrounded by white and lavender gowns and the fragrance of expensive perfume. 'Oh, Papa!' exclaimed the bride, clapping her hands. 'How wonderful!' She turned to address Delilah. 'Ours didn't arrive on time, and I thought we would have to do without. And yours look so pretty! And at this time of year, too.'

'They're grown under glass, madam,' Delilah managed. Was she going to be lucky enough to make a few sales?

'Oh, *please*, Papa,' the bride was saying, but she didn't need to beg – her father was already extracting coins from his pocket.

Delilah was just starting to rummage among the posies to see which ones would be best for a wedding when the man stopped her. 'We'll take everything you have, miss. Will ten shillings cover it?'

Delilah tried hard not to let her jaw drop. It was more than double what she would have expected to get, and the man was genuinely holding out a *gold half-sovereign* to her. It glinted in the winter sun.

Honesty won out. 'That's too much, sir,' Delilah began.

He interrupted, still smiling expansively. 'Young lady, you have made my daughter happy on her wedding day and that's worth more to me than anything – I refuse

JUDY SUMMERS

to quibble. Here, take it, take it – you're our Christmas miracle.'

Delilah curtseyed again, lost for words, and took the coin.

'Now,' he continued, briskly, to his daughter, 'you take whichever you want for yourself, and we'll hand the others around to the lady guests.' He addressed Delilah again. 'Can you do that for us, miss?'

'Of course, sir.' Delilah still couldn't believe her luck. She passed out posy after posy to happy, smiling faces and felt her own spirits lift. Who could fail to feel joy when they were surrounded by so much of it, regardless of their own circumstances? Not Delilah, that was for sure.

Eventually the guests, and then the bride and her entourage, disappeared into the church. Delilah didn't dare peek inside, but she remained outside the door despite the cold, watching as a few snowflakes started to descend. She still had two bunches of flowers left, and they had been paid for fair and square – more than fair – so she wouldn't walk away with them; it wouldn't be honest. Besides, she wouldn't need to continue with her round at all. And she did feel just a sneaking urge to see the happy bride again, this time as a married woman.

The guests came out first and formed into lines on either side of the door, so Delilah stepped back, though she did manage to spot a couple of ladies who didn't have flowers so she could distribute the last two posies that had been paid for. Then out came the bride and groom, bright white and blood red against the grey stone of the church. The crowd cheered as they paused on the step, their faces glowing with shared exultation.

This time it was the groom whose gaze met Delilah's. He whispered a few words in his new wife's ear and pointed; she followed the direction and nodded.

Once they were down on the pavement and had finished receiving wishes of goodwill from their friends, the groom approached Delilah. 'So you're the one who made my wife's happiness complete.'

Delilah looked at the beautiful, smiling bride. 'I rather think that might have been you, sir.'

He laughed. 'Well, I can't thank you enough.' He turned to the best man, who was at his shoulder. 'Have you any coin on you, old boy?' And before Delilah knew it, he was holding out another half-sovereign. She started to shake her head but he insisted. 'With my compliments and those of my dear wife.' He laughed again. 'That sounds dashed odd, but I suppose I shall get used to it in time.'

The wedding party moved off, leaving Delilah standing half in shock at her good fortune and half in the pleasure of knowing that at least one young woman in Liverpool had a father and a husband who cherished and cared for her.

Once some of her amazement had worn off, Delilah realised that she now had the rest of the day free and that she had money in her pocket. Most of it, of course, would need to be put by, saved sensibly, but it was Christmas Eve and there was very little food at home.

The entrance to St John's market was as busy as she'd ever seen it, bustling crowds everywhere. This time Delilah wasn't selling anything so she didn't need to stay outside; she walked right in with her empty baskets just as if she were a respectable housewife out to do the food shopping.

The amount and choice of everything almost took her breath away, just as it had on the other occasions she'd been inside the vast, echoing space. There were larger shops all around the edge, proper rooms with fireplaces and lockable shop frontages, and then five spacious open avenues in the middle, running the whole length of the building and filled with different-sized stalls packed with fresh produce. The high roof was supported by numerous iron pillars, each of which had a gas lamp attached to it, and Delilah thought that the market would look wondrous indeed when they were lit later in the day, banishing the winter darkness.

Delilah examined each stall carefully before making any purchases. She was not extravagant, but she did allow one treat for the family: as well as bread, jam, potatoes and a bit of bacon, she bought the ingredients to make a Christmas pudding and a piece of muslin to wrap it in. She had a brief moment of worry when the stallholder gave her a very peculiar look indeed when she proffered a gold half-sovereign, but she drew herself up and stared at him haughtily until he backed down. She passed it over, the young queen's head clearly visible just as it had been on that long-ago shilling.

On the way out of the market, her empty baskets now full again, Delilah noticed, lying on the floor, a small sprig of holly. It must have broken off a branch somewhere – there were plenty of them around – but nobody was claiming it and if she left it there it would only get trampled. So she picked it up and tucked it into her shawl.

Once she reached home she put the holly on the mantel for luck – the day had already brought plenty of it, after all. She stowed her riches away safely, lit the fire, scrubbed the table and then turned with a will to the currants, peel, flour and suet, the small twist of sugar and nutmeg, and the three precious eggs that she'd carried so carefully. She'd never really been the family's cook – Meg had taken that over from Ma as soon as she could be safely left by the fire, and since they'd lived here they hadn't had much to cook anyway – but all she really had to do was combine all the ingredients into a large ball and then wrap it in the cloth and tie it up. Then it was into a pan of water over the fire, and all she had to do was wait, and think. *You're our Christmas miracle*, the man had said. Well, Christmas miracles and winter wishes were like snowflakes: they were beautiful and lovely to think of, but they disappeared as soon as they came into contact with anything solid. Delilah had long resigned herself to the fact that miracles, dreams and wishes were not for the likes of her.

She tried not to think about Frank, or about Meg, or Rosie, or Jemima, or Ma.

As Delilah watched the pudding boiling – made as it was with real, solid ingredients, not fleeting wishes – her cheer returned and she hugged herself at the thought of the children coming home to find such an unexpected treat. It would need to cook for many hours, but it was not much past noon now so the timing would be just right for when the boys got back this evening, and if they were careful with it there would be some left for tomorrow, their day of rest.

Delilah didn't know exactly how much time had passed, but it was much earlier than she expected when Sam burst through the door like a whirlwind, followed some moments later by an equally breathless Jem.

They'd been running so hard that at first they could neither speak nor sign, and she was left in an agonised suspense. They were both here, Annie was just outside, so had something happened to—

Sam got some of his breath back, gasping as he bent forward with his hands on his knees. 'You have to come. You have to come right now.'

It was so like what had happened on the day that Pa and Jonny had had their accident that Delilah was frightened almost out of her wits as she threw on her shawl.

But Sam's next words stopped her dead. 'It's our Meg – she's alive!'

\* \* \*

Delilah hadn't run so fast since she was a little girl.

As luck would have it, William had arrived back just as she was flying out the door to pick Annie up and follow the boys. She'd had to leave the fire, but

JUDY SUMMERS

she'd pushed all the hot coals to the back of the grate where they could just be left to die down naturally. It was a waste of good heat, but she didn't care.

They were now all hurrying through the cold and darkening streets, she and William taking it in turns to carry Annie as they listened to a breathless Sam explain even as he ran, urging them to greater speed. Meg was alive. A young man who was a friend of hers had found him and Jem at the station. Meg had previously spoken to this youth – or his mother, or something – about her family. She had mentioned two brothers who worked outside the railway station, one of them deaf. She had described what he and Jem looked like two years ago. This young man – Tommy, his name was – had been able to find them by coming to the station and asking around. To start with Sam had been suspicious of him knowing their names, but Tommy had given them such an exact description of Meg, allowing for the time that had passed since Sam had last seen her, that he was convinced. He'd dropped everything and run home as fast as he could to tell Delilah, outpacing Jem in his hurry.

Delilah, thankfully passing Annie back to William, was able to question Sam further. How had this all happened? Had this Tommy said why Meg hadn't come looking for them herself, all this time?

Here Sam was less sure. Delilah could understand that: once he'd heard the astonishing news about Meg's survival, he surely wouldn't have been able to concentrate on the details. What she could glean was that Meg didn't know that Tommy was at the station looking for them, because it was a surprise for her, and she thought *they* might all be dead. Sam didn't know why, but that was why she hadn't come looking herself. 'But anyway,' Sam continued, 'she's alive, she left the workhouse and she's got a job as a maid in a big house.'

'So where are we going? To this house?'

'Yes. You go to that park, he said – you know, that one where you sell flowers on Sundays. If you go right over the other side of it there's a row of big houses. Last one on the left, he said, and go down to the basement door.'

'But . . .' By now Delilah was having trouble speaking and running at the same time. 'Are they expecting us? Does Meg know we're coming? And whose house is it?'

'Don't know,' called Sam, pulling ahead. 'Don't care! Meg's there and nothing's going to stop us seeing her. So come *on*!'

The terrace of houses was enormous – they must be some of the finest in Liverpool, four or five floors high at least. The family stood uncertainly outside the one at the far end. 'Are you sure?' asked Delilah again. 'He really said Meg was here?'

'That's what he said,' insisted Sam, stoutly. 'And I'm going to knock even if you aren't.'

Delilah couldn't let him go on his own, so she led them all down a set of steps to what she knew would be the servants' entrance. She paused for a moment to make sure they all looked as smart and respectable as possible, then took a deep breath and rang the bell.

The door was opened by a girl who looked to be about thirteen or fourteen, but it certainly wasn't Meg.

'Oh,' said Delilah, taken aback. 'I beg your pardon. We were told that Meg Shaw lived here . . . ?'

The girl's reaction was extraordinary. Her eyes widened, then she broke into a huge smile, covered up her mouth in an attempt to stifle a squeal of excitement, and hopped from one foot to another.

When she was able to speak, she burst out with, 'Are you Delilah? Oh, you must be Delilah! And is this William, and Sam, and Jem, and little Annie?'

Delilah was about to reply, thinking that this girl really must know or have known Meg, when a severe-looking woman appeared behind her. 'Sally? What's going on here?'

Sally squeaked and turned to her. 'Oh, Mrs Lawrence, it's . . .' Delilah didn't catch the rest, as Sally was hiding her mouth and whispering.

Understanding dawned on the woman's face as she listened, and she too smiled at them, suddenly appearing much less stern. 'Miss Shaw, is it? Do come in, yes, all of you, the children too. Come this way into the servants' hall. Sally, wait one moment and then go to the kitchen.'

Feeling hopeful but slightly bemused, Delilah followed Mrs Lawrence down a passage and then into a spacious room that contained a large dining table. Mrs Lawrence left them there, making her way up a staircase in the corner, and Delilah stood uncertainly with the others clustered around her.

Before she could even begin to formulate a proper thought, the door to the passage opened once more. Delilah caught a brief glimpse of Sally before the girl stepped back and pushed a neat young woman into the room.

For one frozen moment Delilah and the newcomer stared at each other. Afterwards she was never quite sure which one of them had made the first move, but before she knew it she and her sister Meg were in each other's arms.

\* \* \*

It took some time before Delilah could fully grasp the enormity of what had happened, but fortunately they would now have all the time in the world to catch up with each other. To start with they were all only able to express shock and delight over and over again, and Delilah could hardly take in the words of Mrs Lawrence, who appeared again to invite them – all five of them – to return the next day to have Christmas dinner with the house servants. Delilah's joy was tempered by the sad confirmation from Meg that Rosie really had died in the workhouse, and on the way home that evening she shed many tears again for her lost little sister.

When they got back the room was empty, for which Delilah was thankful as she didn't want to have to deal with Pa – or with Mr Bradley, who had threatened to drop round – just at the moment. The fire had gone out but she lit it again, in the happy knowledge that she had the money to buy more coals, and they were all able to tuck into their somewhat undercooked pudding. Nobody cared about or even noticed the consistency; all their talk was of Meg and of the miracle that had happened. They had thought both sisters gone for ever, and now one had been returned to them. They stayed awake late into the night, all too excited to sleep, before falling one by one into a contented slumber.

The next morning Delilah woke up almost in a panic. Had it all been a dream? Had she been wishing so desperately for her sister that she had conjured up the complete phantom of her survival? But she hadn't – not unless all the others had experienced the same dream, for it was the only subject on everyone's lips.

Delilah spent the morning making last-minute repairs to clothing, aware that her stitches weren't as neat as usual because her hands were shaking. As noon approached she made the boys wash their faces and slick their hair down with water while she tied in Annie's blue ribbon, now rather the worse for wear but still the prettiest thing any of them owned. Once she was sure they were as smart as they could be, they set off.

They were welcomed once more with extreme cordiality, and Delilah could see again how much these people really cared about Meg, how they were delighted that she had been reunited with her family. *They appreciate her much more than I ever did, but I'm going to make up for that from now on.*

The meal was magnificent, the most stupendous spread Delilah had ever seen, and if this was what they ate in the servants' hall she hardly dared think what might be served upstairs. She attempted to remain delicate, not letting her hunger show, and reddened a little when she saw the way Sam and Jem were wolfing down their food and looking around for seconds. Happily Mrs Roberts, the cook, only looked on contentedly and said what fine boys they were and that it was nice to see good food being appreciated.

There appeared to be no hurry for them to leave after dinner. William fell into intelligent conversation with the house butler and footman, Sam and Jem played with a boy who was about their own age, and Annie was being made a fuss of by Sally and another girl, so Delilah had the leisure to sit to one side with Meg and hear everything that she had to say.

Some of it pierced her heart. The trials of what she and Rosie had suffered in the workhouse, the privations and the cruelties – and it was she, Delilah, who had condemned them to it. When she attempted to express an apology, however, Meg shook her head. 'Nobody was responsible for the matron's cruelty except the matron. You weren't to know.' Her tone was firm, mature; Delilah realised again just how much her younger sister had grown up since they had last seen each other more than two years ago.

She was just beginning to feel more reassured – that Meg had forgiven her, that their future was looking brighter – when the blow fell. Meg didn't want to leave her position to come home with them. She was explaining it, saying she did love them but she'd carved out a life for herself here, that she would happily send them her wages, but that she wanted to remain . . . but Delilah didn't hear most of it, so overwhelmed was she by the news. Then the cook said something about Meg having a rare talent, but Delilah wasn't paying attention to that either. All she could think about was her own sense of upset and disappointment and – as ever – how she could best hide it from those she loved.

She tried. 'Meg, you're a grown woman now and you can make your own decisions. And I can certainly admire someone who knows what she wants and works for it.' Did her voice sound as strangled to Meg as it did to her? 'But . . .' She couldn't help but add, her tone a little more desperate, 'you won't forget us, will you? After all, we're you're family.'

It wasn't quite as bad as she'd feared. Meg wasn't cutting herself off from them, but she had a good job and she wanted to keep it. She got Sunday afternoons off every second week, and she would be able to come and see them.

Some sense started to return to Delilah's head. Look at this place! Meg had not just a job – and a steady one at that – but a career with prospects. How could Delilah possibly browbeat her into coming back to live in a single room and maybe scraping a few shillings by sewing or laundering? She must put Meg's interests first.

Delilah found Sam at her elbow. 'See that fella just come in? He's the one what came to the station to tell us about Meg.'

Delilah looked over and, to her shock, recognised the young man she'd sold a posy of flowers to in the park, immediately before Frank had proposed to her. Heat, guilt, shame – *something* – overwhelmed her. She normally made an effort to talk properly to her customers, but she hadn't done so on that day because she'd been distracted by Frank and Bridget whispering behind her. Oh, if only she'd paid more attention! If she'd only asked him what his girl's name was! The answer would have been enough to set her wondering and questioning further, and she might have found Meg earlier. Yet again, she had failed her family.

'That's Tommy,' said Meg, noticing the direction of Delilah's gaze, although thankfully not reading her thoughts. 'We're . . . walking out.' She blushed. Little, buttoned-up Meg!

'Respectably, of course,' added Mrs Lawrence, who Delilah had learned was the housekeeper. 'You've no need to worry about your sister while she's here, Miss Shaw.'

Delilah saw the way Tommy and Meg were looking at each other. 'No, no, I see that.' And then she sighed as she thought of Frank.

*   *   *

The following Sunday Delilah agreed to meet Meg in the park in the afternoon. She could still hardly believe that they might have been walking in the same grounds at the same time without ever encountering each other, but the park was huge and they had generally been at opposite ends of it, or there on different days of the week, so it probably wasn't all that surprising.

In the course of their long ramble – punctuated by fewer sales than usual, but for once Delilah didn't care – she was able to give Meg an idea of everything that had happened to the rest of the family during the last two years.

She ventured into the realms of apology again, but Meg was firm. 'No.' She shook her head. 'Look,' she went on, 'I'll be honest and say that there was a time when I thought you'd abandoned us, but that was all a misunderstanding and it's long past. And I'm just as guilty of not trying to find you – when you didn't come for us I thought you didn't care, so I never went looking.' They walked on in silence for a few moments, and then she added, 'Anyway, going over the past serves no purpose. Tell me about *now*, and tell me about the future. This flower business looks good?'

'Maybe not for long.' Delilah hadn't meant to, but the comfort and relief of having a sister, a friend, to whom she could unburden herself, was just too tempting. She poured it out, all of it: Frank, Pa, Mr Bradley, everything.

After she'd finished there was silence, and Delilah started to worry about what Meg would say.

When Meg did speak, it was in a tone of cold fury. 'So Pa *sold* you.'

Meg had always feared and hated Pa, even more so than any of the others. 'Well, yes, but . . .' began Delilah, aware that this had in fact been exactly her own reaction at the time.

'Don't give me that!' snapped Meg. Then she relented. 'I'm sorry, that didn't come out the way I meant. I can't possibly begin to understand what pressures you've been under all this time. But don't make excuses for Pa, not to me. What he's done to you makes him no better than the workhouse matron who sold me and other girls for her own profit – and she ended up in court.'

Delilah had heard the horrifying tale of the matron and her crimes; the same woman she'd spoken to herself on several occasions. Meg, it disturbingly transpired, had actually been one of the lucky ones.

'Look,' Meg was continuing, 'you're strong. You've always been strong, always there for the rest of us, even if we – if *I* – didn't appreciate it enough at the time. You can be strong now. Don't let your life be ruled by Pa, or Mr Bradley, or any other men. You've got friends and you've got family, and anything you need to help get you out of this, you just say the word.'

It wasn't long after that that Meg had to return to the big house. Delilah walked with her to the steps and then turned to make her own way home, her mind busily at work.

# Chapter Sixteen

Protecting the children had to be Delilah's main concern. That was indisputable; it was the rock on which she'd built her life.

The question that now occurred to her, the one that consumed her thoughts even as she walked and bought and sold over the next few weeks, was this: regardless of her own feelings, were the children's best interests *really* going to be served by her marrying Mr Bradley? She had his word that none of the boys would ever work at the docks if she didn't, and she certainly believed that. But she also had only his word that they would get good jobs if she did, and as time went by she began to doubt that part more and more.

Mr Bradley's evident contempt for Jem was enough on its own to turn Delilah away from the arrangement. If he could care nothing for such a clever, sweet, loving young boy then what hope was there? And the more she looked, the more she examined his behaviour closely every time he came to visit, the more she could see a similar disdain for the others. Annie was nothing more than a nuisance to him, to be ignored, complained about or pushed out of the way as the situation demanded; Sam's burgeoning adolescence was to be taunted and William's intelligence despised.

Whenever she touched on the subject Mr Bradley still assured Delilah that the jobs would be forthcoming as soon as the wedding was over, but she was less and less convinced both about those promises and the ones relating to the security of James Jenkins's position and Abraham's personal safety. The problem was that once Delilah was married to Mr Bradley she would, like all married women, effectively cease to exist. A husband and wife were legally one person, and that person was the husband: Delilah would have no authority to direct him at all, no leverage to ensure he kept his promises, no right even to plead with him. No right to argue if he decided to stop her seeing her family entirely. Marriage to a man one could not trust was worse than no marriage at all – and, although there *was* a man Delilah felt she could trust with her future happiness, Mr Bradley was not he.

Delilah turned everything over in her mind in the days prior to another Sunday afternoon out with Meg, which led her to compare their respective situations. Meg had been sold by the dishonest workhouse matron, and Delilah had been sold by Pa to a man who looked to be equally as devious. Both of them were powerless girls.

But were, they, though? Delilah asked herself on Saturday morning as she stood outside the railway station. Were they really so powerless? Meg had gained her independence through her own efforts, making the absolute best of the situation in which she had found herself. She hadn't needed to be 'rescued' by any man, and her friendship with Tommy had grown out of mutual admiration and respect. Could Delilah be happy with anything less?

She enjoyed running her business. She had to accept that as a fact, and hope that it wasn't influencing her unduly in trying to work out what was best for her family. But it wasn't just enjoyment – it was income and it had the potential to be a career if she worked hard enough and made the right decisions. She was making more money than ever before and was now considering how she might supply flowers for weddings more often once the spring and summer arrived. What she really needed, of course, was a shop – a proper premises that she could call her own and that customers would visit regularly because of the quality of the produce and the service on offer. This was still far beyond her, but it was not quite as unthinkable as it might once have been. In the meantime she could certainly set her eye on a market stall as a reasonable ambition for her next step. Was all this to be given up for the chance to be 'Mrs Bradley', with the uncertainty of prospects for the others, not to mention the odious personal sacrifice it would entail?

'You can do it,' said Meg, the following day.

'Can I?'

'Of course you can. Look what you've already achieved, setting all this up from nothing.' Meg indicated the flower baskets. 'You've supported our whole family all this time, coping with losing Ma, and everything else, and you've already come out further on top than you were before.' Meg looked her sister in the eye. 'You're Delilah Shaw, and don't you forget it.'

Delilah sat up a little straighter. 'I suppose I have had *some* success . . .'

'More than "some". Don't do yourself down, Delilah – if there's one thing I've learned from working with Mrs Lawrence and Mrs Roberts it's that women can succeed on their own terms. They can, I can, and you can.'

Delilah shook her head. 'How did my little sister come to be so sure of herself?'

'Experience, I suppose.' Meg shrugged, a hint of tightness appearing on her face. 'Anyway,' she added, 'sometimes it takes a bit of distance to see things more clearly. I can say all this to you specifically because I haven't been living through it all with you.'

The words *You're Delilah Shaw, and don't you forget it* played in Delilah's head all the way home. She would do it. She would sever all ties with Mr Bradley and she would support her family herself, without needing an untrustworthy man to do it for her. Once she had done it she would try to find Abraham and James to warn them about any possible repercussions; this was the part that worried her most, but they were grown men and in any case she didn't think they'd be any safer even if she did go through with the wedding.

There was no point in putting it off. Tomorrow was a Monday, her day off, and Mr Bradley would be in his office: she would do it then.

\* \* \*

Delilah felt her steps slowing as she approached the docks. But she had to keep going. The scene ahead of her was going to be unpleasant, but better to get it over and done with and then they would be rid of him, of his power and his malign influence over their lives.

The recollection of her previous experience in that office made her stop completely as she neared it. Had it been foolish to come on her own? But all she was going to do was to step in – hovering in the doorway if she could – tell him it was all over, and then leave again. There could be no danger in that, surely.

A figure standing still amid the bustle of the docks was sure to be noticed, and Delilah found herself being hailed by James Jenkins.

He came over and nodded at the office door. 'You're not about to go and see Mr Bradley, are you? On your own?'

'Yes. But I'll only be a moment.'

He looked unconvinced. 'I mean – it's not my business, I know – but when that happened last time I thought . . .'

'It won't be like that this time,' said Delilah, squaring her shoulders. 'I've only to tell him something very quickly and then I'll leave again.'

'Well, if you're sure . . .'

'I am.' Delilah paused, remembering the wider import of the news she was about to give Mr Bradley. 'Perhaps I might see you for a few words afterwards, depending on how busy you are? But I don't want to get in the way – maybe I could walk up and see Ellen instead.' She would find some way to intimate the danger without telling the whole story. And, tempting as it was to ask James to come in with her while she spoke to Mr Bradley, she couldn't risk him finding out the whole story about the overseer's threats – it would cause all kinds of trouble. All Delilah wanted was a quick and fuss-free end to the situation.

'She'd like that.'

Delilah was so distracted that it took her a moment to realise that he was speaking of Ellen. 'Good, that's settled then. Right, off I go.' She was speaking as much to herself as to him; the compulsion to turn around and run away was so strong that she nearly gave into it. But she could not. It was best for all concerned to get it over and done with.

She heard Mr Bradley's voice calling, 'Come in,' as soon as she knocked on the door, so she entered. He rushed forward with an obsequious smile on his face before noticing who it was, at which point he stopped. 'Oh, it's you.'

Her surprise must have shown on her face, as he rushed to explain. 'Not that I'm not pleased to see you, of course – at you coming to see me of your own volition – but I'm expecting a visit from the owner of our whole company. He wishes to inspect his warehouses, and will meet me here so I can conduct him on a tour.' Mr Bradley seemed exceptionally pleased with himself, and Delilah noted that he had on his best suit. She weighed up whether or not to continue, but actually felt that the situation was in her favour: if he was expecting an important guest any minute, he would surely not risk making any attempt to assault her again, no matter how unwelcome her news.

She was so busy thinking this that she didn't really notice that he was ushering her away from the door and shutting it behind her. 'I can only spare you a few minutes – wouldn't be the thing to be seen with guests here, although the future Mrs Bradley is always welcome.'

There was no point in beating about the bush. 'That's just it.'

'What is?'

Delilah took a deep breath. 'I'm not going to be the future Mrs Bradley.'

He stopped in the very act of smoothing down his waistcoat. 'I beg your pardon?'

'I'm not going to marry you, Mr Bradley. The arrangement is off.'

His eyes narrowed. 'You don't mean that.'

'I most certainly do.' Her message delivered, Delilah nodded and turned towards the door.

'Oh no you don't!' He covered the space in a couple of heavy strides and blocked her exit.

Delilah, still buoyed by the expectation of being interrupted at any moment, was angry rather than afraid. 'I've told you now, and there's nothing more to say.'

'There most certainly is.' He began to splutter. 'Who do you think you are, coming here and telling me that you're upsetting my carefully laid plans? I have an agreement with you – and, lest you forget, an arrangement with your father.'

'Whatever you may have discussed with Pa is nothing to do with me. I need his permission to get married, I know, because I'm not twenty-one, but he can't force me to marry against my will. Any vicar, during a wedding, would ask me if I agreed, and all I would have to say was that I didn't. Indeed, you couldn't force me to go to a church at all – I'd fight all the way, and the kicking and screaming would soon give away my opinion.' She stared at him defiantly.

'But you didn't agree just for yourself, did you? Think of your father, your brothers. Are you now so selfish as to forget their interests? And those of your other friends? You really want dear William to spend his life without employment, and Abraham to find himself on a ship to America?' His tone was hardening, but there was edge of some kind of nervousness to it.

Delilah's anger grew. 'The only reason I agreed in the first place was because you threatened them all – their livelihoods, their safety. But the more I see of you the more I'm convinced that you would never keep your promises. And what power would I have, as your wife, to make sure you kept your word?'

'None whatsoever,' was his reply, still sounding anxious. 'But you can be absolutely sure, girl, that I will keep to my promises if you *don't* marry me.'

For the first time in their entire acquaintance, Delilah began to feel that she had the upper hand. He was starting to slide from agitation into panic, knowing that his desires were slipping away from him, whereas her anger was hardening to cold fury. 'You think you can rule all our lives, don't you? Well, you can't. You're not the only man in Liverpool who can hire workers, and you're certainly not the man I'd choose to marry if I have any kind of say in the matter.'

Again she tried to leave, but again she was prevented. This time he actually grabbed her arm. 'Oh no, you don't get away as easily as that. After all this time? All the work I've put into getting you over the years? Not on your life.'

'Let go of me, Mr Bradley.'

He pulled her closer to him, and she could see that by now his eyes were quite wild. 'I've been watching you for *years*! Ever since you developed into a woman, and I said to myself – that girl will be mine one day. I'll have her, you mark my words, that's what I said. And now I've got you I'm not letting you get away.'

She tried to pull away from his grasp. 'I don't care how long you've been watching me. I might have been sorry to disappoint you if you'd behaved better, but as it is your feelings are nothing to do with me.'

'Nothing to do with you?' His voice rose in outrage. 'You don't know the half of it! Finding work for your father and brother, making your family dependent on my goodwill, and me risking my position by employing them when there were others better suited?'

'Again, Mr Bradley, this is not my concern. You needed men to work and they were well able to do the job. Now let go of me.'

'No! I won't let go of you, not now, not ever. Not when I've come so close to getting you in my bed, to being able to touch you whenever I want, to . . .'

He was pulling her closer, his fingers digging into her arm, and she began to struggle in earnest. 'And that was the main thing that put me off,' she spat. 'Lying with you? I could never lower myself to do such a thing.'

His rage and entitlement broke all bounds. 'Lower yourself? *Lower* yourself? How dare you, you little slut! I'm offering you the chance to get out of the gutter you've found yourself in, the gutter I put you in just so I could rescue you from it.'

Once again he must have read the surprise on her face, for he continued, raving now with spittle flecking both of them. 'Oh yes! That's how much I wanted you. Your father wasn't dependent enough on me, so I had to make damn sure he'd never have another penny if it wasn't for me. That accident wasn't easy to arrange, you know – I could have got into real trouble, and yet I did it – I risked everything for you. And I'm not going to be deprived of my prize now!'

Delilah felt herself go limp with shock. 'You . . .' She couldn't go on.

'Oh, now you believe me!' he continued, still attempting to drag her away from the door. 'Now you know how much I love you!'

'That isn't love!' Delilah shrieked. The devastating realisation of what he had just admitted to had not sunk in properly – she still felt it hammering at her, trying to get in. She continued yelling, not even aware of what she was saying. 'You don't know the first thing about what love is! My Pa – you called him a friend and you crippled him! And you killed my brother – and my

311

Ma ended up dead too! And yet you have the *nerve* to talk of love! I hate you, I despise you—'

'I will have you, I tell you! One way or another. You're mine and I won't give you up!' He drew back his hand to slap her, and she tried to duck.

The office door crashed back on its hinges.

Delilah twisted in Mr Bradley's grasp to see a furious Abraham standing on the threshold, with James looming behind him. 'You let go of her right now.' Abraham was incandescent, literally shaking with rage.

But Mr Bradley wasn't going to give up that easily. His eyes were still wild. 'You get out of here, if you know what's good for you.'

Abraham took a step forward, plainly making a huge effort to control himself. 'No. You see, I heard what you just said about John Shaw's accident.'

Mr Bradley sneered. 'And who's going to take *your* word over mine? Yours, and that of this baggage of a girl? Get out, I tell you, and leave her to me.'

'I heard it too,' said James, his reassuring bulk moving to stand at Abraham's shoulder. He looked at Delilah. 'Abraham saw us talking earlier so he asked me what you were doing here. We were worried when you didn't come out.'

Delilah didn't have time to frame a reply before Mr Bradley interrupted. 'Well, you're no better – a coal heaver with some kind of grudge? Status and class count for something around here, and I can convince anyone you might care to summon that you were mistaken and that this is all a conspiracy against me.'

'Is that so?' came another voice. It was one Delilah vaguely recognised from somewhere, though by this stage her nerves were so shredded that she couldn't think straight enough to place it.

An exceedingly well-dressed man of middle age stepped into the room. He took in the scene and then consulted the pocket watch that was in his hand. 'We are five minutes over time, by my reckoning. But the delay has proved . . . informative.'

Delilah looked from him to Mr Bradley. The effect on the latter was immediate and profound – the colour drained out of his face all at once and he really seemed to *shrink*. 'Mr – Mr Ashton! This isn't what it seems – what I mean is . . . this trollop of a girl came here to offer me her favours in return for work for her family. Of course I was simply trying to remove her from the premises when these ruffians—'

'You can stop there,' replied Mr Ashton, still speaking calmly and with an aura of effortless authority. 'I arrived exactly on time, found these men outside your door and enquired what was afoot. I stood with them for some minutes and I heard your confession.' He snapped his watch shut and replaced it in his pocket. 'You are most certainly dismissed without references as of this moment, and the law will have to see to the rest.'

Mr Bradley tried to bluster, but he was deflating like a pig's bladder. 'You can't trust this girl, sir—'

'Actually I can,' replied Mr Ashton. 'I can personally vouch for her honesty.' He turned to Delilah, who was still looking at him blankly. 'Don't you remember? You sold me flowers for my daughter's wedding. First of all you tried to haggle me into paying you *less*, and then when there were some bouquets left that I had paid for, you stood outside in the cold during the whole service so that you could distribute them afterwards. I know trustworthiness when I see it.'

Now Delilah recognised him. But she was still incapable of saying a word. She felt her legs beginning to go from under her.

The rest happened as if she was seeing it from a great distance and with something muffling her ears. Mr Ashton instructed James to apprehend Mr Bradley and take him outside while Abraham went to find a constable. Then he assisted Delilah to a chair and stepped back to give her space. 'I have no lady with me, but perhaps we can find you a female companion from somewhere until the shock has worn off.'

'Oh, no, sir – no, really, I'm fine,' Delilah managed. She wasn't completely sure that she wasn't going to be sick as the realisation of what had really happened to Pa and Jonny washed over her again and again, so she bent her head forward and concentrated on trying to keep control of herself.

She wasn't quite sure how long it was before Abraham returned. 'Begging your pardon, sir, I've brought the constable, and he says would you be good enough to step outside to speak to him.'

'Of course.' Mr Ashton hesitated. 'Do you know if there are any women working nearby? I think the young lady . . .'

Delilah had regained some of her composure. 'Thank you, sir, but that won't be necessary. If I might just sit here a few more minutes . . . and Abraham here is an old friend of my father. I've always felt safe around him.'

Mr Ashton nodded. 'Very well. On behalf of my company, please accept my apologies for Mr Bradley's actions, and know that he will be prosecuted to the fullest extent of the law.' He turned to Abraham and handed something to him. 'My card. If your own employer makes any issue of your lack of work during this hour, please refer him directly to me.' And then, with a last nod at Delilah, he was gone.

315

Abraham hesitated on the threshold. 'Miss Delilah, I don't know what to say. I'm just sorry I didn't get here earlier to stop him hurting you.'

Delilah found, to her surprise, that her wrist was red and swollen where Mr Bradley had twisted it as he gripped her. Now she had noticed it, it began to sting.

'And I'm sorry, truly sorry, about what happened to your Pa and Jonny. If I'd had any clue what was going on I might have stopped it, I might have been able to prevent—'

'It wasn't your fault.' Delilah could hear some firmness returning to her tone. 'Of course it wasn't. You've always been a good friend.'

Abraham hesitated, as though unsure whether or not to go on. Eventually he did. 'I have to ask. About something you – he – said earlier in your conversation. Did you really agree to marry Mr Bradley because he threatened to send me back to slavery if you didn't?'

Some of the earlier events now started flooding back into Delilah's mind, and she felt the heat rise to her cheeks. She kept her eyes firmly on the floor. 'I'm sorry you had to hear that. And please know that in changing my mind and refusing him I wasn't deliberately putting you into danger – I just knew I couldn't trust him.'

'You agreed to . . . for *me* . . .' Abraham was still overwhelmed.

Delilah made an effort to pull herself together. 'You've been so kind to us all over the years. And friends and family stick together – isn't that what you said?'

There was silence for a moment, and then Delilah raised her head on hearing a strange sound.

Abraham was crying.

# Chapter Seventeen

Delilah hadn't realised what a weight she'd been carrying around until it was lifted. She could now get up every day confident in the knowledge that Mr Bradley was not going to appear suddenly at home, that he was not going to threaten her or her peace of mind. She no longer had to calculate how best to avoid his grabbing hands, all the while knowing that the future held the prospect of . . . *ugh*. In short, he no longer had any form of control over Delilah or her family.

She caught scraps of information about him during her daily rounds: he was not going to be convicted of murder, as he hadn't set out with the intention of killing Jonny, but he was facing either transportation or a long prison sentence for arranging the accident that led to his death and Pa's crippling injuries. Delilah was content with this outcome: if Mr Bradley had been found guilty of murder he would be facing the noose, and she didn't want to feel responsible – however illogically – for his death. As it was, the blame for the accident had been correctly apportioned, any lingering suspicions at the docks about Abraham had been put to rest, and Delilah would never have to see or think about Mr Bradley again.

The new information, now she'd had time to process it, had changed her thoughts about the accident, or at least in part. Any sympathy she might have been tempted to feel for Pa swiftly evaporated when he raged and howled about losing out on the money Mr Bradley had promised him for the marriage, but she did experience a softening towards Jonny. He'd been dead so long now that her memories of him were fading, and as Sam grew and began to resemble his older brother physically, Delilah found herself somehow more able to believe that Jonny had been like Sam in character as well. Perhaps he hadn't been quite such a vicious bully as she remembered, perhaps he'd had some redeeming qualities that she just hadn't noticed at the time? He'd looked up to Pa and tried to emulate him, copying all Pa's bad qualities in the belief that this made him a man, but perhaps he might have grown out of it to be himself in time. In any case, he hadn't deserved to die at fifteen at the hands of a man who was prepared to risk the lives and livelihoods of others simply in order to obtain his own selfish desires.

Whatever had been the truth of the matter, Jonny was gone, and Delilah hoped he was resting quietly or that he'd found Ma in heaven. What she needed to concentrate on was the rest of the family, those who still walked the earth and whom she hoped to keep there a good while longer. Now that the constant apprehension about Mr Bradley had gone, she was free to turn her full attention to the matter, and today she was about to take a great leap forward.

A message from Mr Ashton had reached her, enquiring as to her welfare after the incident he'd witnessed at the docks, and in her reply she had been so bold as to ask if he might write a note testifying to her honesty and good character. He had agreed, and it was with this note carefully folded in her pocket that Delilah was on her way to St John's market for the interview that would secure her a stall under its roof.

As she walked she ran through everything in her mind. She had brought with her a basket of her prettiest bouquets, carefully made up by herself and Jem the evening before, as a sample of the quality of the wares she intended to sell. She had her note from Mr Ashton, plus another from a wholesaler confirming that he would be supplying her with fresh blooms – there would be no more leftovers from Mrs Farrell and no more sneaking through the back gate of the flower shop every evening. Delilah also carried the second of the two half-sovereigns that had been given to her on Christmas Eve, carefully saved since that day against future need.

Finally, and ever so slightly to her chagrin, she had William with her. He, of course, was aware that the business was hers, that she was both the driving force behind it and the worker who kept it going, but Delilah remained suspicious that a manager at the market might be reluctant to let a stall to a single young woman. So William strode next to her, wearing his best collar and tie and trying to shorten his stride to match hers.

They arrived and stood for a moment looking up at huge building and the impressive entrance.

'I'm proud of you.'

Delilah turned as she heard William's words. 'Are you? I mean, after everything . . .'

He took her hand. 'Of course I am. You've done everything for us, held us all together – you were willing to give up everything for us. But this is a much, much better solution. You've done this all on your own, Delilah – *you*.' His voice, deep now, wobbled a little. 'So, let's get in there. Ignore the manager if he patronises you or talks more to me – you know and I know that the purpose of this is to get you your stall, so we just need to bite our lips until it's settled.'

Delilah nodded, almost unable to speak. Then she checked over her basket again, ensured she had everything ready and expelled a long breath. 'Let's do it.'

It was easier than she had expected. The manager did address most of his remarks to William to start with, but after William referred them all directly to Delilah he got the message. The letters were produced and approved.

'So,' said the manager, handing the papers back. 'It's just the question of the rent. Two pounds per annum, payable in quarterly instalments.'

Delilah had considered everything very carefully when calculating the costs and benefits of a fixed stall. The large market shops were beyond her budget, but she didn't want one of the cheapest pitches either, the ones that were just a bench or a space to lay out a blanket of wares. She was to have a proper stall, three yards long, in a good position in one of the main aisles. It meant ten shillings off her profits every quarter, but the price was worth it. She would benefit from increased visibility and sales; the fixed address meant that wholesalers would now deal with her and she could choose whatever flowers she thought would sell best rather than having to make do with whatever she could glean from other shops' leftovers; and she would enjoy a greater security. The market had its own guards who patrolled the aisles, and theft was extremely rare.

She was thus very happy with the bargain she was about to make, and she handed over the half-sovereign with an air that was almost regal. 'For the first quarter, in advance.'

It was the shining coin, she thought to herself, that had really clinched it. If she'd produced a great stack of pennies and had to count them all out, the manager might have cooled on the idea of Delilah as a market tenant, but he couldn't argue with a price paid in gold. Once again Delilah thanked her lucky stars that she had been in the right place at the right time on Christmas Eve – and that her honesty had been noticed.

The deal was done, and Delilah was told that the stall would be hers on the following Monday morning once the current trader had vacated it. It was now Thursday, which would give her a couple of days to sell off what she had in hand already, inform Mrs Farrell and the other shopkeepers that she would no longer be purchasing from them, and plan how she would set up her stall.

'Well done,' said William as they left. 'Not just for securing the deal, but for keeping your temper when he asked me to sign the papers instead of you.' He patted her arm and imitated the manager's somewhat pompous tone. 'I was very impressed, young lady.'

'Well, I suppose I'm getting better at learning how to play a game that's rigged in men's favour.'

He laughed. 'Does that mean I can idle around reading Latin all day?'

She knew he didn't mean it. He was still desperate to get a job, a proper one with prospects, but nothing had turned up yet. 'Well, while you're waiting for something to fall out of the sky, why don't you come with me to the station while I try to sell these?' She looked at him slyly. 'If it doesn't offend your male dignity to do so, of course.'

He stuck out his tongue like a little boy, and took the basket from her to carry it. 'No man should be ashamed of honest work, even if it does involve flowers.'

'Don't tell Sam that.' They spotted Sam easily as they approached the station, considerably taller and broader than any of the other street sweepers. 'I wonder,' said Delilah, suddenly.

'What?'

'Well, did you notice the porters in the market while we were there? I don't know if they work for individual fees or if they get wages from the market, but they all had smart armbands, and it would be good, steady work, surely, even if it's daily paid?'

William nodded. 'You might be right. And you know Sam – he'd be quite happy with a job carrying things.' A shadow came over his face. 'In some ways I envy him. He's not like me, getting ideas above his station.'

'Oh, stop that. You're different people, that's all – and besides, you don't get into nearly as many fights as he does! A good, steady job will do wonders for him, but you stick to finding your own path, and educating yourself when you can. Going my own way has worked for me, so why not you?'

'If you say so. Now, where do you normally patrol? Around here somewhere?'

'Yes, here will do.' Delilah let William set the basket down and then rearranged the contents to best effect before picking it up herself. She waved to Jem, who was polishing shoes only a few yards away, and he smiled back without pausing in his work.

A few sales followed over the next half an hour as they strolled up and down, and Delilah was just wondering if she should move on to another location when a besuited man with a well-trimmed beard wandered over from the shoeshine box. He hesitated. 'After you,' he said to William.

William looked puzzled, and then Delilah realised that the man thought he was a customer. *Well*, she thought, *he does look very smart today and his jacket is nicely mended and brushed.*

'No, after you, sir – I was just helping my sister out.'

The man looked at them both with a quizzical expression. 'A flower seller in a collar and tie? What is the world coming to? My, how times and customs change.'

'*O tempora!*' said William, bafflingly. '*O mores!*'

He'd said it almost without thinking, but the effect on the man was considerable. After a moment during which he was taken aback, he rapped out something else Delilah didn't understand and William replied in what sounded like the same language.

'Well, well,' said the man, switching back to English. 'A Latin scholar as well, eh?'

'Yes, sir,' replied William. 'I loved to study it at school so I've continued to read it now, and my sister here encourages me. Education is never wasted, and it's especially comforting while I'm . . . currently between jobs.'

The man gave him a lengthy, considering look. 'Between jobs? Hmm.' Eventually he seemed to make up his mind about something and produced a card from his waistcoat pocket. 'Stephen Hughes, printer and bookbinder. I'm looking for a new junior in the workshop. Needs to be a sharp young man who can read well, and one who can read Latin would be even better.' He handed over the card. 'The address is here. Come to my premises next Monday morning, eight o'clock, and we'll give you a trial – if you're interested.'

'Interested?' William's eyes had nearly fallen from his head. 'Interested, sir? I'd be delighted.'

Mr Hughes smiled. 'Glad to hear it.' He paused, amused at William's stupefaction, and then glanced at Delilah. 'Seeing as you're too delighted to tell me your name or ask me about pay, maybe I should negotiate with your sister. It's skilled work, educated work, and we pay the going rate for the right man. Sixteen shillings a week to start, with the possibility of long-term employment and progression if you do well.'

He was still looking at Delilah, but she remembered her own irritation with the market manager addressing his remarks about her business to William. 'Thank you, sir, but my brother's a grown man and can answer for himself.'

She threw William a significant look, wondering if she was going to have to kick him as well, but he took the hint. 'Of course, Mr Hughes, sir, those terms will be very acceptable. I'll be there on Monday morning without fail. And it's William Shaw, sir.'

'Very well, William Shaw. I'll see you on Monday.' Mr Hughes shook William's hand and then they watched him walk away.

'Did that really just happen?' William still looked bemused.

'You've got the card in your hand, haven't you? Make sure you don't lose it.' Delilah caught his eye and knew that he was thinking the same as she was. 'Latin,' she said, rolling her eyes as a giggle escaped her. 'What use is Latin?'

'That'll never get you a job, boy,' boomed William.

And then, to the great surprise of everyone around them, they both burst out laughing, tears of merriment and joy streaming unheeded down their faces in the middle of the crowded square.

\* \* \*

It wouldn't do to be nervous, thought Delilah when Monday morning came. Not her, not William, not any of them. Today was the first day of the rest of their lives: she had said that to herself on many occasions during the last few years, but this time she really meant it and she could sense that a corner had been turned.

She needed to be the first out, as she was due to purchase from the wholesaler at seven o'clock, but she made sure everyone else was awake before she left. She told Sam to make sure that he left Annie with Clara as usual; Delilah had hopes that she would soon be able to end the arrangement and have Annie with her, but she thought it wise not to attempt it on her first day when there was so much for her to learn about the market and how it worked. She bestowed a few kisses and made her way out, carrying the assorted baskets she'd sourced during the last few days to display her wares to best effect on the stall.

The long winter was over; spring was in the air and in her step as Delilah approached the market. Plans were bubbling in her head, falling over each other in their excitement. The stall would be her base to sell to servants and housewives, and that would form her main income. Thank goodness she wouldn't have to be outside in all weathers any longer, though there was a little pang in losing her regular interactions at the station, the docks and the park. However, in due course she – or rather, her business, in the person of someone else – might be able to pick up on those again. Once Annie was bigger there would be nothing stopping her walking about with a tray and a basket just as Delilah had done. And, in the shorter term, was it just possible that she could kill two birds with one stone?

Delilah missed Bridget. In the same way that she hadn't realised how much the Mr Bradley situation was weighing her down until it was gone, it was only now that she had apparently lost Bridget for good that Delilah realised how great a hole the loss had torn in her life. She felt that she had never appreciated Bridget properly, never told her how much she meant.

The scant information that she did have indicated that Bridget was being forced to stay home and keep house for the family, hardly ever allowed out and kept strictly under Michael's eye, her friendships and interactions monitored. In the past Delilah had sometimes envied Bridget her older brothers, the comfort of having men's wages coming in while she, Delilah, was the eldest of her siblings and had to look after them all. But now she wasn't so sure: Bridget might not have to worry about where her next meal was coming from, but every other aspect of her life was tightly controlled and there seemed no way out of it. There were only really two possible ways she might escape.

The first was a marriage of her own, but Bridget would surely not be allowed to do that until at least one or two of her brothers had wives to take over the domestic duties, and even then Delilah doubted very much that Bridget would have a free choice of husband. Michael might not actually 'sell' her, as Pa had tried to do to Delilah, but he would pick one of his own friends or companions, no doubt someone as involved as he was in the Liverpool underworld. Beautiful, kind Bridget would never get the gentle husband she wanted; she would be tied to a dishonest, violent man and she would sink without trace.

The other alternative was that Bridget could break away from her family, just as Frank had done. Much easier for a man, of course, who could earn enough to support himself, but not impossible for a woman, as Meg had shown. It would have to be approached in the right way – Bridget would need somewhere to live as well as a job that paid some money, and there was the added complication of her mother, whom she would not like to leave. But if Delilah's affairs continued in their upward direction, and especially now in the light of William's earning potential, was it too much to hope for? A shop, maybe, where she and Bridget could work, with rooms behind and above for everyone to live in? The idea that they could all be together and safe almost made Delilah choke on tears, but it was a worthy ambition to aim for.

What did almost make her trip over her feet as she entered the market was the recollection of how close this all was to the idea she had put to Frank on the day he had proposed to her. The notion had seemed so impossible at the time that she had declined his offer and she had lost him for ever. And now here she was, perhaps not exactly within touching distance of achieving it all, but at least with the goal in her sights, and he was not here to share in it.

To think, she might have been his wife by now. Delilah O'Malley. With his comforting presence at her side and his ready wit to carry them through every difficulty. She would be one of those lucky women who actively looked forward to her husband coming home in the evenings rather than seeing it as an event to be dreaded.

A nearby church clock struck seven, and Delilah told herself to stop brooding and concentrate on the matter in hand. Here she was, on the first day of her new business venture and with an awful lot to do, and she was moping over her past mistakes and a man she would likely never see again. She still loved him and she always would, but he had made it quite clear that he took her refusal as final, and he had disappeared without even trying to change her mind or to come up with another solution. If he had loved her as much as she loved him, Delilah told herself, he would not have given up so easily. No, she was on her own and it was time to forget about Frank O'Malley.

\* \* \*

Frank sighed as he unloaded another crate of flowers from the train. Delilah was never far from his thoughts, but seeing flowers always brought her image sharply in front of him.

He had only fragmented memories of that day in the park, of which two moments dominated: Delilah's refusal of his proposal of marriage, and the stupid, idiotic words that had come out of his mouth shortly afterwards. When she'd turned him down, it had been like running into a brick wall, such was his shock and pain. And to start with he'd felt bitterly that she didn't love him as much as he loved her, and that she didn't want to find a way to make it work. That was why he'd spoken so hastily and walked off, unable to get his head straight for hours afterwards.

It was only later that day that his own words had come back to haunt him. *Those children.* You love *those children* more than me. How had he let such words escape, even in the depths of his devastation? Her younger siblings, whom he loved as though they were his own, and he'd spoken of them in such a dismissive way as if they were nothing. Like her Pa might have done. He was embarrassed and ashamed, unable to face her again.

If only he'd gone back. If only he'd not walked out of the park, not gone home and stayed there staring at the wall for the rest of that day and the long evening that followed it. If he'd been to see her and thrown himself at her feet, apologising for his words and the bitter way in which he'd reacted to her perfectly reasonable doubts, they might now have been together. Even if he'd waited until the following day it might not have been too late to fix things.

But he couldn't face her, because he was a coward. So what he'd actually done when the next day dawned was speak to his supervisor about being transferred to another station somewhere along the line. He'd even been tempted simply to gather up whatever money he had, head for the ticket office and ask how far away it would get him, but something stopped him from being quite that reckless. That made him laugh now – was he, the freewheeling Frank O'Malley, developing a sense of financial responsibility?

And so it was that he'd kept his job with the railway company even though he'd run away to hide from his responsibility, and for a while now he'd been based in Manchester. In some respects the work was similar: a big city, a station where ladies and gentlemen alighted from passenger trains and where goods came in from the surrounding towns and villages. Milk, fresh vegetables, all sorts of things that were wanted in the city but couldn't be grown there.

Like flowers.

It was the flowers that reminded him constantly of the one major difference between the cities of Manchester and Liverpool: Manchester didn't have Delilah in it. Of course, it didn't have the rest of his family in it either, and he did also miss Bridget and Mam – if not Michael, Patrick and Gideon to the same extent – but it was Delilah who filled his every waking thought and many of his sleeping ones too.

Delilah had a responsibility that he couldn't pretend to understand – or, rather, that he hadn't *wanted* to understand when he'd said those words. Four younger siblings and she had to look after them all while also dealing with the tragedy of losing the others. She, a slip of a girl with no help from a mother or any man and with that drunkard of a Pa to cope with into the bargain. She was their sister and their Ma rolled into one, and she loved them. She loved him too, he was sure of it deep down, no matter what his mind tried to tell him in the dark of the night. She would have been happy to have him, but she had been prepared to sacrifice her own happiness for her family.

As Frank unloaded another crate of spring flowers, he told himself once again that he should have been admiring Delilah for all this, not criticising her. The fact that he'd been in shock at the time was no excuse.

And she'd also shown similar consideration to *his* family, for God's sake – he could now recall another memory with a clarity that made him want to curl up and weep from shame: she had specifically spoken of Bridget and Mam, and what might happen to them. And he'd rewarded her thoughtfulness by saying cruel words and walking away from her.

'What sort of man are you, Francis O'Malley?' he asked himself, only realising that he'd spoken out loud when several other porters turned to him in surprise. 'Sorry, lads. As you were.'

He repeated the question in his head. Was he the sort of man who stuck stubbornly to his own wants and desires, regardless of those around him? The sort of man to let his shame and his idiotic pride keep him away from his family, his friends and the woman he cared about more than any other on God's earth? When he could be back there helping her, even though she didn't want to marry him? Or was he the sort of man who could put his own personal happiness to one side, in the same way Delilah had, in order to help his loved ones?

These questions, and the possible answers to them, ran through his head all the morning. By the time his dinner break arrived he had come to a decision: Delilah needed him, so he would support her. It didn't matter whether they could be married or not – he would be there for her. A shoulder for her to cry on, a rock to support her, a smile to cheer her, a friend; whatever it was that *she* needed.

Frank went back to his lodgings, collected up his few spare clothes and possessions and threw them all into the sack he'd borrowed from one of the carts he'd been loading. He was paid up with the rent until the end of the week, but it didn't matter and he wasn't about to try and track his landlady down to ask for a refund. Now he'd made his decision he was in a tearing hurry, and he almost ran back to the station.

He found his supervisor. 'I've had an urgent message from my family, sir. Can I get on the next train to Liverpool?'

# Chapter Eighteen

Business was booming. If Delilah had ever been unsure about the wisdom of paying out rent for a stall then those worries had certainly been put to rest; being able to sell from a fixed location in a reputable market had increased her profits even when the rent money was included in the calculations.

She mustn't get too far ahead of herself, she knew: when winter came flowers would be both more expensive to purchase and more difficult to sell, plus they would need to allow more money for coals and so on. But with William's position now seeming secure, they could start to plan. And if Delilah was pleased with her own new work, she was absolutely delighted with his. He was getting on well, learning the trade. His employer was pleased with him and – this was the thing that really made Delilah's heart sing – William was *happy*. He ran out of the door each morning in his eagerness to get to work, and his face lit up every evening as he told her about his day. Bless him. He'd always been different from most of the other boys, wanting to study instead of playing on the streets or fighting, and now he'd found his place in the world. He was healthier now that his slender frame wasn't weighed down with hard manual labour, and the improved food they could afford meant that he had lost that pinched look.

Another boost for William was that Pa had finally ceased treating him like a child. At the end of the first week in his new job William had come home and ostentatiously poured the entirety of his wages on the table. He'd made sure that Sam was between Pa and the coins, just in case, but he wanted Pa to see them, to know what William's much-derided education – the education Delilah had supported and encouraged – had done for them all. Pa had looked, blinked, grunted at his tall son and then dragged himself outside. It had happened during one of his few periods of lucidity: Pa was so far gone in his drink these days that it was increasingly rare that he was even coherent. He'd slipped and got so behind with his oakum-picking work that Delilah had given up on it, allowing him to just eat and sleep in the room and keep himself out of the way the rest of the time. He might be the head of the family in name, but he was no longer in control, no longer able to cow them all with threats of violence. As time passed even Delilah's fury with him over Mr Bradley had dulled around the edges and Pa was now no more than a nuisance to be worked around; she had every confidence that he would stay that way.

Everything, in fact, was going rather well, so why did Delilah not feel happier? She refused to believe that her dissatisfaction was due to the absence of a pair of Irish eyes and their matching, bewitching smile – no, she'd got over that, she kept telling herself. The frequency with which she had to keep issuing this reminder should perhaps have given her a warning that she hadn't forgotten Frank as completely as she wanted to, but she pushed that thought down as well.

She would concentrate on the family she still had with her. That was the thing to do. The next item on Delilah's list of improvements for her younger siblings was Annie's situation, and she had an idea. One Friday evening in April she closed up her stall a little earlier than usual, having sold her entire day's stock already, and set off home. When she reached the court she saw the girls playing and waved to them as she went to knock on the door of the room where Clara lived with her mother and half a dozen siblings.

Bet, Clara's mother, came outside to enjoy the small amount of spring air that made its way into the court. 'Home early today?' Everyone in the court knew everyone else's business; it was impossible not to with so many families crammed close together.

'Can I talk to you about Clara?'

Bet looked over to the girls. 'What about her?'

'She'll be ten later this year, won't she? And I think you said you were looking out for a place for her?'

'Yes, as soon as I can find something. Why, have you heard of anything?'

'Actually, I was wondering if she'd like to come and work for me, at my stall. Partly she'd still be keeping an eye on Annie, as I'd bring her too, but she'd also help with arranging the stall and selling to customers, learning the trade.'

'Paid?'

'Yes, of course.' Delilah hesitated. 'I have to be honest – to start with I couldn't pay much more than she'd get making matchboxes or sewing in a sweatshop, but the work would be much nicer and then when she was older I could pay more. She could go out with the baskets like I used to, and then keep part of any profit she made. And in the meantime she can walk there and back with me so you know she'll be safe.'

Bet stared at the little girls for a while longer before she answered. She was a hard woman, of necessity; a woman born to poverty who had survived two drunken, violent husbands and innumerable childbirths, and she wasn't normally given to displays of emotion. But she did have a soft spot for her youngest child, and her hollow eyes were shining as she turned back to Delilah. 'Done. It would be a good, respectable way for her to earn money, and once they know her face at the market there might be opportunities there even if you decide not to keep her on.' She hesitated. 'She's a bit wild, I know that – all the youngsters have to be round here or they wouldn't survive. But you won't hold it against her that she doesn't talk fancy.'

'She's a wonderful girl,' replied Delilah, really meaning it. 'I'm so grateful to her for looking after Annie all this time.' She was going to start gushing in a minute, she knew it, and she turned away.

'Well then.' Bet's voice also had a catch in it. 'Let's call her over and tell her the good news.'

And so it was that on Saturday morning Delilah set out with both Annie and Clara, the latter with her face scrubbed so shiningly clean by her mother that Delilah winced when she saw it and hoped it hadn't hurt too much. When they arrived she went through the usual routine of dealing with the wholesaler and setting up the stall for the day, showing Clara what to do and keeping an eye on Annie at the same time. Once the market opened for business everything went smoothly; fortunately Annie was quite happy to sit on an upturned crate behind the stall watching people go by and shredding a few dropped stalks. The novelty would wear off eventually, Delilah supposed, but it was a good start.

It was around mid-morning when Delilah looked up to greet a newcomer to the stall and saw that it was Mrs Farrell from the flower shop on Dale Street.

Delilah was immediately on the alert – had Mrs Farrell come with any kind of trouble in mind? Did she now see Delilah as a rival? But she did not seem antagonistic, merely looking through all the bouquets with a practised eye, examining them closely through her pince-nez.

'Chose all these yourself, did you?' she asked, eventually. 'And made them up?'

'Yes, ma'am.'

Mrs Farrell nodded. 'You've got a good eye. I often wondered what you'd done with all the flowers once you'd taken them away.'

'I sold on the streets to start with, out of a basket. But business was good so I was able to take this stall – and start dealing with a wholesaler, as you know.'

Delilah still wasn't quite sure whether or not this was all leading up to some hostile act.

But Mrs Farrell only nodded again. She didn't actually smile, but a movement of her lips indicated approval. 'I like to see a woman doing well for herself.'

'Oh, thank you, ma'am. And . . . may I enquire about you? I hope business is good?'

Mrs Farrell shrugged. 'The business owner died, and we were all laid off.'

'I'm sorry to hear—'

'Don't be.' Mrs Farrell waved a hand. 'I was thinking of retiring anyway. I've got enough saved, and my sister runs a nice boarding house. I'm going to move in with her and help her with her accounts.' She paused. 'We did good business, you and I, and I'm sorry if I was brusque to start with. Like I said, you've done well, and I respect that.'

'Thank you, ma'am, I'm grateful to you for saying so.' Relief began to wash over Delilah.

Mrs Farrell paused before departing. 'The shop's to let, if it's of any interest to you. It's in a good position, though, so it'll probably go quickly.' She nodded and made her way over to a nearby greengrocer's stall.

*The shop.* Not just any shop, but the one Delilah had loved all her life, where she had lingered and watched and coveted, where she had been desperate to work. Where she had seen the shop girls as being infinitely above her. Her heart missed several beats and the thought that it might now be hers.

That idea was at the forefront of her mind all that day and evening. She wanted to talk to William about it, but thought that she should get her own feelings straight first, so she didn't say anything. They were all due to meet Meg in the park the following afternoon, so perhaps then she'd run the idea past both of them.

Delilah always made sure that the family looked smart when they went to Prince's Park, so it was with some pride that she walked with them on their way to meet Meg. There was the usual happy family greeting, Meg looking more petite every time now that both Sam and Jem were taller than her. They walked for a while and then the younger ones ran off to watch the ducks swimming on the lake and the toy boats being sailed. Delilah was amused to see that Sam's new long trousers, a present ahead of his forthcoming thirteenth birthday, didn't stop him from gallivanting with the children just yet. The spring sunshine glinted on the water as the boys swung a giggling Annie between them on their way.

The older three sat down on a bench. Delilah listened for a while to William and Meg enthusing about their work and smiled to herself, feeling the warm satisfaction of them all having got through what was surely the most difficult part of their lives.

When the talk turned to her stall, she mentioned her conversation with Mrs Farrell and the fact of the flower shop premises being to let.

Meg and William were both well aware of how much that shop had meant to her over the years, so it was strange that they should be so silent.

She sighed. 'Just tell me. Whatever it is you're thinking, just come out with it.'

'It's not that I'm against the idea,' said William, carefully, 'but have you considered the cost? It's a big step – we'd move out of the court and into the shop, wouldn't we, so we'd have to be absolutely sure that we could afford it. It would be terrible if we were to start out on that path and then lose it all.'

His use of 'we' warmed Delilah's heart, but she had to be sure that she could manage everything without William's income, when it came to it. He wouldn't live with them for ever; he'd no doubt want to get married within a few years, and then his first priority would have to be his new family. She desperately yearned for the shop, but if it ended up tying William to them for years out of a sense of duty, when what he really wanted was a life of his own, she couldn't do it.

Delilah was already beginning to shake her head at Meg's, 'Like I said before, I could send you some of my wages, I don't really need it all,' when the additional and rather tentative, 'and maybe, if I left my job here and got a daily place somewhere, and paid rent to you . . .' made Delilah jump up with a howled, 'No!'

The others looked at her in surprise. 'No, no I can't. You've got your own lives and your own paths, and I can't have you give them up for me. No, forget I said anything.'

Meg took her hand and pulled her back on to the bench. 'Yes, we have got our own lives,' she said. 'But why shouldn't you have yours, too? You've given up everything for us over the years. For all of us.'

'It didn't do Rosie much good, did it?' said Delilah, all the old guilt returning. Her eyes began to burn.

'Don't,' said Meg, a catch sounding in her own voice. 'It won't help any of us to rake over the past.'

The past. Oh, if only Delilah could go back to that day in the park last year when she'd turned down Frank's proposal of marriage. But then, she'd be a wife, wouldn't she? Unable to run her own business if her husband disapproved, just as Mr Bradley had threatened.

Delilah stared angrily into the distance, dashing away the tears that had come to her eyes. Honestly, she was so overwrought that she could swear she could actually see Frank coming towards them now. She had to get control of herself.

Beside her, William shifted. 'Meg,' he said, in a strange tone, 'shall we walk down to the lake to see what the others are doing?'

'Is that . . . ? Yes, let's do that.'

Delilah watched, bemused, as her brother and sister walked off arm in arm. Then she felt a shadow fall over her, and she looked up to see that she wasn't imagining things. Frank was standing right in front of her.

\* \* \*

Delilah opened her mouth, but no words came out.

Frank had a slightly wary expression on his face. 'Is it all right if I sit down?'

Still unable to formulate a single syllable, Delilah nodded and gestured to the bench. He sat down, a little distance away from her, and cleared his throat.

They sat in silence for a few moments.

'When did you—'

'Who was—'

They stopped. 'You first,' said Delilah.

'I was just going to ask you who that girl was. I spoke to Bridget yesterday when I got back, and she said she'd heard that . . . ?'

'Yes, it's my sister Meg.'

'The one you thought was dead?' Frank crossed himself. 'A blessing from above.' He looked at her properly for the first time, and Delilah felt all the old emotions washing over her. 'I couldn't be happier for you, Delilah, I really couldn't. You deserve every miracle.'

'Miracles often turn out to be caused by people doing a lot of work that you can't see,' she replied, before realising that she was in danger of drifting away. She returned to her original question. 'I was going to ask when you'd got back – did you say yesterday?'

'Yes. I went to see Bridget and Mam first so I could find out from them about what you were doing.' He shook his head. 'I didn't realise Bridget had been kept away from you.'

'Are they all right? Was it . . . was it because of them that you came back?'

Frank paused for a moment and then took a deep breath. 'No.' He looked her squarely in the eye. 'I came back to see you, to tell you that I've been an idiot and a fool, and to ask you to forgive me.'

Delilah had to look away for a moment, aware that yet more tears had sprung to her own eyes.

He inched a little closer, but made no attempt to touch her. 'When I went away, I was angry and ashamed, and I let that get the better of me. It was stupid. You see, I wanted to marry you, more than I'd ever wanted anything in my life. For us to be together, for you to be mine. And when I couldn't have that I said terrible things and then ran away from everything. I was selfish.'

His hand moved forward just a fraction, hovering in the space between them. 'But what I've come to say now is that I've realised there's something that I want even more than that.'

Delilah looked at him in surprise.

'Oh, don't get me wrong, I still want to marry you. I ache for it.' He broke off with a wry smile. 'Will you listen to me, sounding like a bad poet? Still, you haven't walked off yet, so I may as well keep going until I've said it all.' He composed himself again. 'But the thing I want most of all is for you to be happy. I'll dedicate my life to it, marriage or not. Whatever you need, whatever you want. I'll be your husband if you'll have me, and your lifelong friend if not.'

Delilah was so choked that she couldn't speak.

'Say something, please,' he begged. 'Now I've made a fool of myself all over again I need to hear something.'

'You haven't made a fool of yourself.' Delilah forced herself to face him even though she knew that tears were running down her cheeks. 'It's the nicest thing anyone's ever said to me.'

His expression became less wary, though he was still unsure. 'And . . . ?'

She wiped her face. 'Can I ask you something?'

'Anything.'

'If we were married, would you expect me to give up everything for you? To stop my selling and my business, and to just be your wife and keep house for you?'

'Are you joking?'

'Pardon?'

Frank genuinely looked incredulous. 'Delilah, I'm so proud of you, of everything you've achieved. For yourself and for your family, and despite having to put up with me being an idiot.' He waved his arm in a grand gesture that was almost the old, carefree Frank. 'You're the star in my firmament, and I'd be there to support you, not the other way around.'

Delilah's hand, almost of its own volition, moved slowly towards him, and he took it in both of his own. 'Let's find somewhere,' he said, 'where you can live and work in comfort. Your brothers and sisters are mine too from now on – marriage or not – and we'll look after them all. I'll work and bring home wages, or give them to you, while you sell flowers.'

How on earth could he have heard about her plans for the shop? She'd only spoken of it to William and Meg. But then she realised that he hadn't. He didn't know what was in her mind, but despite that, he was *thinking the same thing*.

She had to be sure. 'Can I tell you about something? Actually, two things, though you might not wait around to hear the second once I've told you the first.'

'There's nothing you could say that would drive me away.' He still had hold of her hand, clasping it as though she were about to disappear into thin air.

'On the day I last saw you, I walked home after you'd left to find that Pa had arranged for me to marry someone else.'

His grip tightened reflexively. 'Go on.'

'It was Mr Bradley, the overseer from the docks. Pa had sold me to him. At first I refused, of course I did – but he promised work and wages for all the boys if I agreed and made terrible threats about what would happen if I didn't.' She had to turn her head away again, unable to face the shame as she admitted it. 'So I said I would.'

It was her left hand that Frank held; he now turned it a little so he could look at her fingers. 'No ring.'

'No, I came to my senses in the end and told him I wouldn't, but it took several months, and – oh! All the time I was just wishing I could have that afternoon over again so that I could say yes to you.' She risked a glance at him under her eyelashes. 'If that makes you change your mind, then I'll have to accept that, but I can't be anything other than honest with you. It would be terrible if you found out about it later from someone else when I should have confessed it to you myself.'

'Confess?' His voice took on a more urgent tone. 'You've got nothing to confess, dearest girl. How was it a crime or a sin for you to be bullied into something, and especially once I'd run away and left you with nobody to protect you?'

'Really?'

'Really. Jesus, Mary and Joseph, if only I'd not been so stupid and selfish I would've been here to help you through it and we could have spared you months of pain.'

After a few moments of silence, Frank asked, 'So what was the other thing?'

Delilah was still deep in her thoughts. 'What other thing?'

'The one you just mentioned. Now we've agreed that the first one is of no particular importance, I'd like to hear the second.'

'Oh, Frank!'

'Come on, now, none of that. You're in a public park, and if anyone thinks I've made you cry then I'll look like even more of a fool than I really am.' He stifled a smile. 'And I don't want a fist fight with any of your brothers, to be sure.'

Delilah was beginning to recover herself. She had honestly thought that hearing about Mr Bradley would drive Frank away, but if anything it had done the opposite. He was still here with her, still holding her increasingly warm hand. Her voice became steadier as she said, 'I need to tell you about a shop.'

He seemed puzzled by the change of subject, but went along with it. 'A shop. By all means.'

'Not just any shop. *The* shop. Do you remember, I told you and Bridget about it when we used to walk past it?'

'The flower shop? Your special one, on Dale Street?'

'Yes. It's a long story and I'll tell you the rest some other time, but my business is doing well – I don't know if Bridget told you that I've got a market stall now – and the shop is to let.'

'Is it, now?' His eyes were narrowing as he carried out some calculations in his head. 'Expensive to rent, is it?'

'Yes. Or, that is to say, it's more expensive than my stall and our rent in the court put together. But it's in a good situation so it would mean more sales. And there are rooms to live in – not just the parlour behind the shop but a floor above, and an attic as well, as far as I can tell from looking at it from outside.'

'Plenty of room, then. And are you considering taking it?'

'I . . . I haven't asked after it yet. It would be a risk, and I don't want to get everyone's hopes up about the future only to lose it again. It would be so wonderful! A safe place for the children, and maybe a home for Bridget if . . . but anyway, I'm not sure if they'd let it to me anyway. There are a couple of people I could ask for references as to my honesty and hard work, but . . .'

Frank caught her meaning. The old, impudent glint appeared in his eye. 'Do you think,' he said with exaggerated diffidence, 'that they might be more likely to let it to a married woman than a single one? A woman with a husband in a respectable line of work who brought home a steady wage to add to the income from the shop?'

Now that the moment had come, Delilah felt oddly shy. 'Frank,' she said, after a moment.

'Yes?'

'Would you . . . would you ask me again?'

He stared at her as if he couldn't believe what he was hearing. Then he slid off the bench and down on to one knee. He lifted the hand he had been holding for so long and raised it to his lips.

Delilah felt the touch of them and shivered.

'Delilah, my own dearest love, will you make me the happiest man alive and marry me?'

She laughed from relief and joy. 'Yes, Frank, yes I will.'

# Chapter Nineteen

'No you damned well won't.'

The last couple of hours had passed in a delightful blur. William, Meg and the others had all been overjoyed with the news that met them when they made their way back from the lake. Delilah had been able to introduce Frank to Meg, and she looked forward to hearing what each thought of the other next time they were alone. Frank had exchanged grins and rapid signs with Jem before scooping Annie up on to his shoulder, just like he used to, and they had all walked and skipped their jubilant way between the blossom-filled trees before making their way home.

Pa was there when they arrived, and seemingly in one of his lucid periods. Delilah had shared the good news with him, but his only reaction was to throw a venomous look at Frank and spit on the floor. 'No you damned well won't.'

'I will.' Delilah felt strong with everyone around her. She could feel the waves of their support.

'No, you won't. You're not marrying any damned Irishman, and that's final.'

'You can't stop me.'

'Oh yes I can. You might think yourself a fine lady these days, but you're still my daughter and you can't get married without my permission.'

'Is that true?' Frank asked Delilah.

'Yes,' whispered Delilah through gritted teeth. 'Until I'm twenty-one.'

'And when will that be?'

'Next January. My birthday is New Year's Day.'

He brightened. 'Well, that's not so bad, is it? I mean . . .'

But Delilah was thinking of her shop. Her beautiful shop, a proper home for the children, which had seemed so close. After all these years, to finally have it within touching distance! And now that security for her family was about to be snatched away, and all because Pa hated the Irish. There was no way it would still be to let in more than half a year's time. And anything might happen to separate her from Frank in the meantime – her Pa, or his brothers . . . and what about the children? The safe home she might be able to offer them . . .

While these thoughts were running through Delilah's head both William and Sam started an argument with Pa, the one attempting reasoned persuasion and the other beginning to ball his fists. But Pa, finally able to exert some authority on a world and a family that had got away from him, was firm. He would not give his permission for Delilah to marry Frank and that was that. And the local vicar knew he was alive so there was no point her running to him to arrange a wedding by saying she was an orphan. 'You need a man to sign you over, girl, so you should have paid more attention to the respect due to the head of the house.'

He wasn't going to budge, or at least not here and now, and Delilah stormed angrily outside. She could hear Frank starting to plead, but that was never going to work. Pa's voice became more agitated and eventually Frank joined her out in the court, much to the interest of the many curious onlookers. 'I think it'll be doing more harm than good to keep arguing with him just now.'

She collapsed into his arms, tearful with frustration and at the same time aware of how very comforting it was to be so close to him. 'Oh, Frank! And just when I thought—'

'It's all right,' he said, taken aback at first but then more than happy to put his arms around her and pat her consolingly on the back. 'We'll work it out, you and me together. He can't stop us, you know – not for ever.'

'Yes, but—' Delilah pulled back a little so she could see his face, and belatedly realised she had made a spectacle of herself in front of all the neighbours.

Frank saw her embarrassment and made a loud announcement to them all. 'Yes, ladies and gentlemen,' he said, grandly, 'I'm pleased to tell you all that Miss Delilah Shaw has agreed to become my wife, and that we're overjoyed, regardless of the feelings of certain others.' He bent to speak to Delilah alone. 'May as well get it out in the open – the more people who know, the more normal it seems and the more your father hasn't a leg to— I mean, can't keep arguing against it.'

Delilah nodded, catching the eyes of a few of the court's other women and seeing their nods and smiles. 'You're probably right.'

'Now,' he went on. 'Not to worry for now about your Pa – he'll come round. How about if we go and see Mam and Bridget now, to tell them the good news?'

'Oh yes! I'd like that. But . . . will it make things awkward in your family?'

'If the boys don't like it, they can lump it,' came the firm reply. 'Now we're together I'm not going to let anyone tear us apart.'

Despite her worries, Delilah smiled. Yes. Yes, they would work their way through this, and they would do it together. Her whole future was not going to rest on Pa's whim and his dislike of foreigners. Certainly she and Frank would marry, even if they had to wait until next year, and if they really put their heads to it they might find a way of getting the shop as well. But in the meantime . . . 'Bridget will be pleased, at least,' said Delilah, as they left the court arm in arm.

'Pleased? That's the understatement of the year! She'll be floating on air, just like I am right now. And Mam thinks you're the best girl in Liverpool, too, don't forget.'

Michael wasn't at home when they reached the O'Malleys' rooms, but Patrick and Gideon were both there along with Bridget and their mother. When they saw Frank and Delilah arrive together Patrick whispered something in Gideon's ear and slipped out, but Delilah hardly noticed as Bridget flew to her.

'Oh! It's so lovely to see you! And . . . is it good news?' She hugged Delilah. 'It must be – I can tell from Frank's face. Oh, I'm so happy for the both of you!'

Delilah held Bridget tight for a few moments, the happiness of being reunited with her friend on top of her engagement to Frank being almost too much to bear. Then she stepped back and looked a little uncertainly at Mrs O'Malley, but she received the kindest welcome from her, too.

'Michael isn't going to like it,' said Gideon, casting a shadow on the happy family party.

'Michael can—' began Frank. Then he looked at the women and composed himself. 'It's not his business. I'm a grown man and what I choose to do with my life – and who I choose to marry – is nothing to do with him.'

Gideon looked sceptical, but he said no more.

Delilah spent the rest of the afternoon sitting with Frank and Bridget as they all repeated over and over again how happy they were and tried to steer away from the idea that the marriage might not happen, if both Pa and the O'Malley men were set against it.

'But you've got Mam on your side,' pointed out Bridget, when the subject could no longer be ignored. 'She might be a woman but Michael has to listen to her, out of respect.'

'Oh, I wish my Ma was still here!' The words escaped Delilah before she could stop them. The words she'd forced herself not to say since that dreadful day almost three years ago. Three years of worrying, of carrying the whole family against everything that life threw at them. Of missing Ma every single day but not being able to say so in case she upset the younger ones, or in case it made her collapse into the weak girl she knew she really was underneath. Because it was all an act, wasn't it? Being strong for everybody. Inside she wanted to be a child again, to have Ma's love and the advice of an older woman who knew what life was and who cared for her daughter's future.

'I'm sorry,' she said, wiping away a tear. 'But I just can't help – it would be so wonderful to have a parent who was on my side.'

Bridget took her hand and leant forward to kiss her. 'You poor darling. How much you've had to bear. But you've got your brothers and sisters, and you've got us.' After a moment's thought, she added, 'And you've still got your Ma's friend, haven't you? Ellen, did you say her name was – the one who was your Ma's friend all her life?'

'That's true,' said Delilah, slowly. But she shied away from the idea of going to see Ellen, for fear of how she would feel when she saw little Jemima again.

Frank was urging her now, not quite aware of all the background. 'Yes, that's a good idea – why don't you go and see her, ask her advice? She's known your

Pa longer than you have, and she might be able to come up with an idea you haven't thought of.'

'I'll think about it,' was all Delilah could manage.

She needed to get back to start on the evening meal for Pa and the children, so Frank and Bridget both rose to walk with her. All the way through the alleys Delilah kept thinking that if she could only persuade Pa to give his permission, she would be able to get the whole family out of here, away from the crowds, the filth, the fear of crime.

'Forgive me for asking,' said Frank, apparently reading her mind, 'but is your Pa likely to even live another year, until you're twenty-one? You see him every day, so you might not have noticed the difference, but coming back to him now after months away, I can see how much he's changed. His eyes were always yellow, since I've known him, but now it's spread to his skin as well, and I don't think that's a good sign.'

Delilah sighed. 'I thought it was just my imagination.'

'I don't think it is. What will happen to you all, if . . . ?'

'I don't know. And I don't want to think about it unless I have to.' That was certainly true, because Delilah didn't want to examine her own feelings too closely – what if she found herself *hoping* for Pa's death? That would be a terrible thing, against all family feeling.

Frank hesitated when they reached the entrance to the court. 'Do you want us to come in with you? Or would you prefer to talk to him on your own just for now? I'll do whatever you think is best.'

'Just for now, it might be better if you don't. I don't mean that I don't want you to come in,' added Delilah in a rush. 'Just that . . . it would be better if he calmed down. You never know, I might be able to talk him round.'

'All right.' Frank lifted Delilah's hand to his lips and kissed it. 'Farewell then, my lady. I'll call tomorrow evening, shall I? After work?'

'Yes, yes please.' Delilah turned to Bridget and hugged her again. 'And please do come as well if you can.'

'I'll try.' Delilah knew what lay behind Bridget's hesitancy, and she promised herself again that she'd get Bridget out of her situation and safe as well as her own brothers and sisters. Besides, Bridget was *really* going to be her sister for the rest of their lives, so she owed it to her after all her kindness.

Pa was out, so Delilah didn't get the chance to renew the argument or put her case again. He still wasn't back by the time she went to bed, so it would have to wait. As she lay down – on a second mattress that she had managed to purchase, so that the boys and girls in the family no longer had to share – she tried to keep thinking of Frank, recalling her joy as he had spoken those precious words in the park. But as she fell into an uneasy slumber, it was with visions of Pa looming before her, and herself standing on the street gazing at the precious shop from which she was for ever excluded.

\* \* \*

Delilah had no luck at all with Pa over the course of the week. Nothing that she could say, or Frank, or William, or any of the others – even Bet tried, bless her – could move him. It was the last tiny bit of power that he possessed, and he was going to hold on to it for all he was worth. And he was so adamant that he didn't want her to marry an Irishman that Delilah began to fear, deep down, that he might end up not just delaying the wedding but, in some way that she couldn't yet fathom, actually *preventing* it. Despite the spring warmth, she went cold every time she thought of the prospect, the idea that her hard-won happiness might yet be snatched away from her. She'd had to pick herself up and start again so many times, but she didn't think she'd ever recover from that.

The stall was so busy that there was little time to think during the day, but in between selling and making recommendations to customers, watching Annie and trying to supervise and teach Clara – who had extreme difficulty in remaining still in one place all day – Delilah did manage the odd moment of contemplation. And it was during one of these that she decided that she had to stop being a coward and go to see Ellen.

The question of Jemima and her future had never been properly raised between them, but if she were to go and see Ma's old friend to ask her advice about the marriage, it would surely come up. She needed to have a plan in place for what she would say, how she would approach it. But she couldn't come to any kind of conclusion; she veered wildly from being desperate to have her youngest sister back to worrying that it would break Ellen's heart if she separated them. Jemima would shortly turn three, and she had lived with the Jenkinses for her whole life; it was all she knew.

It was Sunday again before Delilah had the opportunity to walk to Brick Street, and when the day came she found herself making all kinds of excuses to put off going. The room needed tidying, the linens washing. But she knew that she had to face it eventually, and the urgency of the situation with regard to the marriage and the shop overrode everything else. She had been to see the shop the previous evening after work, and knew it was still to let. If she could only find a way to change Pa's mind, it could be hers. Seeing Ellen might help her to achieve that goal, and she had to face the fact that a conversation about Jemima would be part of that. Oh, why were families so complicated?

The front door was open when she got there, as were most of the others in the street on such a fine day, but Delilah didn't need to go inside; both Ellen and James were enjoying the sun as they spoke to their neighbours. Several little girls were playing nearby, and Delilah's heart gave a lurch as she saw that one was Jemima. In theory, of course, she knew that Jemima was nearly three, but somehow she'd been envisaging her as the tiny tot she'd been last time they met, and to see her now looking like a proper little girl was a shock. She looked so much like Rosie had done at the same age that Delilah bit her lip. She stood for a moment, watching the happily shrieking children, before moving close enough for Ellen to notice her.

'Delilah!' Ellen smiled and then her eye automatically sought Jemima.

'It's been a long while since I saw you,' began Delilah, 'and I'm sorry. I wondered if you had a few minutes to talk?'

Ellen and James exchanged a glance. 'Women's business?' he said. 'You go on. I'll stay out here and keep an eye on our lass.'

Delilah didn't think he'd chosen those last two words deliberately, but they still stung. She and Ellen made their way into the main room of the house, identical in its layout to their old home, and Delilah could almost imagine that she saw Ma, setting the kettle over the fire or hanging washing up to air. She shook her head and Ma disappeared. *Don't get distracted.*

Once they were seated, Ellen began tentatively with, 'I heard a rumour – you know how word gets about the place . . .'

'About me getting engaged to Frank?'

'Yes!' Ellen hesitated again. 'I'm happy for you, but I also heard it might not be straightforward? It's only gossip, though, so I'll be pleased if you set me right.'

Delilah sighed. 'That bit's true as well, unfortunately.' Faced with a sympathetic listener, one who had known her all her life, Delilah felt more secure, and she poured out the story of the engagement, the shop, and Pa. It was always Pa, wasn't it? He was the fly in every ointment, the coal smudge on every clean sheet.

Ellen nodded along and sympathised, but when Delilah got to the part about Pa being so obstinate about giving parental permission for the wedding, she looked confused. 'Didn't your Ma . . .'

'What?'

'When she died, didn't your Ma say anything to you?'

Delilah frowned. 'I'm not sure what you mean. She told me to look after the little ones.'

Ellen pursed her lips, as if wondering whether to say something or not. If that was the case then she decided in favour of silence. 'It doesn't matter. You just need to keep at your Pa, remind him that it's what your Ma would have wanted for you.' She sighed. 'I miss her too, you know, every day.'

'I know. And I'm sorry I haven't come to see you more often, but . . .' She trailed off.

'I was lucky,' said Ellen. 'I found myself a good man, a man who cares about *me* as well as having a clean, tidy home and his meals cooked. Your Ma wasn't so lucky, but I hope you'll find a way. I'll come and talk to your Pa, if you like, or James can.'

'I'd appreciate anything you could do to help.'

There followed a silence that threatened to become awkward. It was broken by Jemima running in. She gave Delilah a wary look and skipped over to Ellen. 'Look, Mama – look what I found!'

It was a little flower, Delilah could see, no doubt picked from a crack in the pavement.

'You can have it, Mama,' said Jemima, attempting unsuccessfully to stick it to the front of Ellen's dress.

Ellen gently took it out of the little girl's hand. 'It's lovely, darling. Now, Mama is talking, so why don't you go back outside while the sun's shining?'

Jemima skipped off. They both watched her, and then Ellen turned back to Delilah with tears streaming down her cheeks. 'Once you're married, I suppose you'll want . . .' She couldn't go on.

Delilah felt her heart break in two. She couldn't do it to them, she just couldn't. Much as she wanted to sweep Jemima up in her arms, cuddle her and take her away to be with the rest of her family, she had to realise what effect that would have on the little girl. Jemima thought Ellen and James were her mother and father, and she'd lived with them all her life. To her it would be like being abducted, torn away from her parents and taken to live among strangers. It would be incomprehensible to her and would cause immense distress. Delilah needed to do what was best for Jemima, regardless of her own desires.

And then there was Ellen and James. All those years helping Ma with confinement after confinement, being kind to the growing Shaw brood, and all the while with the heartbreak of having no child of their own. And then Jemima had come along and they had loved her as much as they would have done any child born to them. Was such kindness to be repaid by Delilah taking away the source of their happiness?

Ellen had noticed Delilah's hesitation and was now staring at her with a wild hope in her eyes.

'I—' Delilah choked up and couldn't get the words out. She tried again. 'I think it would be better, if you're agreeable, for Jemima to stay with you. Better for her, I mean – we'd love to have her back, but after all this time with you she'd never see us as her family, and she'd always think we'd *taken* her from her family. From her parents who love her.' She dissolved into tears.

Ellen was sobbing too, and she moved to take Delilah in her arms and comfort her, just as she'd done many times when Delilah was little. Just as Ma had done.

'You're such a good girl,' said Ellen, eventually. She kissed the top of Delilah's head. 'I always knew you would be. How could you not?'

Delilah didn't quite understand, but it didn't matter. She clung to Ellen as though she were drowning.

'Such love,' continued Ellen, dreamily. 'Your Ma was so happy, at least for a while . . . but she'd be proud of you now. Giving up your own happiness for the good of someone you love, leaving them with someone else. Just like your father.'

Delilah started and drew back. 'Pa?'

Ellen's hand flew to her mouth. 'Ignore me. I'm so overcome I don't know what I'm saying.'

But Delilah could see that there was more to it than that; Ellen seemed genuinely horrified. 'Is this something to do with what you said earlier? About Ma telling me something before she died?'

'I told you, ignore me. If your Ma didn't tell you then it's not up to me.'

'So there is something?'

'Yes, I mean no – look, can you tell me exactly what your Ma said to you, that day?'

Delilah sat back and closed her eyes. 'Ma was in the bed. She was in pain, but it was coming and going, and she said, "You'd think I'd be used to it by now." I asked if she wanted anything. She said no, and then . . .' Delilah's eyes opened wide. 'She said, "Listen. It won't be long before the pains come back, and I need to talk to you now, while I can. I've got something to tell you." So she was going to say something.'

'So what happened? What stopped her?'

Delilah tried to think back. She'd been so tired, and that day had been so terrible that she'd tried to erase it from her mind. But she must try . . . 'Meg came in. Yes, that was it – Ma looked like she was going to speak, but the door opened and it was Meg. She came to tell us that William was home and was it all right if they had their tea.'

'And that interrupted your Ma?'

'Yes. After that she said something about how grown-up we were, and I asked her what she'd been going to say. But all she said was that it wasn't import-ant. And then she said, "If anything happens to me, make sure you look after your brothers and sisters," and I said I would. And that was it, really – her pains came back and we sent out for you to come.'

Ellen was nodding. 'I think I see now.'

'See what?'

'Why she didn't say anything. She was scared that if she told you, you wouldn't look after the others.'

'Ellen, I don't understand what you're saying. How could Ma possibly think I wouldn't do everything I could for the little ones?'

Ellen sighed. 'All right. I know now, or I think I know, why your Ma didn't tell you, but I also know that her fears were wrong – you'd never stop loving your brothers and sisters.'

'Will you please just tell me what's going on?'

'Your Ma always meant for you to know one day, and she won't blame me, I'm sure, for telling you now. Not when it might actually help you.'

Delilah was on the edge of her seat with impatience. 'Tell me what?'

Ellen expelled a long breath and straightened her skirts before replying. Then she looked Delilah straight in the eye. 'That John Shaw isn't your father.'

# Chapter Twenty

Delilah blinked. She opened her mouth but no words came out.

'It's a shock, I know,' continued Ellen. 'And I don't want you to think badly of your Ma. It's not like it might sound.'

'How . . . What . . . ?'

Ellen looked at her. 'Tea,' she said firmly. 'What you need is a hot cup of tea with plenty of sugar.'

Delilah sat in complete bemusement as Ellen began to bustle around. Eventually a cup was put in her hand and she sipped without thinking, starting back at the scalding liquid.

'You get that inside you,' said Ellen, a little calmer herself now, 'and I'll tell you all about it.'

Delilah took a few more sips and then felt strong enough to look up and nod.

'Like I said, you mustn't think badly of your Ma. When we were young, she was in love. And I mean really in love, not just a passing fancy. It was at the docks that she met him; we used to have to run down there on and off with messages or food for our Pas. He'd . . . come in on a boat, and he decided to stay and make his home in Liverpool. It was lovely to see them together, how much they cared for each other. They were going to get married; they had it all planned. You have to understand that, Delilah – when your Ma realised she was expecting you, it wasn't some fling, it was with the man she thought she was going to be with for ever.'

Delilah could well imagine Ma's long-ago happiness, but her heart sank as she knew that this story wasn't going to have a happy ending. 'So what happened?'

'Her Pa said she couldn't marry him.'

'Why?' Delilah thought of her own situation. 'Was he a foreigner?'

'Yes, and he had dark skin. Your grandfather didn't like that at all, and he wouldn't let your Ma marry him, even when she said she was expecting his child.'

'Poor Ma,' said Delilah, a wrenching sympathy and solidarity with her mother welling up inside her. She looked at the back of her hand as if seeing it for the first time. Of course, she'd always been a little more swarthy than the younger ones, but it was all of a piece with her having black hair, so she'd never really thought about it too deeply. But now . . .

'But, of course,' continued Ellen, 'they didn't want your Ma having a baby out of wedlock, either – there was plenty of it about, of course, but they were a respectable family. So your grandfather talked to one of his friends who had a son who was looking for a wife.'

'Pa?' Delilah realised what she'd said. 'I mean . . . you know.'

'Yes. And John Shaw was only too pleased to have a pretty girl from a steady family thrown at him.'

'But how could Ma do that? Why didn't she make more of a fuss?'

Ellen shook her head. 'It makes me upset to remember it, even now. She was heartbroken. But they talked it over together and realised that you'd have a better life that way. There was plenty of violence, back in those days, for black men, and especially those who had white wives. The girls were mostly cut off from their families and lived in the worst parts of town.'

'But they loved each other?'

'Oh yes. Don't ever think different. They broke their hearts over and over again, but they wanted what was best for you. Just like you've done for Jemima.' Ellen used the corner of her apron to wipe away a tear. 'I probably wouldn't have said anything if I hadn't been a bit overcome about it all. You'd never have known.'

'I suppose I should feel sorry for Pa. Did he know? Does he know?'

Ellen shook her head again. 'Your Ma never told him – if she had done then he'd never have had you in the house. She was always terrified he'd work it out, but he had no interest in anything to do with "women's business", even then, so he didn't notice when their first child came early. And of course all the others are his: once your Ma made her vows, she stuck to them, no matter what it cost her.'

Delilah sat in silence for a long while. Then she sighed. 'Poor, poor Ma. And poor everybody – it sounds like they were all made unhappy.'

'Yes. But it was a long time ago now, love, and people come to terms with these things. Your Pa certainly got a good bargain out of it, and your Ma found a measure of contentment, in time, especially when all the other children came along.' Ellen sighed. 'It's life, Delilah – we women have to take the best of what we can. But your Ma never went near the docks from the day of her wedding to the day she died – I think she was worried she wouldn't have the strength to keep it up if she ever saw him again.'

A suspicion had been growing in Delilah's mind ever since Ellen's first, shocking revelation, and now it was overwhelming. 'So, he's still around then, is he? This man – my real father?'

'He is.'

There was silence for a few moments before Ellen continued. 'Aren't you going to ask me who he is?'

Delilah got to her feet. 'I don't need to ask – I know.'

\* \* \*

The docks were much less busy on a Sunday, but there were still a few people milling around and Delilah could see another ship on its way in. She had no time to wonder where it had come from, because she was hurrying to her appointment with fate. She was going to meet her father for the first time.

It wouldn't be the first time they'd seen each other, of course, for Delilah had known him all her life. But it would be their very first encounter as family, and she wanted to get it right.

When she reached the warehouse she stopped so she could catch her breath, waiting until her breathing was steady – or as steady as it was going to get – before she smoothed down her dress and stepped inside. 'Abraham? Are you there?'

She spotted him some way off in the cavernous space, inspecting some crates of fruit and making marks on a piece of paper. He hadn't seen her and she was obliged to move further inside and call out again before he noticed her presence.

Abraham straightened and turned to face her. Her *father*. The man who'd loved her Ma, who'd given up his own chance at happiness in order to do the best for his daughter. The man who'd kept his secret for over twenty years to protect those he loved.

She was standing stock-still, just looking at him. He returned the gaze, questioningly at first, and then his expression changed, and she knew that he knew.

He took half a step forward. 'Delilah?' His voice was uncertain.

She started forward, and then began to run. He did the same, and they met in a flurry of arms, warm embraces and tears. 'Oh, my baby, my own sweet girl,' he sobbed. 'After all this time.'

Father and daughter remained clasped together for some time before mutually pulling back so that they could look at each other. Abraham kept her hand in one of his and used the other to wipe his eyes. 'But who's told you? And why now?'

Delilah found her legs giving way. 'Is there somewhere we could sit and talk?'

'Of course, of course. Come.' He supported her as they made their way to a small partitioned area in the far corner of the warehouse. Inside there was a bed, neatly made, a wooden chair and a few bags and boxes. Pinned to the wall were two arrangements of flowers, carefully dried and pressed.

Abraham saw the direction of her gaze. 'My proudest possessions.' He looked about him. 'I'm sorry, it's not much of a home, and I don't get many guests . . . you sit there.' He assisted her to the chair and then moved to perch on the edge of the bed.

They were now separated by the space of several feet, and Delilah moved her chair forwards so she could reach out and take his hand again. 'Abraham.' She hesitated. 'Pa . . . ?'

He dropped his head. 'Stop it, or you'll make me cry again and I'll be good for nothing.' Then he looked up. 'No, don't stop it. Say it again, please.'

'Pa.' Delilah gazed at him. 'It was Ellen who told me, just now, and when she was telling me I wondered – how on earth did I never think of it before?'

Tentatively, he touched a lock of her black hair where it tumbled over her shoulders. 'You got this from me,' he said. 'And your green eyes. And I'm glad. I both did and didn't want you to look like me – it would have made your life more difficult. But it didn't really matter – you're a living, breathing reminder of our love whatever you look like. Daisy's and mine.'

'Daisy?'

'Yes, that's what I used to call her – there are lots of ways you can shorten Margaret, and that was ours. We were the only ones who used it; everyone else called her Maggie or Meg.'

A long-ago conversation with Bridget chimed in Delilah's mind. 'And that's why my name is so different from all the others, isn't it? Ma wasn't just being romantic – she wanted some kind of reminder that nobody else would notice.'

He smiled for the first time. 'She was a clever girl, your Ma. The name had to begin with "D", she said, but it couldn't be Daisy. And it had to be something that reminded her of places far away, not something that was common in Liverpool.'

'And then she went back to more usual names after that. Jonny for her first son, after Pa, and then Meg for her next daughter, after herself.' Delilah nodded. But then she too took up a lock of hair. 'But I don't understand why I don't look more like you. In my face, I mean.'

'I don't know. My father was a white man, like I told you. And although my Ma was a slave, I've got no idea who her father was – he might have been a white man as well, for all I know.' He shrugged, the weight of generations of pain and suffering heavy on his shoulders. 'I don't know how it works, but your skin got the white part of the family and mine the black.' After a pause he added, 'And some people do see a similarity, I think – when I came to your home that time I was terrified that little girl was going to say something when she looked at us.'

'And I think Sol saw something too, when he first met me,' said Delilah, remembering the odd start to their conversation. 'Well, I'm proud of my heritage, whatever it is. Proud for you and for your . . . for my grandmother.'

'Grandmother.' He shook his head. 'How pleased she'd be to see what you've made of yourself. A free woman in a free city.'

'And that's what I am,' said Delilah. 'My ancestors might have come from different places in the world, but I'm all Liverpool. Because that's what Liverpool is.'

He squeezed her hand. 'That it is. And it's my home too.' Another little smile touched the corner of his mouth. 'All you need to do now is marry an Irishman and your children will be the Liverpool of the future.'

She gasped. 'How did you know?'

'Oh, word gets around. I gather there was quite a scene in your court last week, and there's always someone about who works around here, or someone who knows someone.' He looked at her seriously. 'Is that what you want? Is that what would make you happy?'

'Oh yes, yes it is. But I'm so scared it's not going to happen.' She poured out the story, safe and secure in the knowledge that she was sharing her feelings with someone who cared.

His lips tightened when he heard about Pa forbidding the marriage on the grounds that Frank was an Irishman. He said nothing at the time, however, listening to her in perfect silence until she ran out of words.

After some moments of contemplation, he spoke. 'What we need to do is think about how best I can help you. First, I have some money put by—'

'No, no, absolutely not!' Delilah was almost on her feet. 'I didn't come here to – you must know that – what I mean is—'

'I know you didn't,' he said gently. 'Of course you didn't. Look at you, Delilah – you're a self-made woman and I couldn't be prouder of you. But the fact remains that I've got nothing and nobody except you, and I've been getting paid all these years without spending very much of it. It will all go to you when I'm dead, anyway, but if it suits us all better for you to have it now, then it's yours.'

Delilah was shaking her head. 'No,' she said again. 'I came here to see you, to let you know that I knew, to . . . to share everything with you. To thank you. I don't want money.' She paused as something struck her. 'But how would . . . sorry, I'm not being . . . but what I mean is, how would anyone know that, after you're dead? If nobody except Ellen knows that you're really my father?'

'I've got a paper,' he said, proudly. 'I paid a law-man to draw it up, years ago.' He reached under the bed and took out a tin, from which he extracted two sheets. He unfolded one. 'Here.'

Delilah stared for a moment at the handwriting before she could focus enough to read. It was an official-looking thing with signatures at the bottom, confirming that after Abraham's death he wished to leave all his worldly goods to 'Delilah Shaw, daughter of Margaret Shaw now living in Brick Street, Liverpool'.

'I need to get that last part changed,' Abraham noted, watching her read. 'But I didn't know if your court had an official address. Anyway, we can skip that now and move straight on to your shop, once you've got it.'

'But I haven't got it yet,' said Delilah. 'And nor am I sure I'll be able to marry Frank before it's leased again.' She thumped her hand on her knee in frustration. 'And that's got nothing to do with money and everything to do with Pa.' She paused, realising what she'd said. 'I'm sorry, after so long it's going to be difficult to get out of the habit of—'

He was shaking his head. 'You mustn't. Mustn't get out of the habit, I mean. As far as the world is concerned, John Shaw is your father. And it's what he thinks, too.'

Delilah sat for a long moment, considering her complicated relationship with the man she'd always believed to be her father. 'He did support me while I was growing up,' she conceded, 'along with all the others. Whatever has happened since, I owe that to him.'

'And there's your Ma's good name to consider, too,' added Abraham. 'I know and you know what the real truth is, and I know she's dead and gone now, but I can't stand the thought of any notion getting round that she was a loose woman.'

'You're right.' Delilah felt dejected again at the thought of what she now knew Ma's life to have been. 'She suffered enough – let's not do anything to hurt her now she's dead.'

Delilah's problems seemed insuperable, so she thought it best to turn the subject. 'What's the other paper?'

Abraham handled it reverently. It was evidently older than the other, and looked like it had been folded and unfolded many times. 'You know,' he began, 'how it's the law now that births have to be registered with the official records? On top of any baptism record at a church, I mean.'

'Yes,' said Delilah, confused as to his apparent change of subject. 'I remember Ma doing it for Annie, and I had to register Jemima after . . .' She tailed off.

'Well,' continued Abraham, 'you were born before that became the law. So although there'll be a record at a church somewhere that you were baptised the daughter of John and Margaret Shaw, there's no state document anywhere that says who your father is. Your Ma and I, we knew everyone had to know – had to *think* you were a Shaw, but we wanted something just for us. Just to remind us.' He held out the paper. 'I've never shown this to another living soul.'

Delilah took it and unfolded the creased paper with extreme care. And there in front of her was Ma's handwriting. It had been very untidy, as Ma had only ever been to Sunday school as a girl, but she'd known enough to be able to write out bills for the laundry she took in, and to sign her name at the bottom. In splotched ink, faded to brown with age, Delilah read the words, *My daugter Delilah is the child of Abraham Davis, once of Ammerica and now living in Liverpool.* It was signed *Margaret (Daisy) Shaw.*

'Davis?' asked Delilah, still staring at the paper, which for some reason was shaking. 'I don't think I've ever heard that before.'

'I never had a surname,' came the reply, with a hint of bitterness. 'Slaves don't need them. But when I came here I realised I needed one if I was to stay. I wasn't about to use my *father's*' – Abraham's mouth twisted – 'so I borrowed the name of the captain of the ship that brought me here. It was as good as any other.'

Delilah stared again at the paper, at the writing, at the physical reminder of Ma. Abraham was happy to sit in silence, no doubt lost in his own thoughts, so she was free to let all the overwhelming feelings of the day sink in.

She wanted to tell Frank all about it. That was one of her earliest coherent thoughts, and it told her once again that he was the man she wanted to marry. The man she loved, just as Ma had loved Abraham.

The words on the paper blurred and then became clear again. 'Abraham,' said Delilah, slowly.

'Yes, my dear? My own dearest daughter? I can say that while we're alone.'

'Like I said, I didn't come here to talk about money, but there is something you could do.'

'Something that will help you? That will set you on your way to happiness?'

Delilah looked again at the faded words *daugter* and *child*. 'Yes.'

# Chapter Twenty-One

'And that's the whole story,' concluded Delilah, looking at Frank's stunned face.

He ran his hands through his hair. 'And quite some story it is, too.'

They were sitting alone in the Shaws' room, where Frank had come to call as he now did every evening after work. She watched him for a while as he took it all in, pleased to see that his first conclusion was the same as hers. 'So, this paper, you think it will mean that Abraham can give you the permission we need to get married, now?'

'Yes. He took it to both priests – the Catholic one as well as ours, because he knew you were from Ireland – and they both said they'd accept it.'

'And you're sure,' he took her hand, 'you're still sure that being married to me is what you want?'

'It is,' she replied, firmly. 'Shop or no shop, or whatever is to come, you're the man I want to have as my husband.'

'Well then.' For the first time that Delilah had ever seen, Frank blushed. 'What are we waiting for?'

'We just need to organise things so that Pa – and Abraham says I'm to keep calling him that, he doesn't mind – doesn't find out. Like I just said, we agreed that Pa shouldn't know. There's no point in raking over all that now, telling him about what really happened all those years ago. All we need is to get to the church without him knowing, and then once we're married he can't do anything about it.'

'But won't he go to the church and ask why they let you marry without his permission?'

'I'll worry about that when it happens, but I don't think it will. Once he knows there's nothing he can do, he won't waste the energy. He might shout and rave and be angry with us, but that's nothing I haven't had to deal with before.'

'And now you've got me to stand up for you. For ever and ever, until death us do part.' He paused. 'I was going to say, how lucky it is that you found out. But from what you said I gather you wouldn't have heard all this if you hadn't been so kind to Ellen, so it's all your own doing, really. You've made your own luck.'

'I suppose, if you put it like that . . . but I still feel lucky. And grateful.'

He grinned the old impish grin. 'And, to be sure, you only had the good fortune to meet me because you'd been so kind to Bridget in the street that day. Truly you have been rewarded!'

She gave him an affectionate shove. 'How am I going to put up with you for the rest of our lives, Frank O'Malley?'

'Ah.'

She looked at him in surprise. 'What?'

'Well, now we really are close to being married, I wanted to talk about names.'

'You mean, I should have Abraham's instead of being called Shaw? But what difference will it make, if I'm to change it anyway?'

He shook his head. 'Not that. I meant my name.'

'I don't understand you.'

'It's . . . it's difficult to say such things about my own family, but I don't think I want to be called O'Malley any more. You remember when I got sacked from that hotel job when they found out who my brothers were? Well, I've a feeling that's only going to get worse, and having the name over your shop isn't going to do you any favours.'

'What are you suggesting?'

'That when we get married we have a completely new start. We'll both change our names to something else and then go from there.'

'You'd do that? For me, for us? Change the name you've had your whole life, that was your father's before you? And won't your mother mind?'

'Well, if you do, why shouldn't I? Besides, I wouldn't be the first Irishman to change his name, and Mam understands.'

'Out of interest, what would you change it to?'

He laughed. 'That I don't know, not yet. We can decide between us, and be as extravagant as you like. How about "Mr and Mrs Flowerseller-to-the-rich-and-famous"?'

'Oh, stop it, Frank!'

'Well, whatever you think. The main thing is to get married as soon as we can.' He lifted her hand to his lips, as he had done the previous day, and she felt a shiver of pleasure run through her as he kissed it.

\* \* \*

Despite Delilah's fears, the wedding proved straight-forward to arrange. After some resistance she allowed Abraham to pay for a special licence, so that banns did not need to be called for three weeks; Pa didn't go to church, but some neighbours did and gossip was bound to get spread if the announcement were made so publicly. The shop was also secure in principle, waiting only for confirmation of the marriage before they could move in. They had been obliged to put Frank's name on the agreement, but Delilah didn't mind: she had found a man she could trust.

And so here she was, on a beautiful day in May, arriving at the local church. It was very different from the last wedding she'd seen, that of Mr Ashton's daughter: no carriage, no white dress, no hordes of smart guests. But in other ways Delilah felt just as lucky as the earlier bride: she had a father and a husband-to-be who loved her, and she was overpoweringly happy.

She did have flowers, a bouquet that would have graced the richest of ceremonies; Jem had made it up for her and he and Sam presented it just before they set out. Annie skipped along beside them with a smaller posy. Bridget met them outside the church, as did Meg, who had been released from work for the special occasion. William was already inside with Frank: he was to act as the best man, as none of Frank's brothers were expected. As she greeted them Delilah did think that she caught a fleeting glance of Gideon O'Malley further up the street, but if it was him then he swiftly disappeared round a corner.

And there was Abraham, waiting for her in a suit he'd bought specially for the occasion. Delilah had managed to fudge her way round the enquiries of her siblings as to why he should be there, saying that she needed an adult man to give her away, and they'd seemed satisfied. She waited until the others had all gone in before she turned to him.

He held out his hand and she took it. For just one moment they were the only two people in the world as they shared a look that held what nobody else knew. 'Your Ma would be so proud,' he said, before stopping with a little choke.

She squeezed his fingers. 'Shall we go in?'

The church was almost empty, of course, but Delilah felt another wave of happiness when she saw Ellen and Jemima sitting in a pew. Jemima had a flower in her hair and she waved shyly as Delilah passed.

And there was Frank, standing at the front, turning as William whispered to him, as handsome as ever, smiling at her in that way that made her heart sing. Delilah floated her way up the aisle towards him.

The ceremony was soon over, Delilah remembering almost nothing about it later except Frank's face and her hand in his, and the new Mr and Mrs Malling left to start their new life together. Delilah had turned down some of Frank's more outrageous suggestions and, in consultation with Mrs O'Malley and Bridget, had proposed something that at least resembled his old name.

Outside the church Ellen came to say goodbye, Jemima in her arms. Delilah gave the little girl a flower from her bouquet and kissed them both, watching them on their way. The rest of the party headed not for the Shaws' place, but for the rooms shared by Frank, Bridget and Mrs O'Malley in a different court. There a modest but very happy meal was shared.

They were just finishing when the door opened and Michael, Patrick and Gideon stepped inside.

There was an immediate feeling of tension, and Frank rose to his feet.

Michael opened his mouth, but was forestalled by his mother. 'If you've come to say anything other than congratulations, boys, you can leave again. Frank is happy, and we're happy for him.' She had evidently never been a tall woman, but now she looked tiny and gnarled with age as she stood defiantly, facing up to the hulking Michael.

Even the terrifying O'Malley brothers wouldn't harm their mother, and Michael shut his mouth again, merely nodding to them all. Patrick did the same, but Gideon went a step further, smiling at Delilah and shaking Frank's hand. He was the next youngest,

Delilah recalled, so perhaps there was still hope that Frank might have an ongoing friendship with one of his brothers.

Michael was on the verge of leaving when Bridget called out to him, and he paused. 'What?'

Delilah watched as Bridget tried to stop herself shrinking under his gaze. *Go on*, she urged, in her mind.

Bridget drew herself up. 'When Frank and Delilah move into the shop tomorrow, I'm going with them.'

'No you're not,' was the only reply, given in a dismissive tone.

'Oh yes I am.' Bridget folded her arms. 'You're not my father, Michael, you're my brother. It's nothing to do with you. Mam's happy for me to go, and that's that.'

Delilah could see that Bridget was shaking, and she longed to step forward to take her friend's hand, but she restrained herself. She also put out her arm to stop Frank interrupting. Bridget had to do this by herself.

Michael stepped forward, looming over his sister, but she didn't step back. 'You can't leave Mam. She needs you.'

'What I need, Michael O'Malley,' snapped his mother, 'is for you to stop thinking the women in your family are yours to control. Bridget's been offered a good job and a good home there, away from all that's going on around here, and I'd rather see her take it and make something of herself than stay here with me.'

Delilah had to struggle to hide her amusement as she watched the shades of disbelief and consternation pass over Michael's face. Honestly, *men*. How lucky she was to have Frank, Abraham and William all in her life; they showed that a different type of male behaviour was possible.

Gideon spoke in a murmur to Michael, and eventually he nodded. 'All right.' He jabbed a finger at Bridget. 'But you're going because I say you can, you get that?'

'Of course,' replied Bridget, in a deceptively submissive tone. Delilah admired her: she herself might have been tempted to argue the point, but Bridget was clever enough to know that letting him think he'd had his own way was of no importance now that she had carried her point.

The three brothers left, and the party atmosphere was able to resume. Delilah and Bridget embraced, each telling the other how happy and proud she was.

The afternoon drew on. Meg had to leave first, in order to start on the long walk back to Prince's Park. William insisted on going most of the way with her, and it was early evening before he returned. He collected the younger ones, and Mrs O'Malley and Bridget both also prepared to leave – they had arranged to stay with a friend for the night so as to give Delilah and Frank some privacy.

And then they were gone, and Delilah was alone with her husband. She had wondered if it would be awkward, but she felt only love and contentment. The wedding night, the spectre of which had been so horrifying and disgusting when Mr Bradley was her intended husband, was now not to be dreaded but rather anticipated with pleasure.

Frank smiled at her in the firelight, and she stood and held out her hand. 'Shall we?' An overwhelming happiness suffused her as she led him through to the other room and closed the door.

# Chapter Twenty-Two

Delilah was unable to stop smiling the following morning as they left the rooms together and made their way to the agent's office to collect the keys to the shop. It was a Sunday, so they were officially closed, but a helpful young man met them outside and wished them luck.

Before she knew it, she was in Dale Street and standing before it. The flower shop. The place she had dreamed about, had loved for more years than she cared to remember, now hers. *Theirs*.

She squeezed Frank's hand and they made their way inside. It hadn't been empty for very long, so the downstairs rooms were still in good condition, but the upstairs ones were a different matter. Mrs Farrell and the other employees hadn't lived in, so they contained the dust and detritus of years. But they would soon clean up, with a bit of hard work, and Delilah gleefully looked at all the space they would have. One of the two bedrooms would be for her and Frank, and the second a girls' space for Bridget and Annie. Delilah had originally thought that Clara might come with them too, but this was the one part of her plan that had not been a success. Clara, used to a life on the streets, had not taken to working at a static market stall and certainly didn't want to tie herself to living and working in one confined space. Delilah hadn't pushed the point, not wishing to make a young girl unhappy, and she had also noticed the reluctance on Bet's face at parting with her youngest daughter so soon, even for such a good position.

And so Bridget and Annie would have the room to themselves, at least until Delilah's own children started to come along. She thought back to last night and wondered if she might even be expecting already, and how many children she and Frank would have.

But she had no time to daydream. There was a small room above, in the attic, and Delilah had determined that this was to be William's. He was a grown man in paid work, so he would live there almost as a lodger, paying for his board but coming and going as he pleased and not expected to help out with any chores. Sam and Jem would therefore sleep downstairs in the back parlour that also functioned as a kitchen. They wouldn't mind – it would be the warmest room in the house, and she'd already flattered Sam by saying she would be trusting him to guard the place against any potential intruders. Delilah continued to worry that he might end up being drawn back towards the shady underground world that had once started to claim him, but for now he appeared to have escaped it. He had got himself a job at the market just as Delilah was leaving it, but it wasn't far and he'd be back every evening.

Jem would continue at his school – Delilah hoped he might even be able to go three times a week instead of twice from here on – and would, for now, spend the rest of his time helping out in the shop and yard. Jem adored Frank, who had surreptitiously taken him to see the trains another few times, and Delilah had no doubt that this would be a happy arrangement all round. And finally, Annie would be safe and looked after by all of them instead of having to run wild all day. Once she turned six Delilah hoped, with Meg's previously offered financial help, to send her to a proper elementary school.

The boys would have to share their space with Pa. The question of whether he would be invited to live with them had been discussed exhaustively, with Frank leaving the final decision up to Delilah. It was so, so tempting to mark their new start with a clean break and be rid of him completely, but when it came to it Delilah wouldn't leave him behind. He wasn't her Pa, but he didn't know that and neither did anyone else except Frank, Abraham and Ellen. He had done terrible things, of course he had; Delilah wouldn't ever forgive him for selling her to Mr Bradley. But as he had become less violent and more ill, the old shades of sympathy had come back. He'd been crippled because of Mr Bradley's unhealthy obsession with Delilah, losing his job and his self-respect through no fault of his own. And although he hadn't ever been any kind of ideal father he had been the family breadwinner for all those years, and he remained the father of Delilah's brothers and sisters. She would never think of them as her 'half' siblings; they were all family. 'And family,' she had concluded to Frank, 'is complicated.'

'Tell me about it,' had been Frank's reply, along with a kiss, and Pa was to stay. When she spoke to him later today Delilah hoped to assuage some of the anger he would feel about the wedding by showing him his new, more comfortable living arrangements. With Frank, William and Sam all living in the house he wouldn't dare to be violent even if he still found himself physically capable of it; and she could keep the shop's takings upstairs.

She would worry about Pa later. There was an awful lot to do if they were to be ready to open the shop first thing tomorrow, and Delilah was glad it was a Sunday so everyone was free to help. Frank, Abraham, William and Sam moved in what furniture and household goods they had managed to acquire: no bedsteads – not yet – but mattresses enough for all, a table and chairs and various other items such as cooking pots and the kettle. She and Bridget made a start on the cleaning while Jem fetched and carried and kept Annie out of everyone's way.

It was just after noon when Meg turned up, accompanied to Delilah's surprise by her friend and fellow maid Sally. They were dropped off by Meg's young man, Tommy, driving a cart. He stopped only long enough to help them unload and carry in several large boxes, then apologised and said he had to return the horse. Delilah watched him drive off competently and felt glad that Meg had found someone so steady and pleasant. She still had trouble thinking of Meg as anything other than her little sister, but Meg would be sixteen this year – the same age Delilah had been when she'd had to take on most of the responsibility for the family.

'I didn't know whether you'd be able to come, as you were allowed time off yesterday,' she said, picking up a surprisingly heavy box. 'And what's in these?'

'Ah,' said Meg. 'All in good time. Where's the kitchen?'

'And Sally, too?'

'The family's away, so Mrs Roberts said it was her wedding present to you that she'd manage everything for the afternoon and let us both come.'

'That's very generous, but it seems harsh that Sally should spend her afternoon out doing more work for us!'

Sally thumped down the crate she'd been carrying. 'It's a treat to come out with Meg, it really is.' She surveyed the kitchen corner of the back parlour and reached for a broom. 'And if there's one thing we know about, it's cleaning floors!' She caught Meg's eye and they both giggled.

The unusual sound gave Delilah pause, as she struggled to recall if she'd *ever* heard Meg laugh; if she had, it was years and years ago. Delilah looked at Sally, already hard at work but with a beaming smile on her face. Meg had told her, during the course of their Sunday chats, of her friend Sally's tragic history and sad life in the workhouse. Since that time Delilah had been glad for Sally that she had Meg for a friend, but she could also see that Sally was doing Meg good, too. There was more than one way to make a family.

By mid-afternoon the kitchen corner was sparkling and Meg was beginning to unpack food from the boxes they'd brought.

'What's all this?' asked Delilah, coming down to empty a bucket of dirty water, Bridget just behind her. 'Surely you didn't . . .'

'I thought you might not have had time to get anything in,' explained Meg. 'I don't have to pay for rent and food so I don't spend much of my wages. And I got a good price from Mr Jones the grocer, where Tommy works.' She saw Delilah about to speak. 'So don't argue.'

'And this is a present from both of us!' exclaimed Sally, pulling away a cloth to reveal a large cake. 'We paid for the ingredients ourselves and made it after all our other work was done, so we could bring it.' She gave a little excited skip.

'Oh, it's wonderful! Just what we'll all need after our day's work.' Delilah hugged them both. 'Sally, I'm sure Meg will say the same, but you're always welcome here, either with Meg or without – you're one of the family.' She held out an arm and Bridget, who had been looking on with that gentle smile, joined them in the embrace. *Sisters all,* thought Delilah, *wherever we started from.*

The kettle was just boiling when Frank, Abraham, William and Sam arrived with the last few bits. 'Nothing left in the room now except what was there when we arrived,' said Sam, as Delilah went into the shop at the front to meet them. 'Pa will find it empty when he gets back from wherever he's drinking today.'

'Don't worry, I'll find him before that and talk to him,' said Delilah. 'Now, wash your hands under the pump out the back and come and see this wonderful food Meg and Sally have brought. There's cake!'

Sam's face lit up, and he and William made their way past.

'You too,' said Delilah to the others. 'Now we've got our own pump there's no excuse to sit down with dirty hands.'

'Just one moment,' said Frank. He exchanged a glance with Abraham, who was carrying a cloth-wrapped bundle. 'We wanted to give you a present.'

'A present? Oh, there's no need for that.'

'I beg to differ, madam,' said Frank, grandly. 'And it's from both of us.'

Abraham put the bundle down on the counter and stepped back. Delilah unwrapped it and then gave a gasp of astonishment and joy: it was Ma's old clock.

'It was Jem who told me about it, a while ago,' said Frank. 'He's a sharp one for noticing things, isn't he? So I wanted to get it back for you, but I didn't know which one was yours. So I wondered if Abraham might recognise it . . .'

'. . . not realising that it was me who gave it to your Ma and Pa as a wedding present, all those years ago,' finished Abraham.

Delilah stroked the familiar wood with a loving hand. 'Oh, Ma,' was all she said. Then, after a moment, she looked through to the back room to check nobody could hear her and murmured, 'How lucky I am to have such a father and husband. The luckiest, happiest girl in Liverpool.'

They both shook their heads simultaneously, as if in a mirror, making each other smile. 'No,' said Abraham. 'Not lucky – deserving. Now, I'll leave you to it. The pump is out the back, you say?'

He left, and Delilah and Frank faced each other. 'This is your shop,' he said, gesturing at the space, 'won by your own efforts, and ready to be filled with flowers and love. And that in there – that wonderful collection of all those different people – that's the family you built. You did all this, and I couldn't be prouder.' He bent his head. 'Or more in love.'

'Come on, Delilah!' came Sam's voice from the back room. 'We can't cut this cake until you get here!'

Delilah broke off the kiss with a smile. 'Duty calls.' She took Frank's hand and they went through to join their family.

Find out what happened to the younger members of the Shaw family in Judy Summers' next novel, coming soon.

Dear Readers,

I'm delighted that you've chosen to join me in the world of the Shaw family. Some of you might be familiar with it from having read *The Forgotten Sister*, and others among you might be new here, but you're all equally welcome.

Liverpool was an exciting place to live in the 1840s. It was growing rapidly both in population and in size, with grand buildings being erected and new opportunities for commerce springing up all over the place, while the railway and the docks offered the possibility of travel throughout the country and across the seas. These opportunities and possibilities, of course, were not evenly distributed: the rich had more than the poor, and men had more than women. When I decided to write a series of books set in Victorian Liverpool, I had some choices to make about who my protagonists were going to be, but those decisions were not difficult: I knew straight away that I wanted to write about the poorer half of the population, those for whom life was a struggle no matter how hard they worked, and that my main characters would be women.

The Shaw family developed out of these ideas – they're fictional, but they represent those who lived in this particular time and place, proud Liverpudlians who are determined to make the best out of life for themselves and those around them. We heard Meg's story in *The Forgotten Sister* (I won't give away any spoilers here in case you would like to read it!), so now it's Delilah's turn. She is a very different character to her sister, so I wanted to explore how she went about things in her own way, recognising that being on the outside of the workhouse could sometimes be just as challenging as being in it.

The lives of working-class women in the Victorian era were hard, even without all the additional trials Delilah has to endure. Marital rape was legal, and there was almost nothing in the way of contraception, so frequent pregnancies and large families were to be expected, while rates of both infant and maternal mortality were horrendous. The only jobs available were those classed as 'women's work' – which inevitably meant exploitative and unrewarding – and labouring in a commercial laundry for six days a week was about as tough as it got. I must admit that my practical research for *A Winter's Wish* didn't go as far as attempting this myself, although I am old enough to remember living in a house without a washing

413

machine, my mother soaking, scrubbing, rinsing and wringing the laundry in a sink and hoping for good weather to hang it outside so we didn't end up with sopping wet clothes draped all over an unpleasantly damp and steamy house.

Carrying out this sort of labour all day every day, on a much larger scale, must have been almost unbearable and it's no surprise that Delilah wants to move on from it. However, any other paid work she might have been able to get would have been equally exhausting and equally badly paid. Women were deliberately (and perfectly legally) paid less than men, because the idea was that each family should have a male 'breadwinner' – the clue is in the name – who would earn enough to support a family. Unfortunately for that family, it was completely up to him what he did with his money once he had it; if he chose not to hand much of it over to his wife and children, they could do nothing about it and had nobody else to appeal to. A man was considered the head of his family, and that was that.

Delilah, of course, needs to bring in an income to feed her family, and is prepared to work hard, but there was no point in me pretending that she could walk into a nice desk job somewhere. Such positions were not only the preserve of men, but of men who had benefitted from proper schooling, which was by no means the majority of the male population of Liverpool. Retail was a possibility, because women could and did work in shops, but generally only in the lowest positions; manageress-level jobs like Mrs Farrell's were very few and far between.

Entrepreneurship therefore seemed to be Delilah's best bet, and here 1840s Liverpool was exactly the right time and place for someone with ideas and determination. It was the railway that came to my rescue when I was considering exactly what she could do: the easy links with, and decreased travel time from, the surrounding countryside meant that fresh farm goods could be delivered into the city every morning in a way that had been all but impossible before. Delilah saw this opportunity at the same time as I did, and she grabbed it with both hands.

\* \* \*

One of the reasons that Liverpool's population grew so rapidly at this time was the arrival of hundreds of thousands of starving, desperate refugees. The Great Famine that devastated Ireland in the second half of the 1840s resulted in around a million deaths and the emigration of a further one and half million men, women and children. Liverpool, the nearest major port, was the destination for a large proportion of these people – for some only as a stopover on their way to the USA, while others had the intention of making it their home.

Liverpool was already a cosmopolitan, multicultural city by the time this happened; with ships docking daily from all over the world there were inevitably many who decided to stay, and the city was home to thriving communities of people of different national-ities, colours and religions. The sight of people with dark skin wouldn't raise an eyebrow, despite what the viewers of some TV period dramas might choose to believe. The extremely rapid increase in immigration during the 1840s (the population of Liverpool rose by 100,000 people in ten years) did cause a great deal of pressure, resulting in jobs and housing becoming scarce and rents increasing. The system of parish 'outdoor relief', whereby the poor could be supported to remain in their own homes, became unsustainable, resulting in larger workhouses that soon became the only option. Some existing inhabitants resented the new arrivals for all this – job adverts genuinely did often end with the words 'No Irish need apply' – but in the main the city and its people opened their arms, and within a generation the new arrivals were as proudly Liverpudlian as those whose families had been there for decades.

One of the most fascinating things I learned during my research was that it was around this time that today's characteristic Scouse accent developed – up until the mid-nineteenth century Liverpudlians apparently sounded much like the people living in the rest of Lancashire, but the influx of new accents and dialects, particularly Irish and American ones, made everything melt and fuse together into the distinctive voice we know today.

*   *   *

I hope that you like my picture of 1840s Liverpool and the girls and women who built their lives in it. Those of you who know the city and its history well may spot the odd small anachronism, and if so then I hope you will forgive me. Once again I have to confess that I have deliberately placed locomotives inside Lime Street station, which in reality did not happen until later (at this time the engines were detached at Edge Hill and the carriages made their way in via gravity and brakes, to be hauled out again by rope). But my choice to do this was for the benefit of the Shaw family. When Delilah, Sam and Jem make their first visit to the station it might have been less exciting and magical if they had only been able to see carriages: I wanted them to experience the full exhilaration of the wonderful world of modern technology.

New technology, as it happens, is going to influence how Annie makes her way in the world, along with Jem and Sam as they grow up, so I hope you will join me and the Shaw family again soon.

Yours truly
Judy Summers

# About the Author

Judy Summers is an avid reader, historian and mother of three. Her forebears – some of whom probably entered England via Liverpool in the Victorian era – were miners, labourers and domestic servants. She finds these lives far more interesting than those of the upper classes.

Judy lives in the English countryside with her family and is a keen baker and gardener.

# WELBECK

PUBLISHING GROUP

## Love books? Join the club.

Sign up and choose your preferred genres to receive
tailored news, deals, extracts, author interviews and
more about your next favourite read.

From heart-racing thrillers to award-winning historical
fiction, through to must-read music tomes, beautiful
picture books and delightful gift ideas, Welbeck is
proud to publish titles that suit every taste.

### bit.ly/welbeckpublishing

WELBECK

ANDRE
DEUTSCH

MORTIMER

MORTIMER

WELBECK